When Bad Things Happen to Rich People

When Bad Things Happen
to Rich People

A Novel

Ian Morris

SWITCHGRASS BOOKS   NORTHERN ILLINOIS UNIVERSITY PRESS   DeKalb

© 2014 by Switchgrass Books, an imprint of
Northern Illinois University Press
Published by the Northern Illinois University Press,
DeKalb, Illinois 60115
Manufactured in the United States using acid-free paper
Design by Shaun Allshouse

This is a work of fiction. All characters are products of the
author's imagination, and any resemblance to persons living or
dead is entirely coincidental.

Library of Congress Cataloging in Publication Data
Morris, Ian, 1961-
When bad things happen to rich people : a novel / Ian Morris.
pages cm
ISBN 978-0-87580-709-6 (pbk : alk. paper)—
ISBN 978-1-60909-167-5 (e-book)
1. College teachers—Fiction. 2. Advice columnists—Fiction. 3. Publishers
and publishing—Fiction. 4. Ghostwriting—Fiction. 5. Chicago (Ill.)—
Social life and customs—20th century—Fiction. I. Title.
PS3613.O7724W44 2014
813'.6--dc23
2014007746

For Zelda

Acknowledgments

For their emotional, professional, and sometimes material support, I would like to thank Mary Zerkel, Wilma Morris, Marya Morris, Laura Leichum, Rudy Faust, Joanne Diaz, Michael Thomas, Richard Fox, Kevin Kaempf, Mark Heineke, and the Ragdale Foundation. A version of Chapter 15 originally appeared in *Crab Orchard Review*.

The trains roared by under smoke gray skies.
Lake Michigan rose and fell like a bird.
                                    —The Handsome Family

Part 1

Wicker Park (June 1995)

1.

Nix was balancing a ledger when he heard the shots. The accounts were uncomplicated, a single column of credits and debits along the left-hand side of the page, the months of the year arrayed across the top. Under *Income* he entered the amounts of his wife's paychecks, which were deposited electronically every two weeks, and his from the college, which bled in monthly, between agonizing clots during summer and Christmas breaks. Under the these entries came *Expenses*, below which he'd written out headings for each of their bills by groups, each heading topped by the bill requiring the biggest monthly payment, such as for *Household: rent*, then *AT&T, ComEd, Peoples Gas, the Water Department*; next *Student Loans* (one for him, from a credit union; two for her, one from the *US Department of Education* and one from the *TrustCon Bank* of Reno, NV); then *Credit Cards* (seven between the two of them, two *Visa*, one *Mastercard, American Express Gold* [subsequently devalued by the introduction of cards named for more precious metals], *Amex Premia* [whatever that was], *Shell Oil*, and one for a beaded boutique on Clark called *Hubba-Hubba*). When the ledger book's binding had become flimsy from too-frequent openings and closings, he'd shored up the spine with a coarse, pleasing twine. Such care imbued him with a sense of practical efficacy, in the same way he was sustained by the scratch of honed pencil point on the stiff paper of the Optic Lo-Glo Green pages of his National columnar pad. Nix was left-handed and dragged the heel of his palm across the fresh characters as he wrote, smearing the graphite to an eyeliner-sheen beneath the glare of his halogen desk lamp.

He'd begun keeping these accounts the previous year, after he forgot to enter a check in the checkbook register. The result of this lapse was pandemic. Checks bounced, overdrafts that took—given the state of their savings—months to restore and almost caused him and then soon-to-be wife Flora to break up. Nix had stormed out of the house one gray afternoon, driven to the Office Giant, bought the ledger book, and spent an evening charting their finances across the page. Before then, they'd written checks for bills on a need-to-pay basis only, meting out minimums on the credit cards, haggling with the jerks on the student-loan phone banks: adjusting, deferring, forbearing. The introduction of the ledger had given him an immediate satisfaction. In the posture of a Victorian scrivener, he huddled over the ruled, sectioned pages on a spare desktop, scratching *pd.* beside the bills for which he'd written out checks and sealed them in windowed envelopes. He'd logged his first entry in the previous April, grinning at the sight of his first completed column, and thereafter he nursed each month's entries, as though the numerals themselves were federally insured funds in their account at the Industrial Bank of Chicago.

Yet it was sham. For whatever his flair for configuring Arabic numerals, Nix could never make what came in become more than what went out. Every month they aspired to a Shaker economy—stretching the staples in the cupboard, buying coffee in cans, wearing ragged shirts under sweaters, going only to matinees at the second-run theater. Every month they fell short, snared by costs that lurked outside of the narrow lines of the ledger. They'd cover these gaps with one of the credit cards. And, once the card was out of the wallet, they'd rationalize a reward for their prior discipline—dinner out at a someplace cheap or an article of clothing they could otherwise almost afford. Nix then spent the next three months massaging that card's balance below the limit, while the balances of the others spasmed upward. He'd then tend to the worst of those, in a Sisyphean rotation. By this method they slouched toward bankruptcy.

Their wedding the previous June had briefly swelled the *Income* side of the ledger. In exchange for the donation of a Creole pig to a Haitian farmers' collective, they were married on the terrace of the Jens Jensen pavilion in Columbus Park, by a Guatemalan lay nun in a serape decorated with Mayan hieroglyphs. The notices in the papers would have declared the event to have been as complementary to the surrounding prairie as was the structure in which the ceremony was held, had Flora ever—or Nix still—been the sort of people about whom such observations are printed on the Style pages of the *Tribune* or the *Sun-Times.*

After the linens were returned to the commercial laundry and the deposit refunded, they had broken even and were—while driving north for a camping honeymoon in the woods of northern Wisconsin—in the very act of congratulating themselves on their thrift, when Nix noticed blue smoke seeping from beneath the hood of their Honda. Being just nine miles short of the Sweetheart Suite of the Land O' Nod Motel in the Wisconsin Dells, Nix elected to drive the remaining distance with the heater on high and the windows rolled down, lifting his wrist from the steering wheel every tenth of a mile to glance at the temperature gauge.

A rebuilt engine swallowed the $800 they'd saved for the trip and another $800 on the credit card, which inspired a dinner of lavish but ordinary perch at a country club, served by a waitress who begrudged the couple the time they cost her away from the sunburned largesse of a golf outing at a neighboring table. The girl was young and resented Flora and Nix for not hollering "When you gone to show yer tits?" nor trolling dollar bills across the floor like muskie lures, and she tore herself away from the golfers' glass-eyed ribaldry just long enough to chide the newlyweds for ordering a red with the fish.

Flora, shoulders crimson from the hour passed on the roadside waiting for the tow truck, shrugged. "We're from the city," she said.

There were six in all—the first tentative, then four in succession, bap-bap-bap-bap, the last an afterthought—followed by the requisite shouting, "Take that mother-fucking shit, cocksucker," then shrieking rubber, first to the intersection, then the higher pitch of tires cornering at speed.

By the time Nix had looked up from the pale-green page and turned toward the window, the street had grown silent. Nothing for seconds, then a voice, young and male, strong and at the same time uncertain. "Help," it said. Nix listened for an answer from a companion or family. "Help," the voice said again, "I'm shot in the head."

Nix put his pencil down, stood, walked to the window obliquely, as they'd become accustomed to doing on nights like this, and pushed the curtain aside with the back of his hand.

The boy lay in the street, knees to his chest, his palms flat on the pavement, as he struggled to lift his head, which remained pinned to the asphalt, as though anchored by the weight of the bullet. A glistening black presence inched toward the gutter from his hair in a narrow trickle.

Should he call the police? Nix asked himself the same question after every shooting. Always he assumed somebody already had, but couldn't help worrying what would happen if everyone assumed the same. He heard a door slam. Roland Wede, the sculptor next door appeared in the cone of light from the street lamp. The man, bearded and shirtless, stood over the boy and sipped on a bottle of beer. If the victim spoke, Nix couldn't hear, but Wede craned closer, as if listening, then straightened, as the first squad car rolled into view, followed by another and a third, lights flashing, wriggling out of the narrow alleyway like silverfish.

Nix walked the length of the apartment, through the dining room, which they'd yet to furnish, except with their bicycles, down a hallway of warped, painted floorboards, to the bathroom. He glanced at his face in the mirror above the sink long enough to notice he needed a haircut, twisted the faucet knob to staunch a persistent drip, then doubled over the toilet, his stomach knotting toward his throat.

Bracing himself on the toilet seat, he turned his head to breathe and saw a dead cockroach plastered to the linen-closet door. The bug had been there for days. Its death was a mystery because Nix hadn't killed it, and he didn't believe Flora would have and then left its corpse where it died. Yet the presence of the remains was materially undeniable. Nix reached for the toilet paper to wrap the carcass in and retched again.

He was anticipating a third attack when Flora called from the bedroom. He stood, splashed water on his face, passed through the kitchen, which still smelled of smoke from the morning's fire, and ducked his head in the bedroom doorway. His wife sat at her computer, knees up, wearing a flannel shirt of his, frayed at the cuffs. She looked up from the screen, blew her bangs out of her eyes, and pushed the headphones back from one ear. "What?"

"Drive by."

"Where?"

"Out front."

"Oh my God. Anybody hit?" They talk like this.

"Some kid got shot in the head."

"Man," she said and darted ahead of him down the hall, slowing as he had as she neared the window, approaching it from the side, and peered out from behind the curtain.

"Is it Juan?" she asked.

Whenever there was a shooting, Flora worried the victim was Juan. Despite the fact that—as far as Nix could tell from his view of the street outside their window—Juan was executive officer of the gang who peddled crack on the block, Flora was fond of him, ever since the time he'd help her fix a flat tire on the Civic. Nix had left for the day. Fortunately for Flora, she had discovered the flat during the seven hours a day that Juan could be found engaged in commerce in front of the elementary school across the street. He jacked up the car, rolled the wheel up the block to All Day Tire to get plugged, and they'd become friends, chuckling over her bad fortune and, Nix assumes, over how her husband was not good at things at which husbands are supposed to be good.

It was not Juan who'd been shot, nor was Nix certain he'd ever seen this boy before. Nix wasn't friendly with the neighborhood youth. He wasn't friendly with the neighborhood itself. Nor did he think the neighborhood had much use for him.

The ambulance arrived more slowly than the squads had. The medics—a man and a woman with a bulky ponytail—both thick set and lethargic, dismounted from the cab and—snapping rubber gloves as they walked—approached the victim.

Flora watched as the paramedics chatted with the police. "Why aren't they doing anything?"

"He might be paralyzed," Nix said. The woman leaned over the boy, without kneeling or crouching, talking into his ear, as the sculptor had, while her partner retrieved a backboard from the rig and tossed it to the ground, the sound echoing down the street, then became so involved in conversation with one of the cops that he had to be nudged twice before sliding the victim onto the board. As they did, the boy convulsed, a straightening of his limbs, and Nix felt an unexpected relief that the kid was still alive.

The ambulance left as slowly as it had come, without sirens or lights, as if not wanting to disturb the quiet of a Sunday evening, no matter how close to death its charge might be. One by one, the squad cars rolled away. In standard form, a detective would be by their building the next day after Nix and Flora left for work. He'd leave a calling card with his name, rank, badge number, and precinct in their mailbox, with a scrawled inscription on the back,

> Call # with info pertain
> to shoot on eve/morn of 6/7–8.

They'd received such cards before and refused to call, as a sort of protest against this indolent mode of police work.

Nix had a dozen papers yet to grade for his 9:30 class the next morning but now was in no mood. He always had papers to grade when he sat down with the ledger book. He'd planned to get through them before he went to bed, knowing he wouldn't, and would resolve to finish them in the lecturers' office when he got to work, knowing equally well that he'd more likely squander his time talking with Nestor or one of the other adjuncts he liked.

In the kitchen, Nix was relieved to see their pyramid of specialty tea boxes on the shelf above the stove had survived the blaze, and he dug through them looking for those laced with valerian. A bad socket had sparked the conflagration, which claimed the toaster, a packet of festive paper napkins left over from the wedding, and Flora's bagel—the precipitating agent. Despite their morning grogginess, they'd faced down the threat with daring and skill. Nix retarded the blaze with dry buckwheat pancake mix, while Flora moved in with the fire extinguisher, spraying at the base of the flames as she remembered having been told to do. The fire snuffed, they stood panting their way back to calm. Nix tossed the empty box of pancake mix into the sink, sighed deeply, and said, "I wanted to shoot the fire extinguisher."

Flora sat again at her computer, which she'd propped on an old typewriter table that looked too small to support the weight of the machine. She hadn't noticed him come into the room. This drove him nuts about her. Nothing short of gem cutting would have preoccupied him enough not to know his wife entered the room. Yet Flora could become sufficiently engrossed in a commercial for deodorant to not notice he'd hung himself from the ceiling fan.

He passed behind her and glanced at the screen.

> Dear RN,
> While we were in Cambodia picking up our new daughter, I slept on a hard mattress and hurt my back. I made an appointment with a chiropractor, but a friend suggests naprapathy. Which would you recommend? Or acupuncture?
>
> Signed,
> My Aching Back

Flora stared the screen, rotated her shoulders, and tapped,

> Dear MAB,
> There is no single answer to your question. A lot depends on the nature of your pain, your budget (are you insured for all of these through your organization's plan?), and the availability of qualified practitioners in your area.
> Get all the information you need in order to make an intelligent choice, and as you begin life with your new baby remember to take care of yourself as well.
>
> Fondly,
> RN

"You didn't really tell her anything," Nix said.

Flora swung her arm behind her to hit him without looking around. "Sure I did."

"You just told her to get more information."

"Which was the right thing to say. People want to be heard," she said.

And she had proven herself right. Flora had come to the Center for Employees of Non-Profit Organizations, CENPO, with a newly printed diploma from the University of Chicago School of Social

Policy. She believed that her inclination toward hard work and her agreeability would endear her to the organization. For this conviction she was rewarded with hard work that she was obliged to undertake agreeably. She learned early on that she needed to watch out for herself as much as for those she had been called to serve. CENPO was reorganizing, and without allies Flora was in danger of being let go almost as soon as she was hired. When hoping to get into the organization's Global Action Initiative, she'd been asked instead to fill in on the Reluctant Nurturer column for *Non-Profit Parenting,* one of CENPO's publishing properties, after its creator decamped suddenly for a morning television show.

The original woman behind the persona was a clinical psychologist and mother. The Reluctant Nurturer addressed the anxieties of a class of professional women who put job satisfaction ahead of wealth and, as such, were inclined to worry or struggle with issues surrounding the raising of children. While Flora did not have children, the training to treat, nor an authentic interest in, the psychological difficulties or personal problems of the people who wrote to her, she was able to synthesize a grace and generosity that registered with her readers. Reluctant Nurturer became RN and became for Flora more than a persona but a calm voice in her head that she'd started to hear in quiet moments when she pondered her own personal crises. The authenticity lay in her own genuine reluctance.

When the fulltime columnist position was listed, she went to Marcia, her assignment editor, touting the spike in subscriptions and inquiries about syndication. Marcia in return pointed out that the one strike against Flora was that she didn't really have children.

"Of course," Marcia said, "there's always something you could do about that."

"What do you mean?" Flora had asked.

"Think about it," said Marcia, combing the surface of a cup of miso broth with a lacquered, wooden spoon. Twelve years on the New York fashion books had left her stomach lining raw and bleeding. NPP was supposed to be a step out of the fast track, but in spite of herself, circulation was soaring and somehow there was buzz. NPP had found that most elusive of sought-after quantities: an untapped audience. Reader surveys had shown that the Reluctant

Nurturer was a large part of the periodical's appeal, though these were reader surveys that Marcia did not make Flora aware of. "Our demographic is women twenty-five to forty-five working for not-for-profits or NGOs who find themselves raising children under challenging personal and geopolitical circumstances. Your story could be an inspiration."

Flora picked at the nap of her favorite gray wool skirt, as Marcia spoke. Exhausted by the humiliation of being considered and possibly rejected for a position she felt she deserved, she understood that the etiquette of her profession all but demanded that she resign her column if she were passed over.

"Would it be enough to be pregnant, or do I have to hope they don't fill the position before I deliver?"

Flora was joking, but Marcia considered the question, lifting the cup to her lips between tangerine nails. She had two kids of her own, a teenaged girl from a first marriage and a toddler with her second husband, a man who had once steamed her drapes. "I think a good faith effort would be sufficient."

Flora and Nix had talked about having kids before. Both agreed they wanted children—just not enough to conceive one. Still, she'd asked Nix what he thought about the idea when she got home, expecting another money lecture, but he'd said, "Sure, what the fuck."

In the months since then, her diaphragm case languished in the medicine cabinet beneath a dusting of spilled foot powder. The magazine had been as good as its word and hired her, even though she and Nix had yet to fulfill their end of the arrangement. Neither Nix nor Flora said anything to the other, but both viewed the possibility of parenthood in their current circumstances with more dread than joy. Months later, reflecting on the wreckage of the summer, Nix would look back on this shooting as a beginning of their trouble, not for any sense of danger but for a lingering nausea that foretold woe.

From down the alley came a staccato report.

"They're shooting again," Flora said, and they listened together in the dark.

2.

On his way to the El the next morning, Nix passed a stain on the asphalt, maybe a foot long and in the shape of Lake Michigan, dry, black, indistinguishable from oil or transmission fluid. Rain was forecast for the afternoon. Even a sprinkle would erase this last trace of the night's violence. Nix's only chance of knowing the boy's fate would come from overheard conversation as he walked down the block. These days, drive-bys had to boast multiple kills to rate a mention on the TV news. Just as well, he thought. If the kid lived, it would be nice to hear—otherwise better not to know.

Nix hated the subways for their modest squalor. In a dank corner of the platform, he leaned against a tiled pillar, out of sight of the other waiting passengers, as was his habit, listening for the scraping murmur of steel on steel. On the tracks below him, a rat slalomed between the support ties of the third rail. They play, do the rats. Whenever you get two or more of them together, they frolic and chase each other's tails. Theirs is not the quotidian existence that the proverbial race suggests. Say what one will, Nix would've welcomed the liberty of leaping around with his friends at eight in the morning. Instead, the train rattled to a stop and he stepped swiftly on board.

Being just four stops from the Loop, he rarely found a seat and had come to regard the Blue Line as a horizontal elevator. He pressed through to the center of the car and assumed the posture of the Man of His Station, his left hand gripping the vertical bar, the RAF satchel he'd brought at Uncle Dan's Army Surplus slung across his shoulder. He wore an ivory Oxford shirt, last year's khakis, scuffed Nikes, the uniform of his station: the untenured academic, a man of some character and more reflection, with no more idea than the rats hurdling the third rail what agency or actor brought him to be clutching a handrail on the Douglas train at 8:30 on a June morning.

Carnelius College occupied a six-story Louis Sullivan knock-off in the South Loop and was spreading like a pathogen to the other buildings on the block and adjacent side streets. Founded as a communications college, there was a major in Television but not English, Sound Recording but not Physics. The interior exuded a bourgeois anarchy, carpets pocked with cigarette burns beneath No Smoking signs yellowed with nicotine, graffiti covered any surface more solid than a coffee cup. Nix strode these halls like a colossus. Four years earlier, when he started at Carnelius, he had been the last of thirty-four adjuncts in seniority. Now he was fifth. When he'd received, earlier that week, his course listing for the fall semester— Devel. Eng. 1012, Dearborn rm. 703—along with a 1099 tax form, he'd wept, for there were no classrooms left to conquer.

Now, two weeks to the end of the term, Nix was already gone. By the standard of his student and peer evaluations, he was a better than good instructor of English Composition, but lately he had a sense that he was coasting. After all the lectures he had delivered to his students on the cardinal virtue of giving a shit, Nix used to believe it was his job alone to make them care about what he was teaching them, if only because they so rarely did. Yet this semester he'd felt even that mote of idealism fade as he and his students circled in each other in an improvised fandango of mutual disappointment.

The Carnelius office for adjunct faculty in the humanities was a depot of surplus institutional furniture that the part-time teachers had fashioned into a clubhouse for the marginally employed. When Nix entered, there was one other instructor in the room, a woman, if he could call her that since she looked like she was just out of high school. Nix knew her only by sight. He was friendly with, even reasonably close to, many of the teachers who had been around a few semesters, but he'd learned to recognize and avoid the ones who he didn't think would last.

She looked up from her book. Nix nodded, affably he hoped, and sat at his desk. Technically, adjunct faculty were not assigned desks, but given Nix's seniority, and the fact he'd gone through the trouble of constructing a Fortress of Solitude behind a bank of filing cabinets, he'd been granted squatter's rights. He pulled up the stool he used as a desk chair and anguished at the heft of the stack of essays he pulled from his satchel. As usual, he'd read and graded the essays written by his best students first, then put the others off until the last minute.

He opened the first, "The Gap: A *Sweet* Shop, Not a Sweatshop," by Ronny Blevins, Section 1. Nix winced. Ronny was assistant manager of the flagship Gap store on State St. and his essays all went on like this. Nix shifted Ronny's paper to the bottom of the pile and started on the next, "Sex Sells," by NyQuelle Morton. NyQuelle had an odd habit of talking about herself in the third person in her essays. This one began, "What follows are NyQuelle's opinions on the subject of the use of sex in advertising. It is NyQuelle's opinion that television has an effect on most viewers."

Nix scrawled *Really?* in the margin and was breasting the ensuing swells of Ms. Morton's profundity when he heard a familiar jingling drawing near and looked up to see Nestor Jay, dreadlocked, bangled harlequin of domestic discord standing beside his desk.

"Nix," he grinned, his customary pretense of surprise, since Nix was always in the office at this time of morning. Nestor settled on the edge of the desk, knocking the paper sack containing Nix's lunch to the floor as he did.

"What's this, persuasive?" he asked, his bracelets ringing as he snatched the first paper off the top of the pile.

Nix nodded. "Week fifteen—persuasive."

Nestor read the first paragraph in the newscaster's voice that he employed when mimicking Caucasians, "'What's the deal with handicap parking spaces? Have you ever seen anyone really messed up ever park in one?' See," he said, "this is why I don't give writing assignments."

Nix laughed. "An end theory of the rhetorical pedagogy."

"You're joking," Nestor said, "but you're more right than you know. Usually, I set them loose in the library and tell them 'don't write anything down.' Pretty soon they're coming to me and saying 'Mr. Jay would it be acceptable to you if I was to record my impressions of this here photograph of'—you know, whatever—'in the form of an essay?'

"After a while it's not enough to write. They crave an audience and since, after all, I *am* an adjunct lecturer in the instruction of composition, they think, 'Why not run it by Nestor? See what he has to say.'"

"How do you grade?" Nix asked, knowing as soon as did that he'd regret it.

"On the quality of the writing. How do you think?"

"Don't you have to give a lot of A's? I mean if they're writing out of an organic need to share their thoughts, it hardly seems fair not to—"

"I give very few A's. Why would you think otherwise?"

"If you say—"

"I said not letting them write makes them eager to do it. I didn't say it made them any good," he said, scanning the essay in his hand. He tossed the paper back on the pile. "They're better than this, usually. How's Flora?"

"Fine," Nix said. It was his custom to reveal little about his wife to Nestor, because Flora and Nestor's wife, Veronika, were friends and anything he said would get back to Flora in the worst possible light.

There was a rap on the metal cabinet behind Nix's head. Josie, the department admin, said, "Steve wants you."

"Uh oh," said Nestor.

"Is it about summer school?" Nix asked.

Josie's eyelids drooped. "How should I know?" Josie was the bassist for a girl group that gigged at least four nights a week, which didn't leave her much time for sleep or patience.

Nix watched her fingernails strum the filing cabinet. "What do you call that color?" he asked.

"Black."

Steve—illuminated only by the ultraviolet lights over his bank of aquariums—sat perched upon his desk chair with the alert, serene bearing and elongated neck of a flightless bird. He wore his red hair in a broad Afro and favored dashikis when the weather was warm. As was his custom, he waited until Nix had knocked, entered, and sat before turning from his computer. "Have a seat, Nix," Steve said.

Nix indicated his seated form.

"No summer sections this year. I wanted you to hear it from me."

Filters and air pumps whirred. "I thought I was a lock."

"You were," Steve said, "before I started banging Carrie Thayer."

Nix glanced over his shoulder to make sure he'd closed the door. "Who?"

"Carrie. First-year adjunct. You know her. Yellow hair, young looking."

"Why my section?"

"It was the only time she was available. If I don't give her this, I don't want to think of what kind of trouble she could make." Behind Steve's head, silk-tailed fish circled and lurked. Nix realized with some certainty that Carrie Thayer was the woman he'd nodded at in the office that morning.

"Why tell me?"

"Figured I owe you. Besides there's something else. Trout's got his hook into a benefactor threatening to drop a surreal pile of cash." Trout was Felding Trout, department chair.

"So?"

"She met Trout at a development luncheon. She would like to endow a chair in Trade Periodicals and thinks it's time somebody wrote her memoirs. Trout asked me to pick somebody. I suggested you."

"What did he say?"

"He left it up to me. I'm not sure he knows who you are, if that's what you're getting at."

"He reviewed my book."

"He's reviewed a lot of books."

"What's her name?"

"The money? Zira something—"

"Zira Fontaine?"

"You know her?"

"*Of* her. She publishes money magazines. Is she still alive?"

"As of whenever Felding asked me to do this."

"There was a divorce. What was it?"

"Before my time," Steve said.

"Aren't you older than me?"

"Am I?"

"What's it pay?"

"That would be for you to work out. This is isn't a Carnelius thing. This is a between you and her thing."

"Whatever," Nix said and stood to leave.

"Of course," Steve said, "I don't have to tell you that any difficulty would reflect negatively upon the college and ultimately upon your appointment here, as far as Trout is concerned."

"He doesn't talk to me as it is."

Steve laughed. "Oh yeah, I was supposed to talk to all of you about that." He handed Nix a slip of paper. "Trout doesn't want to be engaged physically by students or part-time staff. I'll send a message via electronic mail."

When Nix got back to the adjunct's office, he was relieved to find Nestor gone. He studied the number on the slip of paper Steve had handed him, Fontaine, 847-338-9——. Written in whose hand? Hers? No, a man's. Trout's? Could be. Nix had never seen his handwriting, nor any trace of the man beyond his silent presence. The Romantic scholar Trout was resented (or its superlative synonym) by the full-time Carnelius faculty for the Ozymandian salary with which he'd been lured from Swarthmore. He ruled from a pleasure dome of a corner office, the door of which Nix had never seen open or being closed, and communicated only through Steve, his mortal oracle.

Nix had a class to teach but couldn't concentrate on his topic of the day, James Thurber and the Inverted Pyramid. On the essays he'd yet to grade, he wrote "see me." Then, as class ended, he invented a faculty meeting and dove into the office before any of the six students could actually *see* him. Sitting at the one desk in the room with a phone, he retrieved the slip of paper Steve had handed him from his shirt pocket and had a hand on the receiver when he heard a throat being cleared behind him. Fearing Ronny or NyQuelle, Nix turned and saw Carrie Thayer standing with the freshman reader clutched to her chest. "Excuse me," she said, "I'm teaching American Survey this summer and Dr. Seeger said you'd have a syllabus."

"Dr. Seeger?"

"Steve."

In his second semester of teaching the course, Nix had developed a syllabus, which he'd shared at a faculty retreat. It had garnered broad praise, more than he was comfortable with, and had been adopted semiofficially in the teaching of the course since then.

"He's right," Nix said.

"Oh, wonderful," she said, twisting the binder of her book. "—may I look at it?"

"I don't keep a copy on me," he said. "I can bring one in for you."

"You could?" she said, tilting her head in gratitude. "That would be terrific." She smiled and Nix noticed she was wearing braces. *My God,* he thought, *do yourself a favor, Metal Mouth. Run for your life.*

Flora sat perched on a stool at the far end of their kitchen table, wearing one of his sleeveless Ts and looking, as she ate red grapes off a clay plate, like an advertising supplement in the *New Yorker* for travel in Tuscany. "I thought she died."

"Nope."

"Is she some kind of crank?" she asked.

"Why would assume that?"

"She's having somebody write her autobiography for her."

"Rich people do that sort of thing all the time. It's a genre."

"A genre?"

"A subgenre."

"Sort of a strange time to have somebody write about you, if you're a money person, I mean. Maybe, it's an alibi."

"An alibi?"

"That's not the right word—apology? Maybe she wants you to write an apology."

"I think it's just personal, where she came from, what advice she has for other women who want to be like her"

"Would that make you a ghost writer?"

"I guess."

"Is that something you want to be?"

Given the chance at a paycheck, Nix felt he had the upper hand in this discussion. Just the same, he waited until she was in the shower to make the call.

A man answered. "Yes."

"Nix Walters," Nix replied—believing the syntax of business to be one of immediacy and action, lacking copulative verbs—"calling regarding a request Ms. Fontaine placed to Dr. Trout of Carnelius

College pertaining the writing of her … personal reflections" (this last improvisation being due to Nix's fear that the word "memoir" suddenly struck Nix as dirty).

Silence on the other end of the line, then: "This is not a matter to which I have been alerted. May I call you back?"

"Swell," Nix said, gave his number, and hung up. He walked to the kitchen, but hadn't finished pouring a cup of coffee when the phone rang.

"Larson Anders, calling on behalf of Zira Fontaine. Mrs. Fontaine will see you at ten o'clock tomorrow morning at her home," he said and spoke the address. The street was in a northern suburb Nix had passed on the expressway but lay shaded behind rows of hedges and sound abatement walls. "Will you require directions?"

"No," Nix lied.

"Well," he said to Flora, as she passed through the room with a towel turbaned on her head. "That's it."

"What is?"

3.

As the Union Pacific Northern Line train gathered speed, Nix crossed and uncrossed his legs and traced his finger along the columns of the train schedule, checking and double-checking the times of the returning trains. This was not the first time he had traveled further than dignity permitted in pursuit of a few pieces of silver. He'd ridden the Green Line to the most remote outpost of the City College system to substitute for a colleague for a promised $50 he'd never managed to collect; he'd once borrowed a car and negotiated a choked tangle of expressway interchanges to attend a day-long seminar devoted to the opportunity of making "literally hundreds of dollars a month" tutoring high school students for standardized exams. ("Repeat after me," the pitchman barked, as he tore off his blazer, rolled up his sleeves, and leapt on a chair, "I *can* make a difference!" Loudly, the call was repeated. "I *can* teach!" the man yelled, drawing out the *a* in *can*. "I can teach," the reply, this time, less certain. A final call: "I *can* provide for my family." The response to this last, a murmur.) As the two-flats of the North Side gave way to squat, light industry, and eventually to the green stolidity of the northern suburbs, Nix set down the schedule, opened his portfolio case, and looked over the résumé he and Flora had worked on until well after midnight.

He'd spent an hour skimming the color-illustrated book of résumé templates that Flora bought during her last job search, paging rapidly past recommended formats for graphic designers—lavender paper with floral appointments in the corners and chatty headings, like Good At: and Likes To: He also rejected the bland rigor of the gray-papered "Project Manager," lined and charted like a spreadsheet, and chose instead the most constipated of options, the "Entry-Level," featuring the Courier font on 100% white cotton bond. Nix struck a further note of authenticity by dragging his father's Underwood out of their second bedroom where it served as a doorstop.

Flora was exasperated. She said that the typewriter would take twice as long as her computer. (In the end, five times was closer to it.) Then they'd quarreled about what to include. Nix had worked six or seven minimum-wage jobs in high school and college and felt that they constituted something of a track record of dependability, particularly the summer at the grocery before his senior year, where he'd been named assistant manager after only two weeks on the job. Flora was against it, saying such entries made him look desperate and under-qualified. They'd compromised. He left out Hillman's Fine Foods but included in his Cardinal Sheehy Award, bestowed at Loyola upon the writer of "Best Freshman Essay on a Topic of Secular Preoccupation."

Following this entry he'd typed an asterisk, corresponding to a footnote at the bottom of page two: *As Walter Nixon. (For before the publication of *Life During Wartime*, Nix Walters had been Walter Nixon.) Flora opposed this, too, claiming it made him sound "like a mob rat in the Witness Protection Program."

A conductor approached with a proprietary air, scanning the seats for new riders.

Seeing Nix, he tipped his cap. "Morning, sir."

"Lake Forest," Nix said, "round trip."

"I can only sell you one-way on the train, sir," the conductor said. Nix noticed under that the care-worn expression and thick glasses the man was not much older than he was. Nix handed him a twenty, which was the only bill in his wallet, and which Flora had bestowed upon him that morning with an uncharacteristic reluctance. *("Don't lose it." "Why would I lose it?")*

"Ah," said the conductor, shaking his head, "a North Shore single," peeling bills off a roll and slapping the change machine on his belt with his thumb.

"It's all I've got," Nix protested, glad in a way to be taken for a native of the prosperous land to which he traveled, if only mistakenly. But the conductor, snapping out the requisite holes on the ticket with a flourish of his puncher, moved on with a wink to make sure Nix knew this was a man who recognized one of his own class, no matter what the guise or circumstances.

Nix put his change in his wallet and the wallet into the pocket of his jacket and was slipping his résumé into the portfolio case when something caught his eye. He wasn't sure what, a sense of lurking cataclysm. Scanning the page, he saw nothing, looked again, tracing a finger down the left margin and *shit* there it was: the last heading on the page read <u>Educatipn</u>—the tail of the *p* nearly obscured by the underscore. Nearly, but not completely, and once he'd seen it he could see nothing else. No matter where his eyes wandered on the page, they were drawn back to the error like iron filings to a magnet.

He didn't know what to do. He could say he didn't have a résumé, that he didn't think one would be necessary. That had been Flora's idea anyway. But how would he handle that? To announce upon his arrival that he didn't have a résumé would certainly seem suspicious. On the other hand, to wait until she asked to tell her he hadn't brought one would make him appear ill-prepared. The question then was whether to try to fix the error or leave it and hope Mrs. Fontaine didn't notice. The second option was impossible because he couldn't tell her after she'd spotted it that he'd known the error was there all along. A well-placed drop of Liquid Paper would've solved his problem—if he had any. Instead, he uncapped a narrow-tipped black marker and, with the precision of an engraver, fattened the bottom of the *p* into an *o*. The thick paper wicked up the ink and it settled in the depression of the character on the page. He held the paper at arm's length and realized with certainty that his correction was far more noticeable than the error had been. Nothing else for it, he decided. Better for her to think he was conscientious than perfect.

The Lake Forest station platform was deserted at that hour of the morning, as Nix stepped off the train and looked around for the bus stop. By some sleight of hand Nix had brought the wrong shoebox home from the Payless and hadn't realized his mistake until he was getting dressed that morning. He'd tried on a size nine brogue, which was too small. The tens fit, and he'd meant to buy them but must have grabbed the wrong box and had come home with the nines. Flora—who didn't like the idea of buying twelve-dollar shoes to go with a thousand-dollar Italian suit (a relic of his one-and-only book tour) in the first place—was not sympathetic. "What are you going to do?" she asked, as she watched him pry loose the index finger he'd gotten wedged between his Achilles tendon and the heel of the shoe.

"What can I do?"

"Wear your sneakers. It's not a job interview exactly."

"What is it if it's not a job interview?"

"An audition. How many actors wear suits to auditions?"

"Just the ones who think it might help their chances," Nix had said, not realizing until he took a step just how constricted his toes were. He was only able to walk by bending his knees and taking short, flat-footed steps, like one of the flamingo-legged, acid-mused figures of his father's comics. The pain from the scraping of skin and the twisting of toes was excruciating, making the heat seem worse. After a block, he took off his jacket and draped it over his arm.

The bus stop was marked by a sign on a corner lot, a trapezoidal skirt of lawn, fronting a ranch-style hacienda. He leaned against the signpost and checked his watch every fifteen or thirty seconds as if to signal to the owner peering out her picture window that he was waiting for the bus and not casing the house. The bus, when at last it came, was empty except for the driver and two round-faced, middle-aged women who sat with their enormous purses on their laps. Nix took a seat by the back door and looked out the window as the bus hurdled through surprisingly shabby suburban neighbor-hoods, the driver rarely bothering to tap the brakes at each stop, as he knew there would be no one waiting to get on, no kids on their way to the library or swimming lessons, no commuters on their way to the train, despite the fact the route was clearly intended to carry residents to the station, rather than housekeepers and day laborers. This wasn't mass transportation, this was transportation as a last resort.

Nix slid his shoes off his feet and peeled back his socks from blis-ters on each heel and on the big and smallest toes of each foot. Real-izing he couldn't treat these wounds without a first-aid kit, Nix tried to put his shoes back on, only to find that his feet had swelled. After several painful attempts he was able to get them back on by remov-ing the laces, sliding the shoe on, then re-lacing the lower sets of holes, and tying a square knot with the remaining ends that weren't long enough for a bow. When he looked up again, he saw that the bus had left the neighborhood of modest homes and modest yards for one in which houses fell more accurately into the category of estates and lawns that ran for acres before running up upon anything more solid than a lawn jockey.

Upon debarking, Nix limped along, as though looking for water on the surface of the moon, wondering how far he could walk like this, through this neighborhood, before somebody called the police. At last he reached a broad expanse of brick wall, bearing—embossed in an antique-looking tin—the street numbers Nix had written on his paper. Nix found an open door within a larger wrought iron gate and stepped through to find a two-story house, fabricated of the same red brick as was the wall, with white shutters on each of the four windows that gave the house a welcoming, anthropomorphic regard.

Nix put his jacket on, tightened his tie, and pushed his pants an inch lower on his waist so the cuffs covered his shoelaces, whispered an oath of admiration to the woman's lack of pretension, to live in so modest a house, and tapped the brass knocker. Hearing no reply, he knocked again. This time he heard a child crying and a woman's voice call out something that sounded like, "In it?" The door opened and the possessors of both voices stood before him—a woman of perhaps forty, auburn hair creased by a gray part, with a cigarette threatening to drop from her lips onto the head of the black-eyed girl who was clutching her leg.

Nix couldn't remember if he ever knew what Zira Fontaine looked like but felt sure this wasn't her. Just the same he asked, "Mrs. Fontaine?" in a neutral way that could have been either a direct address or a question about the woman's whereabouts. The baby stared with such intensity that it was the pacifier and not the woman's cigarette that fell to the floor. The woman picked it up with a hard sigh, plugged it back it the child's mouth, and said, "'Round back."

"Pardon me?" Nix said.

"This is the coach house. The residence is around back."

"That's funny," Nix said. "I bet a lot of people make that mistake."

She looked him up and down, the pinched shoes, the crescent of sweat spreading from his collar, and said, "You're the first."

The driveway ran between two stands of pine. As Nix passed the first, an astonishing landscape was revealed, a hill, sloping into a small vale and, in that vale, a grand manse. Nix knew little of architecture. This was not Gothic nor Victorian nor Edwardian, more exactly it was Wagnerian, an earthbound Valhalla, with a center parapet and wings stretching unapologetically in both directions. The drive ended in a traffic circle surrounding a circular patch of grass, a round hedge, and in the center, a prancing nymph, too preoccupied with the execution of her plié to notice that her shift was riding up on her thigh or that water gushed from the pitcher she held before her in an outstretched hand.

Nix didn't hear the bell ring inside. He stood before a door the size of that on St. Patrick's Cathedral, wondering if he should push the button above the No Solicitors sign again, but the door then opened, apparently by itself, as they do in horror movies. As Nix stepped toward it the face of a man Nix's age, blond and recently barbered, appeared from behind it.

"Mr. Walters?" he said.

"Yes," Nix said, vaguely aware that he had bowed.

"Larsen Anders," the man said. "Glad that you could come." Nix stepped onto the stone floor of the foyer. There were rooms to his right and left, and in front of him a broad stairway of dark wood that split halfway up with flights running in either direction. "You're four minutes early."

"Am I?"

"This way, please," Anders said, and showed him to a door adjacent to the grand stairway that led to a narrow hallway down which they walked. His footfalls on marble floor echoed, the irreducible sound of wealth. They passed paintings in expensive frames, chairs, and side tables of past eras Nix also didn't know the names for, several open doors to what looked like work or storage rooms, and an institutional kitchen. Nix was careful to walk a step behind Anders to conceal his worsening limp. "It's good you are on time."

"I took an early train," Nix said.

"You took a train?" Anders said, glancing at Nix over his shoulder.

"And a bus," Nix said.

"How resourceful." As they neared the end of the hallway, a much larger door on the right revealed an enormous high ceilinged room with gold and white striped wallpaper and chairs placed in ordered rows along the wall.

Nix laughed. "And here's where Colonel Mustard killed Professor Plum with the lead pipe."

"You are a comedian," Anders said and nothing more. The door at the end of the hall opened on yet another much shorter hallway, at the end of which waited a glass door, whose beveled panes functioned like a kaleidoscope of brilliant greens, so stark and pervasive that he felt as though he were enveloped in the color. Anders opened the door onto a greenhouse, dazzlingly lit by the sun on glass, warm and wet and lush with plants and flowers of all genera, scents, and hues. The woman as well wore a dress of solid green, vivid as the surrounding leaves. Her hair was white, precisely parted and styled in a flip, circa 1963. She sat completely still at a small, wrought-iron table, as though posing for a portrait. This impressed Nix, who could not have sat that still if he were dead. He noticed the table was set for two and beside it a rolling metal teacart. Anders closed the door quietly and Nix, combating an urge to tiptoe, followed him.

"Your appointment," Anders said.

The woman smiled as she turned her head, her gray eyes, young, quick, it seemed to Nix, despite their color and the age of their owner, settling on him square. "Sit down, Mr. Walters," she said.

Nix held out his hand for her to shake, which she ignored, and he was only able to save himself some embarrassment by using the hand to hold his tie flat as he eased into his chair.

"Any trouble finding us?"

"None at all, thank you."

Nix took his résumé from his portfolio case and handed it to her with one finger over his correction. Mrs. Fontaine held up a hand to stop him.

"Not necessary," she said. "I called Dr. Trout. He offered an unalloyed endorsement of your qualifications as a teacher, which of course I have no use for. And he characterized your writing abilities as able."

"Able?"

Mrs. Fontaine started at the question, but appeared to consider her reply thoroughly. "That is what he said."

"Did he mention my book?" Nix asked. Behind him, something between a cough and a laugh burst from Anders's lips.

"Anders was kind enough to read your novel for me last night," she said. "The skills necessary to the writing of a work of fiction are rather different from those of writing a work of fact, are they not?"

"Somewhat."

"Then I am satisfied to rely upon Dr. Trout's recommendation— unless you can think of some reason why I should not do so."

"None at all," Nix said.

"Tea?"

"Why not?" Nix said because he could think of no reason why not, but then she looked at him severely and he added, "Please. Why not, *please.*"

She went still again as Anders poured the tea, and she waited until he had taken a seat in a corner of the room amid the orchids to speak. "My family fled to this country to escape a gypsy's curse," she said.

Nix nodded. After a pause of a few seconds Mrs. Fontaine said, "Write that down," with such urgency that he was startled into dropping his spoon.

"I didn't expect to start today," Nix said. "I use a tape recorder. It's hard for me to write fast enough."

She let him finish, smoothed her dress with the palms of her hands, and said, "The purpose of this arrangement is for me to organize the details of my life in such a way as will make a book. The salient fact in that sentence is that these are the details of my life and therefore it will be necessary for you to write down what I tell you to write down."

Nix felt the urge to argue, but wasn't sure of the grounds: he had no theory or approach to the writing of biography, much less the transcription of autobiography. "Okay."

"The fee we're offering is twenty-five thousand dollars flat. Half now, half when the manuscript has been delivered to me. All rights to the book will be mine, including subsidiary paperback and film rights." Nix made a noise here that he later imagined sounded like a man swallowing his tongue. She raised a hand unadorned by jewelry. "Before you interrupt me to negotiate, I should tell you that it is the practice of my company to pay people more than they are worth. This practice was established by me. Therefore, holding out for more money will serve no purpose on your part. You were not the first I have interviewed for this position."

"Maybe that should tell you something," Nix said. He meant it rhetorically, but she looked at him puzzled and clearly annoyed. "The why that you are having trouble finding somebody."

"In each case, it has been that the applicant has had an unrealistic understanding of his role in the project."

It was that last that did it. Nix may have been broke but he was no one's scribe. "Then I'm probably not the person you want, either."

She looked at Anders for a moment as though she were expecting him to translate. Anders shrugged, and she said, "I don't understand."

"I mean I think you can see this, too."

"I have chosen you," she said, as though that settled the matter.

"I appreciate that," he said, "but, as I said, I'm not your man. I can't even be certain from what you've said who your man—or woman—would be."

"As a habit, I don't work with women."

"Well, man, then—or not. I'm not sure you need a person at all. You seem to have an idea of want you want to say."

She looked over her shoulder at Anders. "My schedule wouldn't permit the necessary investment of time ..."

"How much?" Nix said.

"Twenty-five thousand dollars," Anders said.

"He is not interested," Mrs. Fontaine said.

"Thank you," Nix said, though he was less certain than he'd been a few seconds earlier.

"Larson," Mrs. Fontaine said, "will you make sure Hector isn't blocking Mr. Walter's car?"

"He took the bus," Anders said.

This caught Mrs. Fontaine's attention. "There's a bus?" she asked.

Nix's soles clicked on the marble floors as he hurried to the door ahead of Anders, who yelled, "Thank you for coming."

"Blow me," Nix said, over his shoulder.

Nix strode up the driveway with a determined finality, or so he hoped. Having never endeavored to stride before, he couldn't be sure he got it right, and his feet were killing him. Once he was out of sight of the of the manor and the coach house, Nix sat on the curb and pulled off his shoes. The blisters had broken and skin hung in loose flaps. He torn off ragged skin from both heels with no small amount of agony and decided to walk the remaining block and a half to the bus barefoot, the feel of the warm asphalt on the soles of his feet a comfort, even as he became aware of curtains being drawn back as he passed each house on the street. At the stop, Nix reached in his hip pocket for a wallet but didn't find it, nor was the wallet in pocket on the other side. A frenzy of turned out pockets followed, as he patted himself down, realizing with relative certainty at some point early in the search that his wallet must have fallen out of his pocket when he'd taken his jacket off.

The bus stopped. Before trying to board, Nix told the driver he had no money and then watched the taillights grow dim with distance. "At least it can't get worse than this," he thought to himself, as the rain began to fall.

In fact, it poured. As sheets of water bore down on him, Nix hoisted the shoulders of his now ruined jacket over his head and hobbled eastward toward the tracks. The housekeepers and nannies on the platform, glanced at the sodden, barefooted Nix but didn't stare, likely being accustomed in their jobs to overlooking all manner of excess and behavior from their employers. When the train came, Nix mingled among them, matching their steps as they boarded.

As the rain etched trails in the windows, made opaque by the breath of a dozen passengers, Nix stared at the near-nothing visible to him and grew certain that there was something Greek in this humiliation, leaving him to wonder which gods he had offended and how, his intentions being, generally, benign and his actions being, far more often than not, determined by the actions of others. Indeed, even the vocation of writing, he believed, had chosen him on a beach that fronted a Long Island beach house owned by the uncle of one of his roommates, where he met and fell for April March, the daughter of an airline executive. They'd shared a summer of weather and white wine, of sleeping on the beach and sailing on the sound, of gliding from one lawn party to the next, and, one Friday night in late July, to *The Rocky Horror Picture Show*, to which April went dressed—despite her height and honey-hued hair—as Magenta.

In August, she dumped him. She returned to Smith, which was how she had known all summer it would end between them and which she assumed young Walter had known, too. He had not. Walter had languished for a week after April left, drinking gin in his underwear. Then over the Labor Day weekend, while his fraternity brothers sat on the porch, draining a steel keg of Michelob one plastic cup at a time, Walter Nixon wrote a novel. On a Smith-Corona borrowed from Brother NoDoz, he banged out a remarkable two hundred and fifty pages in thirty-five hours of continuous typing.

The plot concerned Howard Wilkie, the son of a deceased underground cartoonist, who falls in love with daughter of a printing tycoon. She loves him back but leaves him because her father has threatened to write her out of his will if she doesn't.

Despondent, Howard makes a Faustian deal with a Hollywood animation studio, selling the rights to his father's artwork for millions. Learning that he has made himself rich, the girl returns and they live a dissolute, tabloid life until our hero, disgusted by what he has become, plants a false rumor in the press that his father had been an FBI informant. Its franchise destroyed, the studio sues, wins. Howard ends up penniless, though drunk with integrity.

Walter titled the novel *Life During Wartime,* after a song by the Talking Heads—having no idea of the connection but liking the title better than any he could come up with—and sent the manuscript to April, hoping she would read it and regret her decision to leave him (this being the reason he wrote it in the first place). She did read the book (mostly) and—out of guilt as much as anything else—sent the manuscript to a book agent named Leonard Spitz, a cousin of her roommate, and the rest, as they say, was publishing.

A young, black conductor brought Nix back to the present with a gentle rap of his punch on the metal seat rail.

"Look," Nix told him, "I lost my wallet. I've got no money. I'm sorry I should have asked you before I got on the train, but I did that at the bus and she wouldn't let me on so I thought if I got on the train I could explain to you I mean look I'm soaked I had to walk two miles in the rain so if you have some kind of thing where I can sign a piece of paper I'll do it."

The man looked upon him with a measure of amusement and curiosity. "It's all right, sir," he said, appearing to wonder how anyone could think he would collect money from a passenger in such a state, "get you next time," and walked on down the aisle, leaving Nix shivering in the air-conditioned car, rainwater pooling on the Naugahyde seat.

4.

He'd changed. That was the first thing she noticed. As Flora watched him push open the battered door of Urbis Orbus, she saw he'd changed back into the jeans and the blue work T-shirt from J.C. Penney he wore every day of summer like some kind of a uniform. This made her sad because she liked him in a suit. When she met him she knew that he had worn suits once, and she hoped selfishly he would again. She had faith in him, more faith than he had in himself. He was smart but, she worried, easily put off, too eager to settle. All of which was not to say that Flora was interested in money. That had never been her thing. After all, when she'd first met him she was operating—at the top of a broom handle—one of eight papier maché hands on an enormous octopus with an Uncle Sam head, constructed for a demonstration to welcome a global economic summit to town. He'd come down to the march with Nestor, who was Veronika's boyfriend—it being Veronika, also Flora's best friend, who manipulated the system of clothesline and pulleys that clenched and unclenched Uncle Sam's gaping jaw. Nix had walked beside Flora for blocks before he turned with a warm, curious smile, and asked, "Who are we mad at again?" So, no, it wasn't the money she wanted, though the poorer they got, the less sure she was of that. What she wanted was for him to matter, to others, if not to himself. He had once, or nearly, and she wanted that for him again, or for the first time.

She pulled the chair out and sat sideways so as not to wrinkle her skirt. "How did it go with your lady?"

"You were right it was a waste of time."

"Did I say that?"

"You thought it," he said, as Angie, their usual waitress—having designated herself their usual waitress because she had a crush on Flora—leaned over the table, showing as much cleavage as gravity, flexed biceps, and wonder bra could conjure.

"What'll it be?" she asked Flora, her elbow inches from Nix's nose.

"Coffee," Flora said.

"Excellent choice," Nix said.

Angie wrote the order on her pad, flashed Nix a murderous glance, and walked to the counter.

Nix let Flora talk because he was feeling as though he had made a big mistake. She talked about her job, which didn't make him feel any smarter, but he was used to hearing her talk about her job. And so he listened, remembering the brief moment that afternoon when he felt like a hero. When she'd finished her coffee, Nix said, "Let's celebrate."

"What?"

"I'll tell you when we get to a restaurant."

"Fine. I'm starved."

"Let's use your card. I'm cleaned out," Nix said.

"What happened to the twenty I gave you?"

"You what?" Flora said so loudly a man at the next table dropped a shrimp dumpling into his tea.

"I didn't do anything."

"Back up. They what?"

"They what what?"

"They offered you $12,000."

"Not exactly."

"What exactly?"

"They showed me a check for $12,000 as a down payment. They offered me $25,000."

"What?" she said again, this time loud enough to summon Mrs. Nguyen.

"Your order is coming," she said.

"No hurry," Nix said.

"We're sorry about your window," Flora said. On this night the intimate ambience of the Perfume River restaurant was attenuated by the plywood boarding that covered a shattered plate glass window. It was elegance, rare in this neighborhood, that made the restaurant a target for local anti-gentrification guerrillas.

Mrs. Nguyen smiled and bowed. "It's not nice," she said. Madame N. had come from Saigon when it became Ho Chi Minh

City and, as such, was used to fixing things after Americans broke them and would have to again.

Flora ordered the pho. Flora always ordered the pho. Nix generally ordered off the specials card, with a sense of superiority, though, when it came to international cuisine, Flora was the more adventurous of the two of them. Mrs. Nguyen brought two bottles of Vietnamese beer. Mrs. Nguyen liked Nix and Flora because they were regulars and because they didn't seem like the kind of people who would break her windows or spray-paint *No Yuppies* on the bright red enamel of her front door.

Flora fixed a measuring glare on Nix and asked, "Why did you say no?"

"I thought you wanted me to say no."

"That was before I knew how much they were offering."

"You're saying I should take the job for the money?"

"You're saying you shouldn't?"

"I *did* tell them I wouldn't."

"Can you call her back?"

"And say what?"

"You'll do it."

"I doubt there's still an opening."

"How do you know? You said they were having a hard time finding someone."

The Perfume River's central air-conditioning system sent a chill through Nix as he realized that Flora was not going to back down, while he could imagine nothing more humiliating than calling to ask for a job he'd already turned down. "I may have burned a bridge there."

"What did you say?"

Nix was spared for a moment from reliving the Fontaine incident by Mrs. Nguyen's return to the table with their check. Nix left a thirty percent tip, wishing he could say something sharp like "Buy yourself a new window, sweetheart," but couldn't think of anything that didn't sound patronizing, and they walked out into a warm early-summer evening.

They walked without speaking. Nix knew she was waiting for him to answer her question, something he had no intention of doing unless she asked again.

"I'm glad I wore a T-shirt," he said.

"I wish I had a jacket," Flora said.

They were the Jack and Mrs. Sprat of temperature.

As they neared their building, Flora said, "What's that car doing on this block?"

In the dark, Nix didn't recognize the sedan he'd earlier seen in the circular drive of the Fontaine estate until the rear window went down to reveal Mrs. Fontaine and Larsen Anders. "Hello, Mr. Walters," she said. Not cheerful exactly but with the urgent cordiality of someone asking directions of a pedestrian before the traffic light changed.

"Hello," Nix said, too confused to sound surprised.

"Is this your wife?"

"Yes—Flora, this is Mrs. Fontaine and—I'm sorry, I forget your name."

"Larsen," said Anders, with air of suspicion, perhaps thinking, correctly, that Nix was only pretending to have forgotten his name.

"Nice to meet you," Flora said, sounding for all her socialist proclivities, as though she meant it. "Are you coming up?"

"Pardon me? Oh, we haven't the time," Mrs. Fontaine said. I've come by to apologize for how we left things this afternoon and to present you with a counter offer. Mr. Walters, will you come over here please?" Nix did as he was asked. "Larsen," she said, "will you give him the sheet?"

Anders handed Nix a folded piece of letterhead. Nix unfolded the paper and turned it toward the streetlight to read the sum written out in hand in the center of the page, accompanied by no other writing: $40,000.00.

"Would that be acceptable?"

The hand holding the paper began to shake. "One moment."

"Of course."

Nix went to Flora, who for some reason had chosen to remain on the sidewalk several paces away. "This is what they want to give me," he whispered.

She looked and did an admirable job, Nix thought, of suppressing a gasp.

"What are her terms?"

"Terms? How should I know? I mean forty grand, aren't those her terms? Do you I think I should ask for more in writing."

"I think," Flora said, somehow looking at him and the car at the same time, "that you should tell her you'll take it."

"That," Nix said, "was what I was going to tell them." He walked turned to the car and said, "You'll make a new contract?"

"There will be one waiting in the morning. In the meantime can you sign that piece of paper indicating that we've agreed in principle to that amount?"

Nix looked at Flora. She shrugged. He asked her, "Do you have a pen?"

"Not on me" Flora said.

"I don't have a pen," he said.

"Larsen does," Mrs. Fontaine said.

Nix pressed the paper against his knee and signed. He handed the paper to Mrs. Fontaine who passed it to Anders without first reading it. "You can be at my home at 10:00 tomorrow morning?" she asked—or stated, Nix wasn't sure which.

"I can," he said.

"Splendid. Hector," she said and the car drove off and sped nearly to the stop sign at the end of the block before it screeched to a stop and came toward them again in reverse at nearly the same speed.

Again the window came down. "May we have Larson's pen back?" she said.

"Excuse me?" Nix said.

Anders leaned across Mrs. Fontaine. "My pen," he said.

Nix put his hand on his T-shirt pocket and realized he had, in fact, taken Anders's pen. "Oops," he said.

"Yes, oops," Anders said, snatching the pen away from Nix, placing it in his shirt pocket and patting it for good measure. Again they were gone. Nix turned and saw Flora, watching the car disappear down the street as though she expected it to do something more remarkable than drive away.

"Happy?" he said.

"I'll live," she said.

By the time Nix was out of the bathroom Flora was asleep or, at least, in bed with her eyes closed. He had hoped that the prospect of conversation on the subject of himself and all that had happened that day would've been enough to keep her up. Lately, Nix suspected that she had begun to pretend she was asleep when he came to bed, but he couldn't be sure and had never tried to prove it. Their initial liberation from the forethought of birth control had sparked a spree of spontaneous sex, with physiologically impressive frequency, in rooms other than the bedroom, and once in a stairwell at Non-Profit Parenting. In the weeks since, frequent sex had become infrequent sex, which had become talk about having sex, usually Flora saying "We'll have to have sex tonight." Though this was in reality a pretext to not, as if she was saying, "Look we both know that we haven't done it in a long time, and neither of us is exactly sure why that is, but as long as we act as though we want do it, we don't have to confront the reasons why we're not doing it."

Nix sat on the couch, listening to the sounds of the street. (The rapid pulse of impending bloodshed that had been present the night before was gone, carried off by the ambulance and the squad cars and a cold front.) He paged through a back issue of *O-Gauge Railroader* that he'd snatched up at a corner newsstand, just as his bus was arriving.

Nix had never owned a model railroad, though he'd grown up in the same house as an elaborate set-up that, over a period of years, his father had constructed—miniature by miniature—and had forbidden him to touch. By the time he reached the age of eight and was thus chronologically sanctioned by the Lionel Train Co. to operate their HO-scale systems, Floog had added a complex switching mechanism that the young Nix hadn't known how to use, and it was thus that the control of his father's railroad console had receded from his fingertips until he was in his teens and no longer interested.

The set had occupied an entire gabled second-story room of the rose-colored Victorian they rented in Rogers Park. Floog, Nix's father, constructed a Grovers Corners of balsa and glue, through which an eight-wheeled steam locomotive pulled six cars and a caboose in an unending loop, up to the chicken wire replica of the Green Mountains, through a tunnel, and on into town, snagging the miniature plastic mailbag on its way past the station, as the toy fireman on the locomotive shoveled plastic coal into the firebox.

This month's feature article concerned the rusting of boxcar hinges. (No small feat given that each hinge in O gauge was smaller than a nit.) His attention drifted from the text to the magazine's cover, which featured a color photo of the *Injun Joe* diesel engine drawing the gleaming cars of the old *Mark Twain Zephyr* past the moss-covered ruin of a plantation with classical columns. Compared with the tranquil Yankee idylls of his father's set-up (a landscape his father had never known), this was a revelation, a scene straight out of *Light in August*. The energy of this revelation inspired Nix to imagine miniature landscapes themed not just to Faulkner, but to all the great works of American literature: a Long Island Railroad commuter steams past a yellow Cadillac and the HO-scale corpse of a woman, all beneath the eyes of an ophthalmologist's billboard; beneath a trestle over an upstate lake, a tiny pair of white legs kick white foam beside a man in a rowboat; or the freight cars in a verdant California valley drip water and lettuce leaves.

Or, thought Nix, why not scenes from his own life: the Amtrak Chicago to Houston line past a one-room shack in a Kudzu-choked hollow of a fecund Arkansas town, to which Nix had traveled at the end of his short, unhappy life as a celebrity author, after he had decided (not entirely incorrectly) that the failures of his career had all been because he wasn't a very good writer.

Never having been south of Joliet, he had expected living in the South to be something like joining the Peace Corps—his early impression of the fabled region having been drawn from his father's

Weevil and Stroon comics (vol. 4, no. 3), in which Weevil inherits a plantation from his great grand-uncle Colonel Beauregard Weevil along with—as the conventions of the genre dictated—forty acres of hemp. While harvesting—and sampling—their windfall, Weevil and Stroon fall in the mud and come up black-faced, just as the fat county sheriff is driving by. All seems bleak for the hemp-headed Duo, until the white-hooded lynch mob is overcome by fumes, when the ole boys burn the crop. In the last panel, Weevil, Stroon, and their would-be executioners scarf potato chips and spin Canned Heat LPs, while serpentine plumes of smoke and musical notes the size of buzzards rise into the Dixie sky.

In reality, Nix loved the South. He loved biscuits and gravy purchased at a lunch counter for seventy-five cents. He loved the ice tea that flowed perpetually, as if from a struck rock, into glasses the size of wastebaskets. He loved the smell of magnolia and hot road tar. Stillwell College was a liberal arts school nestled in the Ozark Mountains that traded on its isolation as an opportunity for the young writer to hone his craft far from the reach of the urban critic. By the time the semester began, Nix had furnished a modest pied-à-terre with discarded furniture, had gotten to know the town on foot, and had grown to appreciate—after his first unnerving experience with the custom—the way strangers greeted him on the street. He arrived for the first day of orientation not having accounted for the possibility that a room full of aspiring writers in their twenties and thirties might remember Nix's debut effort better than an indifferent civilian population. Even as he struggled not to doze during the department chair's introductory address, he was aware of whispers and of elbows being tugged, of stares and nods.

In the months that followed the other candidates circled him warily. None of them was rude to his face, though it was several weeks into the term before he learned that his colleagues met nearly every night at a bar in town.

For his students, Nix played the distracted bookworm, sporting cardigans, suggesting corny puns as mnemonic devices for grammatical principles, correctly deploying the subjunctive mood. As salve for his sense of isolation and loneliness, he took enthusiastically to the grammar study course required of new English instructors.

While the Others chafed at the superannuated nomenclature and the rigor, Nix found what he'd been looking for: neutrality. While the Others spent their nights in town and their days in their classrooms, exercising their egos at full gallop, Nix studied rules for determining pronoun case in phrases and clauses.

The Others wrote small, earnest stories about precocious, feral boys who lived in trailer parks or about sage, scraped-kneed little girls who lived among secretive and elderly relatives. Eager to blend, Nix wrote "The Bauble," a story about a young man who sleeps with a girl whom he despises for loving him and, on his way out the door as she lay sleeping, steals a glass heart from her dresser. He based the story on an incident from his life—in the months following his abrupt fall—in which he stole, for no reason he could ever explain to himself or anyone else, a glass globe from a fan of his book with whom he'd slept but didn't like. Although in the story the tchotchke in questions turn out to be a relic passed down from the girl's great-great-grandfather, a deposed central-European duke and worth many thousands of dollars, and the main character is sentenced to a decade behind bars. Nix saw the story as a morality play of covetousness and regret. The Others chose to read it as a red flag waved limp-wristedly by a fey Yankee matador.

Clarence Pettijean, the workshop leader—whose sharecropping saga *Solomon's Acre* was as admired by the students of the program (for whom it was literally required reading) as it had been ignored by the New York publishing establishment—presided over a verbal reenactment in miniature of the libracide Nix had suffered at the hands of the national literary press. Pettijean (whom Nix liked and trusted) mitigated the assault only once, interrupting one particularly bloody goring at the horns of Nix's peers just long enough to suggest to the class that they "best remember that Mr. Walters may be unaccustomed to sincerity."

Nix, suffering by then the literary equivalent of the Stockholm Syndrome, was eager to believe him, but came to feel that the Others were slaves to an internal emotional realism, writing fictions solely grounded in their own stubbornly narrow experiences, shackled by the persistence of fact. As it was with Madame Loisel of "The Necklace," it is hard to know what might have become of Nix had he never hung on the stocks of critical pillory. What callow plots might have sprung from his pen? This was a question Nix would never have to answer. If he didn't feel he'd paid a dearer price than the vapid solipsism of his youth had warranted, it was only out of fear that to suggest such a thing would be to invite an even sterner karmic retribution.

He dropped the magazine on his desk and looked out the window at the spotlit circle of street where a body had lain the night before. He would—he resolved with a triumphant finality that made him smile—write Mrs. Fontaine's life story for her, if that's what she wanted, and take her money for the trouble of doing it. Having decided upon this destiny, he crawled into bed beside an authentically snoring Flora and stared toward the ceiling in the dark, picturing his father sprawled on the floor, his aquatic girth seeping toward the mug of Ovaltine and Scotch that was always present whenever he drove his train, his thick fingers fondling the potentiometers that impelled the locomotive through landscapes of chicken wire and flock.

5.

The next morning Nix was up before Flora, rooting though his desk drawer for a miniature tape recorder. He'd bought the device at Radio Shack after the editors of *Spy* magazine approached him about doing a series of interviews of the Famous for Being Famous, but they'd abandoned the idea once they decided that Nix was no longer seen by anyone as being famous for anything, much less nothing, and he'd forgotten all about the recorder. He found it eventually and was further relieved to see there was a tape in the bay. Once he replaced the dead batteries, he hit *play* to see if he'd taped anything worth saving and heard only himself counting and his voice saying "I think it—" then static.

When Flora got up, he said little to her because the new Nix who wrote for commission was stoic, a cipher, and besides he was pissed at her for falling asleep when there was so much about him that remained to be discussed. Reaching the door at the bottom of the stairway, he saw Juan standing on the far sidewalk, staring at something on the street. Juan's mother left early for work, so Juan was out on his corner a good three hours before his competition and therefore able to catch the drive-up traffic from workers off the overnight shift. Nix couldn't tell what Juan was looking at until he reached the porch and saw Mrs. Fontaine's black sedan and her driver standing beside an open rear door. "Morning, sir."

"Morning?"

"Hector."

"Hector," Nix repeated and raised a fist of solidarity to Juan who whistled from across the street. Hector looked in Juan's direction and then at Nix in the rearview mirror with undisguised disapproval.

The back of the car was upholstered with a rich-smelling, wine-dark leather. "What are you doing here?" Nix asked.

"Mrs. Fontaine doesn't want you taking the train no more."

"That's nice of her. How long have you been waiting?"

"What's that, chief?"

"How long have you been here?"

Hector shrugged. "An hour."

"Gee, I'm sorry," Nix said. "You have to do a lot of that? Huh? Waiting for people to come out of places?"

"There's a newspaper," Hector said.

Nix had never imagined there was an art to chauffeuring until he observed Hector's driving. He was never in the wrong lane, never pushed a yellow light. On the expressway he drove ten miles over the speed limit but didn't change lanes often. Nix found himself enjoying the ride, as though it were a reward in itself. Hector barreled down the Fontaine driveway and brought the car to a stop expertly in front of the mansion's door without squealing the brakes.

"Thanks for the ride," Nix said as Hector opened the car door. Hector didn't reply. Instead, he opened the front door, ignoring Nix again when he thanked him a second time. Anders met him in the foyer and led him through the house to the conservatory where Mrs. Fontaine sat at the same table as the day before, wearing a summery dress, as she had the day before, this time in yellow. She asked him to sit, as she had the day before, without standing or offering her hand to shake, and asked if he wanted tea. He accepted, as he had the day before, placed the tape recorder on the table and opened his notebook to a blank page.

Anders poured the tea and left them. There was a silence as Nix waited for her to speak and when she didn't, he said, "It's good."

"Yes, it is," she said.

"I'll record our conversations with your permission," Nix said, "and make notes reminding me of certain phrases or points that I'll want to highlight—"

Mrs. Fontaine raised a hand. "I'm going to stop you. It will not be necessary for you to tell me what you are doing or about any difficulties you are having in doing it. What I'll expect to see is the completed manuscript. If I have questions about your process or procedures, I'll ask them. Otherwise you need not presume there is anything about what you are doing that I am curious. Are you ready to begin? Yes? As I said yesterday, my father came to this country to escape a gypsy curse. He had been an officer in the Hungarian army. This was after the war, the first war. Hungary was no longer a great

European power, but my father was successful at a young age and handsome. He was engaged to my mother. It was during a visit to her estate that a great aunt, rumored to be a gypsy soothsayer, took a dislike to my father, thinking him to be too certain of his own good fortune and told him, 'Your first heir will die young.'" Mrs. Fontaine stopped and raised an eyebrow to signal the solemnity of the event. "The premonition didn't worry my mother, who knew what an eccentric her aunt was, but according to the family story, my father saw something in her eye that made him believe she was telling the truth and was so frightened that when my mother became pregnant, he insisted they leave the country."

Nix listened impatiently. Her stilted manner of speech made him wonder if she had rehearsed this opening or at the very least was speaking in a diction she believed to be appropriate for a biography but was, in actuality, annoyingly stiff. But she had warned him and so rather than interject, he nodded and—to quell his anxiety— wrote random words that she spoke on the page—*pregnant, truth, as*—not so much to look as though he were paying attention as to keep himself from crawling out of his skin.

"They sailed for America in 1927."

"There was a son?"

Mrs. Fontaine stared at him, unsure of how to take this interruption. "Yes there was a son, my brother, Victor. He lives in Phoenix. The specific details of my family's journey to America have never been related to me in any detail. If it is helpful I can have them researched."

Nix, not certain what to say about this, shrugged. "My father," she continued, "had two cousins in America, Stan and Mike living in Ohio, Lorain, where there was a sizable Hungarian community, and that is where my mother and he went."

"Lorain?"

"Near Cleveland on Lake Erie. Steel was the primary industry."

"And your cousins? They were steel workers?"

"They worked on the periphery of the steel industry."

"The periphery?"

"My uncles maintained what you might call a community presence. They were involved seasonally in construction, importing, and they ran a private lottery through the Polish-American Alliance."

"Why Polish?"

"There was no equivalent organization for the Hungarian community. Mr. Walters, I did not intend for these sessions to be interviews, in the usual sense. Why don't you let me say what I have to say, and if you have any questions, you may present them in writing when you are preparing the manuscript?"

"I might have questions of clarification not fact."

"Ask them at the end of the session."

"That may be awkward."

"It will be your job to see that it isn't, no? Where were we?"

"Your uncles were running numbers."

Mrs. Fontaine's eyes narrowed. "I beg your pardon?"

"It was a numbers racket, yes?"

She lifted her tea to her lips and regarded him over the rim of the cup. "As I said, my uncles were well known in their community. My father took a position with U.S. Steel. He had brought with him a significant wealth but was determined to earn a salary. He said that in America even the well-to-do work for a living. As a result of his refinement and education he learned to speak English quickly and was moved to the business office, where he became responsible for negotiating contracts with the iron mines in Minnesota and the shipping firms that transported iron ore along the Great Lakes. This was before I was born."

"You were the oldest?"

"I was the eldest, yes. Born June 11, 1931 at 9:37 a.m. at St. Joseph's Hospital, Cleveland, Ohio, the first of my family to have been born in a hospital. The doctor spanked me on the rear end, and I did not cry. Mother always insisted on this fact. I believe it to be an aspect of family mythology. What would it mean for a girl," she added, though Nix noticed that she watched to make certain he wrote a note in his book.

"I grew up in a white house on Euclid Avenue with a broad back lawn with an oak in the center with a swing and maples edging the property. My parents soon were happy in America, or Father was. Mother came around. I never heard her speak of Hungary, but that she missed her country was something of which I was sure.

My father collected cigarette lighters and other small objects made of steel or brass—things that felt heavy and cold in his hands. I'm aware it's popular these days for people of my generation to mine their childhoods for explanations for their adult failure, but I have nothing that I can conceivably complain of, not anyway before the age of six.

"What happened then?"

"Victor."

"Your brother?"

"Well, you see, six years no longer seems to be a great age difference. For me then, being in the first grade seemed like a very old age to be becoming a sibling. And then there was, of course—the curse."

A chill went through him when he heard those words, not merely for the portent but for the delivery. Nix choked. "Ye-*as*," he said, "the curse."

Again, Mrs. Fontaine regarded him sternly, apparently sensing the capacity of irony in his position and manner. "From the start there was never anything wrong with Victor. Mother knew it, but Father was petrified. He worried every day that something would happen to my brother. I wasn't allowed to touch him until long after he learned to walk. Father never permitted Mother to let him out of her sight. Only when Father went to work could she get a moment's peace. She would have Betty, our maid, sit with Victor as he slept, while Mother sat on the back porch.

"It was the only time she had to herself during the day. She never had to tell me not to bother her. Father insisted Victor be bathed in a room heated to ninety degrees and that he wear a hat, even in the middle of summer. He wasn't allowed to ride a tricycle, to use the swings, or to swim."

As she spoke, Nix looked down and saw through the glass tabletop that his left leg was bouncing furiously. Mrs. Fontaine didn't seem to notice, though Nix didn't see how she could fail to, except that the leg was vibrating so fast, it may have appeared as a blur to the casual eye. He managed to stop this involuntary movement only by pressing his foot to the ground, but as soon as he went back to taking notes the leg began bouncing again. For the next hour his attention alternated between his note taking, which was essentially a pretext to maintain concentration, and his recalcitrant leg.

He'd finally solved the problem temporarily by wrapping his foot at the ankle around the leg of the chair, when Mrs. Fontaine said, "Time for lunch."

The meal was served in the dining room. They sat at the end the long table he'd noticed the first time he and Anders passed it, made to seem even longer now by the fact that places were set at the head of the table and the chair on the side immediately adjacent. Turkey sandwiches and iced tea were brought in by a maid in uniform.

Nix dreaded sitting down alone with her for fear that he would have nothing to say. At the Nixon dinner table, conversation centered exclusively on the meal being eaten, accompanying facts about the ingredients, trivia about the nutritional value of common staples. ("Eat your oatmeal," his father would say. "It is a surprising source of iron." Or Nix's mother would say of the tomatoes in the salad, "I was all set to buy the Romas, but the bagger Henry told me the beefsteaks were three cents cheaper a pound and could be served in a salad, if sliced into narrow wedges.") In contrast, Mrs. Fontaine seemed unlikely to know any more about the price of tomatoes than about what brought the rain.

The sandwiches were arranged on the plate with a potato salad and orange slice garnish like a restaurant. Nix ate the first bite in silence and took a sip of the tea.

"You are going to tell me the tea is good," she said.

"I was. I don't often drink iced tea," Nix said, suddenly aware that he was sitting with his hands on his lap like a figure in a nursery rhyme engraving.

"You don't?" she asked. "What is it that you drink?"

"Water," Nix said, though this was in no way true, but water seemed a noble drink.

"Yes, well, I'm sure we have that," Mrs. Fontaine said, "if you'd like."

"Tea's fine," Nix said. "So you were saying that your father was protective of Victor..."

Mrs. Fontaine shook her head. "After lunch," she said.

They finished their lunches in silence—Nix pretending to admire the complicated woodwork while Mrs. Fontaine carved her sandwich

into pieces and lifted them to her lips on a napkin. When he'd finished, she said, "There's a kiwi pie."

"Couldn't eat another bite," Nix said, though he had never seen
kiwi pie, but the thought of prolonging the lunch even long enough
to try it was too agonizing to contemplate.

Back in the conservatory, Mrs. Fontaine returned to the story of
her life: "There was an epidemic and suddenly my father's worst
fears had a name."

"An epidemic?"

"Polio." She waited for him to write the word in his notebook
and, while he was at it, to change tapes. "Are you sure the machine
is working?"

"Yes, it's voice activated, which means—"

"Which means that it's started by the sound of a human voice,"
she said. Had he looked up, Nix would have noticed she was smiling. Had he even been just as perceptive as he generally was, Nix
could have gleaned from the comment about the water at lunch and
about the tape recorder that Mrs. Fontaine not only had a sense of
humor but was making an effort to make him feel more comfortable. Nix was, however, too nervous and too eager to be intimidated
to notice these overtures or, for that matter, to notice that, as Mrs.
Fontaine had suggested, the tape recorder was, in fact, not working
properly, which Nix would've learned if he had ever used it before.
The machine did possess a voice-activated feature, but it was defec-
tive, or more accurately relatively deaf to sounds in higher register
so that very little of what Mrs. Fontaine said was recorded, while it
did catch every one of Nix's questions.

"Suddenly Father was afraid for both of his children. We weren't
permitted to go to the fair, or the beach, or a public swimming pool—
anywhere people gathered. There were no birthday parties, no pic-
nics. When we came home from school each day my mother would
put us straight in the tub. It wasn't just my parents. Everyone's parents
were afraid. It's hard to recall this fear now—or maybe not so hard.

"In the middle of that fear, a funny thing happened. Victor started
slipping out and running loose in the neighborhood. This was when

he was five. It was a game for him. He would take any opportunity to escape, from the maids, from my mother when Father was at work. No matter where they looked or whom they enlisted to help in the search they never found him. He would return after dark, dirty and extremely happy with himself and often in the back of a police car. Of course, my parents were frantic but they were not about to punish him, at least not physically. They tried locking him in his room, but at an early age he was good with locks, and he was able to get himself out. Shortly thereafter he taught himself how to ride a bicycle—or learned, with the help of the neighborhood children—they all thought this was tremendous fun, this game we played with Victor—and then it was anyone's guess where he might go. Of course they feared more than anything he'd go to the lake.

"Father, at one point, even bought him a bicycle of his own on the condition that he only ride it on the block and only then with superstition ..."

"Do you mean *supervision?*"

"What did I say?"

"Superstition."

"That's funny. Yes, of course, *supervision*. In any case, that didn't work very well so they took the bicycle away, and Victor screamed so loud and for so long, they worried he would have a brain hemorrhage."

"But he didn't?"

"Of course not. Once, I remember"—she laughed—"when he was locked in his room under house arrest, he jumped from his window holding his bed sheet over his head as a parachute. He landed in Mother's rosebushes and was scratched all over."

"He didn't break anything?"

"No."

"And he never contracted polio?"

"No, not him," Mrs. Fontaine said. She had stopped laughing. "I did."

6.

At the end of his first year as chair, Felding Trout invited the members of the Carnelius adjunct faculty to join him for a beer—his reaction, it was presumed, to murmurings from the faculty (tenured and temporary alike) that he was aloof. The magnanimity of the gesture was diminished to some extent by the fact that he delegated the inviting to Steve and by the fact that Trout had once written a book titled *Against Beer*. Nonetheless all of the lecturers said, yes, they'd love to come, and they did—whether thinking that this was an opportunity to get in good with the boss or suspicious that this was a test of their loyalty or both. Trout arrived an hour past the appointed time, threw back a dram of cognac, and then passed before the ranks of faculty gathered along the bar rail, looking so much like a military officer addressing troops on parade that—when Nix's turn came—he half expected him to ask, "Where you from, private?"

Rather Trout had asked Nix his name, which Nix told him and then repeated at Trout's request. Trout asked him which class he had taught. "The American Short Story, sir," Nix said. Trout asked him, "Did you find the students satisfactory?"

"Satisfactory in what way, sir?" Nix asked and realized his mistake upon seeing the genial expression on the chairman's face change to one of impatience and, before Trout could reply, Nix added, "They were eager to read the stories, sir, and generally completed the assignments on time."

"I see," Trout had said, as Nix heard Nestor snort with suppressed laughter, and the chairman proceeded down the row with an operatic flourish of his cashmere overcoat.

In the semesters since then, attendance had diminished steadily, as Trout did not come again, despite the fact that Steve continued to extend the invitation on Trout's behalf. Each time there was an excuse as to why Trout didn't come, and generally the excuses were authentic, as Trout was as likely at any moment to be in London or Frankfurt or Washington DC or L.A. as in a Carnelius College classroom. While Nix and Nestor had been no less wise to the likely absence of consequences for noncompliance than any of their colleagues, indeed wiser than many, they had been the only two who attended every year, other than Steve, who was largely the reason that Nix and Nestor were there, having, out of familiarity or gender or closeness in age, become adjutants to Steve in his position as director of the Carnelius's undergraduate rhetoric, and feeling therefore obligated. Besides, on this particular Friday evening, neither had anywhere else he particularly had to be.

They had reserved the "party room" of O'Flaherty's Irish Pub. There are a lot of authentic Irish bars in the city, but O'Flaherty's wasn't one of them. That much was obvious from the fresh drywall, the electric dartboard, and the tin sign on the wall that said *Est. 1994,* in what was intended to be a Fenian pub script. Beneath this sign Steve sat across from Nix and Nestor, leaving the seat at the head open for Trout at a long table set up with thirteen chairs, and wondered if the cocktail waitress remembered they were there. They didn't have to worry long before Maeve (by the name tag on her right breast) entered the room wearing a Kelly-green polo and khaki shorts that were too short and too tight, not that any of them were complaining, saying "What'll it be, boys?"

"Hi Maeve. This is Nix, Nestor, and—"

Maeve gave him the hand. "No names," she said.

"Beer," Nix said. "Warm, black, flat Irish beer."

"Have a scotch," Steve said. "Everybody scotch." Which is how it began. The first drink was scotch. Nix would order a second, with a splash, because he liked the taste.

The talk was about work, while not being exactly about work because everyone knows that talking about work with people you work with is strictly for losers, just as they knew that if it weren't for work they would have nothing to talk about. At several points they stopped when they heard new voices and sounds of laughter from the bar beyond the door and waited in expectation for more of their expected party to join them. Before long, though, they realized that the voices belonged to the O'Flarherty's coed softball team, who were trickling in after a win, and Nix and Steve turned back to Nestor who was talking about Veronika's bathing suits. (He and Veronika were going over to Michigan beaches, and he was weighing the prospect of Veronika "showing a little more ass." It is something he would like to see but knew it was something men who weren't him would like to see, too.)

Nix was not sure what to say to this. He didn't doubt Veronika would look great in a bikini, but he didn't want to side with all the imagined leering perverts Nestor had conjured. At the same time what if he didn't pay Veronika's physique some compliment? Whenever he talked with Nestor about domestic matters Nix was aware of Flora's disapproving presence. Whenever they spent an evening with Nestor and Veronika, Nix and Flora came home and fought. Whether Nestor was actually the domestic toxin Flora thought he was or if he was merely a scapegoat for Flora's own insecurities Nix didn't know. And so he was careful what he said. By the time, the second round of drinks arrived, they'd given up even the pretense of expecting Trout. Just the same, Nix wondered why no one else had come. Surely there had to be more than a few of their colleagues who would rather Trout wasn't there and be more likely to attend knowing he wouldn't. Certainly, had they all come, including Trout, they could've sat, polite and tongue-tied, until Felding beat an early exit. As he was thinking about this, a tanned woman with sun-streaked hair and a dirt-smeared softball uniform neared the table and waited politely.

"Hello," Nestor said to her, as though she had left the crowd in the other room in search of them.

"Hi," she said, smacking her gum, "are you using, like, all these chairs?"

"Go ahead," Nix said, before the others could object. To his surprise she grabbed two, half curtsied, and left.

Nix watched her go, still facing them as she dragged the chairs out of the room. Steve said. "Carrie quit."

"Quit what?" Nix asked, half listening.

"Quit work. What did you think?"

"She's adjunct," Nestor said "It's the end of the term, so she didn't quit really."

"She's not coming back," Steve said. "In bed last night, she took my cock out of her mouth and said, 'I quit.' And I said, 'Don't quit, baby, keep going,' and she said, 'No, I quit my job. I don't want to work for you anymore.'"

"Woah," Nestor said.

"Ouch. She say why?" Nix asked.

"Just that it was all my fault."

"Man, how is it your fault?" Nestor asked.

"She's says I'm a creep."

"Then, yeah, it's your fault," Nestor said.

Nix unexpectedly found himself envying Carrie Thayer. Over the last few days, he had been imagining what life might be like beyond Carnelius College. When Steve had brought up the Fontaine assignment, he had worried that accepting might be a breach of his personal if not professional ethics. Now, the life of the adjunct instructor seemed a lot less admirable.

"Give it to me straight," Steve said. "Am I a monster? Is what I do, what I want for all of you, so wrong?"

Nix shrugged, not knowing the sum of what Steve had done nor what it was Steve wanted for him. No man is a hero to his valet, but Nix had a sympathetic fondness for weak men, which made him less his father's son than the son of his particular father, and which is why he liked Steve and had since the first time he met him at his job interview.

Steve had sat with his bare feet propped on a radiator, lobbing softball questions that suggested to Nix that Steve was either desperate for hires or an incompetent interviewer. Nix had pretended to ponder each question and gave answers that must have satisfied Steve, for Nix was hired and had worked hard ever since to earn the money he was paid, turning his grades in on time, suffering excruciating faculty meetings, and—whenever asked to—celebrating diversity.

Celebrating diversity was significant preoccupation at Carnelius College. There was, it seemed, a dance troupe for every grievance. Half of each semester's Mondays were lopped off the calendar to commemorate colonial atrocities Nix had never hear of; murals were commissioned, honoraria were paid, interdisciplinary writing assignments were shoe-horned into the curriculum. It was all good-natured—if vaguely ominous—and Nix found that he enjoyed celebrating diversity a great deal. Certainly it was hard not to argue that the voices of the oppressed were more compelling, if not more accomplished, than the petty preoccupations of the establishment. Steve liked to think he was not part of the establishment, and still he looked upon the heterosexual, female cohort of the Carnelius temporary faculty as his personal secular harem.

Another member of the softball team came into the room and put her hand on one of the empty chairs. "May I—"

"Sure, honey," Nestor said.

"Honey?" the woman demanded.

"Take it," Nestor said and the woman somehow managed to wrangle three of the chairs out the door.

"Objectively," Steve said, "it would behoove me as a professional to take a broader view of this event aside from whatever Carrie's personal motivations might be. You're saying I have to assume a more active leadership role."

A third softball player came in, and before she could ask, Nestor bellowed, "One." The girl burst into tears and hurried out of the room, clutching a single chair to her chest.

"That can't be it. Everyone knows you're in charge," Nix said.

"That's right," said Nestor, "but nobody thinks he acts like it."

Rather than considering Steve's dilemma—or even listening, for that matter—Nix was trying to decide at what point he could leave. It wasn't that he didn't enjoy talking to Steve and Nestor, but he could do so any weekday of a semester, and if he left soon he could get home at a decent hour on an evening he wasn't expected to, which would mean he could score some points with Flora, while walking out early of a dull situation. He had thus resolved that there was plenty of advantage and no downside to leaving when Josie walked in with her guitar case slung upside down on her back, followed by a girl who looked too young to drive much less be in a bar. She had short red hair, wore—in contrast to Josie's black hoodie—a bright orange vinyl raincoat and matching boots, and held, twisted among her fingers, a pair of drumsticks.

"This is Margaret Alice Dunleavy," Josie said, indicating her friend, the orange raincoat, and the bob.

"M.Alice D., to you all," said Margaret Alice.

Maeve came swiftly into the room as though she had been trying to head the girls off. "I'd like a can of Old Style, please," Josie said.

"Me too, please," said M.Alice.

"Can I see some IDs?" Maeve asked, her left foot tapping.

Josie found hers and held it over her shoulder impatiently. Maeve studied it far longer than she would have had she believed it for a second to be legit. "What about you, junior?"

M.Alice asked, "If I get a Coke can I sit here?"

Maeve looked at the three men sitting on the other side of the table and then again at the two girls. "Now, why would you want to do that?"

"They work for me," Steve said. "I can vouch for them."

Maeve rolled her eyes and left.

"So are you guys coming out tonight?" Josie asked.

"Wouldn't miss it," Steve said.

"Me, either," Nestor said.

Nix said, "Didn't know about it. Where is it?"

"Dreamerz. It was in the *Reader*," Josie said. "Critic's Pick."

"Never pick it up," Nix said. "What's the name of your band?"

"M.Alice D. Tokeless," said M.Alice.

"So does that make you like a front man?" Nestor asked

"I *am* the front man," M.Alice said diffidently.

There was a silence or as close as anyone could manage to silence among O'Flaherty's inebriates until Nestor asked, "Hey, have you ever heard of Josie and the Pussycats?"

"Let's see. My name is Josie and I'm in a girl band."

"Does that mean yes?"

And Nix could see that they'd crossed over a line. The girls were not interested. Each of the guys seemed to realize that in turn and, as he did, the more pointless the questions became. If he were single (as Steve was and Nestor pretended to be) Nix would have thought nothing about talking to these two girls about music or school or anything else while waiting for a train or in line at the Jewel, but he would never have approached them in a bar. And, not wanting to be taken for the kind of man his age who would, he'd already resolved for a second time to leave, when Nestor said, "You know, Singapore Slings are a two dollars until 7:00 at Trader Vics." Which is how such evenings are extended: the suggestion of a second location, a point beyond which all who remain have abandoned the pretense of

putting in an appearance and are officially in for the anarchic possibilities of a night beyond the pale of obligation. From a payphone
in a replica London call box, Nix tried Flora at home and got the
machine. "I'll be home by ten," he said, cupping the mouthpiece.

A lush draft blew down the side streets from the direction of the
Sears Tower, as the party walked up Wabash. The windows of Mar-
shall Fields rattled with the sound of car traffic and the El clambering
overhead. It was the first day of summer and the longest day of the
year. Whose idea was that? Nix wondered, the second day of summer
shorter than the first, the death of the season explicit in its astronom-
ical configuration. It was literary, a paradox. Nix was sure somebody
had written about it. As sure as he was about the fact that he never
had, or would. When Nix did write, that wasn't the sort of thing he
wrote about—nature as metaphor or nature at all. Such subjects were
beyond his range. "Smells are the hardest thing to write about," a
writing teacher told him, so Nix never tried. Or maybe it was another
student. The phrase had the pithy quality of reported speech.

The crowd was two parts after-work, one part couples from the
suburbs catching a drink before a show, and one part hotel guests.
They had all come to Vic's looking for something among the rat-
tan and the palm fronds, halved-cocoanut guacamole dishes, and
ceramic mugs with humping-monkey handles. Groups of young
women stood around high tables while groups of young men gathered at the bar. The yearly output of Big Ten schools disgorged into
the city, into a dozen corporate headquarters. Management trainees
and junior sales associates huddled, clinging to hedonistic collegiate
affectations. Ten years from now they would be scattered among the
suburbs with children and major appliances, but for now they en-
dured days of sterile drudgery for their nights among each other.
Nix had never lived like that, having thought himself destined for
something less conventional and more rewarding, and at this moment wondered when those possibilities evaporated, even as he was
realizing for the first time that they had.

"Carrie quitting means two unstaffed developmental sections,"
Steve said. "You want to split them?"

"Christ, developmental," Nestor said.

"Nix?"

"Have to check the calendar."

"Are you going to make me beg?" Steve asked.

"It's the theme of the evening: hierarchy and relationship," Nix said. "You're our boss and yet you rely very heavily upon us for so many things."

"If by that you mean—"

"By that I mean where would *you* be without us?"

"Don't make me find out," Steve asked.

The last thing Nix would remember of the night the next morning was the cash machine. He and Flora had a rule (or rather Flora had a rule that Nix was obliged to obey under penalty of relentless sulking) that they only withdraw money when they were together: a restriction Nix felt, under the present circumstances, entitled to ignore. He pushed buttons operatically, intending to withdraw twenty dollars, but his finger lingered too long on the 0, so it was two hundred, and he listened with a sexual dread as the robot shuffled bills into the hopper.

The rest of the night passed like a dumb show performed behind an opaque shower door. They drifted from one bar to the next, each place promising some sort of diversion that the last had failed to. The fact that he was a man in a group of three men—a most depressing configuration—loose in the city on a Friday night shouldn't have distressed Nix who, after all, was married—and still he found himself seeking affirmation, or at least indifference, in the female faces that floated before his heavy-lidded eyes, but saw—and was this he wondered (hoped) a reflection of his state of mind?—only disgust. Perhaps it was only his proximity to Steve and Nestor, who had perfected the art of lounge lizardry to the point of parody that made him feel this way. Though what, Nix asked himself, was true of them that wasn't true of him?

He remembered the cab, getting out at Division and Ashland, walking distance from his house, though he wouldn't be home for hours. He remembered tossing in a couple of bucks and an argument about the tip. Did he remember saying to Nestor, "No wonder cabbies never pick up black dudes"? He thought he did, anyway, at least as well as he remembered his surprise that Nestor couldn't take a joke. He remembered the klezmer ska band at Phyllis's Musical Inn, and was the Irish barfly who tried to pick a fight with Steve at the Gold Star really named Mick? He remembered wondering whether people buy cat-eye frames even if they don't need glasses, and was the frosted blond in the booth at the Rainbo Liz Phair or some sad girl who wished she was Liz Phair. He didn't remember the walk up Damen to Dreamerz, after having told Nestor and Steve at each station of the pub cross that he had to go home, but did remember looking at his watch one moment to see that it was 10:30 and was relieved to know that he could be home reasonably near his self-appointed time, and then having looked again what seemed like seconds later and seeing that it was 2:00 a.m.

The light on stage dimmed to black and spectral figures followed glow sticks about the stage until they were scattered by the striking of a single chord and then the lights came up bright and unfiltered white, as lead singer M.Alice D. sauntered to the front of the stage and banged on the single snare drum that was set up beside the mic, while guitarist Georges Sand Jr. ground razor sharp power chords beside her. It was a good show, good enough to take Nix's foggy mind off anything else, as Josie, in a sweat-drenched white tank top and leather hip-huggers, bounced around the stage on the balls of her Keds. After an hour of howls and thrown bottles, the girls gathered around a microphone to turn a hokey cabaret ballad into a crash test in eight-eight time. Nix stood with Steve and Nestor in a mob wrung dry of sensation, watching Josie, wearily strum the Rickenbacker on her hip, like a lab-engineered hybrid of Gidget and Joan of Arc, some pure manifestation of girlhood and salvation.

If you love her then you must send her
Somewhere that she's never been before

He didn't remember Steve walking him home, nor a word either of them said to each other, but he will remember at some point the next afternoon and will never be able to forget ever after finding Flora asleep on top of the Mexican blanket on the futon curled around the phone.

7.

"Nothing in this house belongs to me," Myrna Nixon once told the young Walter. Proof, to her, of willing self-sacrifice. She would not be tarred with the beatnik brush by her husband's Stroonies who, years after the apogee of the Floog Fenomenon, persisted in slouching up the driveway at a mean rate of once a month.

"Your bra," said Walter, who, being six, thought that when his mother said "nothing in this house belongs to me," she meant that nothing in the house belonged to her, and who, being six, was eager to speak the word *bra*. He had only the time to get the words out of his mouth and beam broadly before his mother had knocked him off a high stool onto the kitchen floor, with a backhand to his mouth. It was the first and only time she ever hit him. Nix knew not the nature of his crime nor why the offense elicited so violent a reaction and was too stunned to ask. Even if he had, Myrna was unlikely to have had an answer for him, except to guess that in that moment she saw a replica of Floog at six and was desperate, on some unconscious level, to convey to her son that his father—blood not withstanding—was no one to emulate.

His mother had always managed an admirable economy. Around and about Casa del Nixon, Myrna sported cuffed jeans, sweatshirts, sneakers from the five-and-ten. She tied her hair with rubber bands and talked about nothing, as far as Nix could ever remember, that happened south of Lawrence Avenue or north of Howard. Her outlook was no less a mystery to a son than were the origins of the Floog Sensibilities—long the subject of idle (and—no shit—*academic*) speculation—to scholars of his oeuvre. Even the uninitiated (i.e. not high) eye ascertained an authentically Okie aspect to the panels of *Weevil and Stroon*: the rag-mended tires and geysering radiators, the stickered steamer trucks, the bristly, bulging Adam's apples, and drooping woolen socks. Contrarily, the psychedelia and the leering sexuality (taken often, perversely, for a political argument where none could reasonably have been said to exist) would not be explained by a Great Plains uprising, nor by four years slapping it in Greenland in the United States Air Force. His life among the banjo pickers and dope-smoking street poets of Old Town offered tantalizing context, and yet Rutt Comics (always thus, never *Comix*, with an X, as erroneously cited in one of the three unauthorized biographies—specifically, *Floog: Illustrateur de l'Enfer Americain, par* Phillipe Riviere) emerged whole, mere months after his first urine-soaked night on a Lincoln Park bench. It seemed that the ways of Floog's mind that spawned *Yarns of the Fragrant Barn* would long remain knowable yet unknown.

"Sprung me from the booby-hatch." Floog's creation myth. Good for a laugh. Lead with the punch line. What the Walter of his boyhood asked in the way of details, Nix doesn't remember. He did remember that it was the drawings that his mother said distinguished Floog among the hollowed-eyed and opened-robed on the ward. He inked caricatures of the staff and of the attending psychiatrists (though not of the other patients; forbidden following an incident) that suggested to Myrna the possibility of a stable, if solitary life, beyond the reinforced windows of the facility. Charcoal portraits for a dollar or five a piece at church fairs and for the tourists on State Street, she believed could add up to a respectable income without the necessity of getting oneself to the same place at the same time every morning and transacting in a socially acceptable way with coworkers—two skills, Myrna knew, Floog would find difficult to master, despite the electric shock and the capsules.

Nix lay in bed, his stomach and throat feeling as though he'd drunk Liquid Plumber, wondering why that particular memory had come to him at that particular moment. He was taking stock. Something his father could never do. "Floog, you should be happy," his mother had said. "Take stock. Look at all that you have." To which Floog would reply, "I don't trust the stock market." That Floog could not have worked for living, even if he wanted to was a given, even among the extended Nixons. Just as surely, Myrna was determined that Nix would, whether he liked it or not. What choice was there? He would never have the luxury of indulging his idiosyncrasies even if he had any idiosyncrasies to indulge. Still, he had not sought out—was incapable of finding, it seemed—jobs that paid enough money to live upon, thus had condemned himself to a purgatory in which he could run in place all the way to the bread line.

He slunk to the kitchen, drank half a quart of orange juice from the carton, vomited in the sink, and went looking for Flora. She wasn't in the bedroom, he knew, nor did he find her in the bathroom, nor the spare bedroom—as she sometimes was among boxes of snapshots and fabric—nor the front room.

Passing the dining room window Nix looked out upon Wede on his back porch, with a girl on his lap. They were sharing a breakfast of scrambled eggs and Olde English. Not yet aware he'd slept past noon, Nix clucked at the idea of drinking in the morning.

Nix stood in curtained shadow feeling a hot breeze from the window, pondering the opposing notions that he may have to endure a life without Flora and that he might be suffering a fatal case of alcohol poisoning. Often he'd thought about how Flora would leave him—how, never why. He'd assumed, knowing her, that she'd tell him in person, stand bravely weeping at the door, present her list of charges, set the parameters of future contact, then leave to a waiting taxi. Nix was equally sure that if the time came for him to do leave her, he'd sneak out when she was asleep, leaving his clothes, computer, and what little he actually owned behind.

Nix took to his desk with the intent of beginning the Augean chore of transcribing Mrs. Fontaine's recorded *pensées* on the computer but instead succumbed to the lure of the ledger book. There were no bills left to pay for the month. Nix had paid the last of the credit cards in full, but he returned to the book to gaze upon the transformed landscape of the grid: seven lines of two- and occasionally three-digit figures stretching across the pale-green page, arresting at diagonal slashes in the lower right corner of the square.

Though he'd dreamed, in the way most people only dream about money, in the dreams he'd been slow in getting around to paying the bills off. Flora's talk of buying a couch had jolted Nix into action, for Nix knew that no couch ever entered a house by itself. Thus, while he had scratched out the checks, humming as he did "The Battle Hymn of the Republic," Flora had sat next him at the kitchen table, not glumly but less enthusiastic than Nix about turning over more than $18,000 to seven multinational corporations who had done nothing for them but sap off thousands of dollars in interest and service charges. "Free at last, free at last, thank God almighty we're free at last," he'd testified as he licked the last envelope.They'd hugged, she limply wrapping her arms around him, the fact of his increasing exuberance sapping hers. Nix ran his hand across the page a last time, closed the book, then went to the bathroom to throw up again.

On the way back to the living room, he glanced out the window. Wede and the woman had finished breakfast and were smoking and gazing out over the back porches of the buildings across the alley. The malt liquor bottle lay empty on the deck, and they'd moved on to Bloody Marys without the tomato juice, served directly from a quart bottle of Gordon's vodka.

Nix snapped the first of the three tapes he'd filled at Fontaine Manor into the miniature tape recorder and pressed *play,* the cap-stans stuttered and caught. Muffled voices growled from the speaker. He turned up the volume on Mrs. Fontaine mid-sentence, in this case discussing the agricultural bounty of the northern Ohio truck farm. Nix's stomach churned in panic. He double-checked the tapes to make sure he'd loaded the first tape, rewound, and realized with a gut-knotting certainty that, as Mrs. Fontaine had speculated, the recorder *was* broken, and that he'd captured only fragments of her rambling recollections.

To salvage what he could, Nix transcribed what he had and in-terpolated the missing passages from memory. He filled several pages of lowercased phrases punctuated by ellipses. By the time he'd completed the first tape, however, he grew calmer, relieved even, as he realized that he remembered the missing words the tape had failed to record quite well, or let's face it, well enough and, gradually, he stopped using the ellipses entirely and typed all words, whether existing or imagined, as the spoken gospel of Zira Fontaine. As this anxiety subsided, Nix was able to appreciate fully the disgust he experienced at the sound of his own voice. He was stunned at its graceless abruptness and affectation. What he could hear of Mrs. Fontaine by contrast sounded at ease, comfortable in the role of subject.

Wondering if the problem with the recorder might just be the batteries, Nix rummaged through is desk for a new set, from the back of the drawer he pulled a battered business card that he didn't recognize at first, then realized belonged to Lenny Spitz, his agent. Nix hadn't talked to him for four years, the last conversation rising to a simultaneous slamming of phone receivers.

Lenny had blamed Nix and Nix did, too. Foyl schmuck. Foyl baybek schmuck, Lenny screamed. Ah, but, they had begun well. Lenny had sold *Life During Wartime* to a New York publishing house of which even Nix, who knew nothing of the business, had heard. An editor was assigned who set about excising every adjective and adverb, re-wrote the middle section and the ending, leaving the beginning more or less intact (aside from adding a new first paragraph to serve as a coda). The publishers were in such a hurry to get the book out—to beat two others of near identical plots rumored to be in develop-ment at rival houses—that the one chapter of back story was titled "TK" and consisted of three blank pages. (It was an editorial decision aesthetically consistent with the rest of the book, which consisted of prairies of white space sparsely populated with two-sentence paragraphs and seraphic ornamentation.) His editor's nervous break-down and subsequent firing from the company for which he'd worked for thirty years (something that Nix assumed was a long time coming but was in fact triggered by this assignment) further ensured there'd be no delays in the book's expedited production schedule.

"Now the problem of your name," Lenny said, "Walter Nixon sounds like a feed salesman from Omaha."

Not for a moment did Nix balk at Lenny's suggestion that he change his name. Bearing the surname of a disgraced president was albatross enough, but Walter had always thought *Walter* was all wrong as well, not just a name from his father's generation, but a name for the sort of man of his father's generation that Nix's actual father never associated with, unless he happened to be an adored uncle (as was the case with Floog's Walter). Wally had been a non-starter because of "Leave It to Beaver" reruns. And he had eventu-ally learned to get by on the proletarian, if retrograde, Walt.

Nix—as a gag—had suggested Nix Walters.

Lenny loved it.

Within days—as Nix Walters—he was posing, in white briefs, with the young stars of the TV networks' fall line-ups in *Vanity Fair,* chatting about his father's career as an underground comic book writer with Terry Gross on "Fresh Air" on NPR, appearing on Charlie Rose with a panel of authors under twenty-three, what Rose called, "the voices of a misplaced generation." He hoped April March was tracking the arc of his career. And she *was* passingly aware, having read on a flight from London to Rome a capsule in *Time* magazine in which Nix Walters was asked, along with the year's other it-celebs, to handicap the Oscars.

In the days before his novel was released, Nix thought for the only time in his life that he might be on the verge of something, that he would be, at the same time, a witness and a participant in an important passage.

Then the book came out.

The savaging was bestial. Anthony Saccora in the *New York Times Book Review* called it "torture." Joan Didion, in a five-thousand-word essay in the *New York Review of Books,* catalogued the Noble Failures of our Young Authors, before concluding that what separated *Life During Wartime* from the other books she'd treated was its lack of humanity. Felding Trout, in another batch review for *Critical Inquiry,* asked if "post-post-modernism has spawned a generation of writers who, in their ignorance of literary convention (to say nothing of the conventions of grammar) [are] digest[ing] the school itself … as their internally-directed aesthetic nihilism dissolves form like bile on a ham sandwich." Even the glossy entertainment weeklies, whose reviewers are generally content to cull the press packets for material, joined in the pummeling. At Yale, the book was the central text of a course called Bildungsroman as Commodity. At the University of Minnesota there was a Write Like Nix Walters contest, for which the winner received a copy of *Life During Wartime.* (The runner-up received two.)

Lenny was ecstatic. "This is fantastic," he said.

Nix was less sure. More and more, when appearing on "Booknotes" on C-Span or on shock-jock morning radio shows, Nix was asked to talk about the scorn his novel had inspired and not the book itself. Such assaults, whether high brow, middle, or low, Nix had a hard time defending himself against, largely because he had no opinion on the subject. While writing the book, he'd ripped off every trope, device, and convention he could recall from any of the universally reviled and thereby commercially successful popular novels against which his work was now being compared as proof of the Death of Literature. Most troubling was that the sales were not what Lenny told him they'd be. In the years that followed, Nix never encountered anyone familiar with his career who didn't believe he'd been made rich. In truth, remainder tables of every bookstore Nix went into groaned with copies of *Life During Wartime.*

Then one night, while in a hotel room in Phoenix awaiting an appearance the next morning on "A.M. Arizona," Nix heard Jay Leno, joking about a federal prisoner who was suing the government for confiscating his writing materials, say, "Gee, why couldn't they have done that to Nix Walters," and he realized the end had come. His feeling on the matter being that whenever one's livelihood can be reduced to a concept so searingly simple-minded as to be comprehensible to whichever constituency of Americans looks to the Leno show for cultural wisdom, it was time to quit.

"It's a first book," Lenny had said. "First books are tough. But you earned out. You know what that means? It means there's going to be a second book."

Nix picked up the phone and started to dial the number, then remembered it was Saturday. He was about to hang up when it dawned on him that Lenny likely wouldn't take his call during the week, either. So he left a message that sounded so suitably familiar, warm, and irritated that this assistant would put it through to him.

"Lenny," he said, hitting the L hard. "It's Walt, Nix Walters, your buddy from the *Life During Wartime* wars. I've got a project you might be interested in. Give me a call." Then hung up. He lifted the receiver and was about to call Nestor to see if Flora was over there. When he heard a sound coming from the kitchen. He walked warily down the hall and realized the noise was coming from the back porch, which was so flimsy, neither of them liked to set foot on it.

The door shuddered and opened and Flora pushed her way in, clutching glossy shopping bags in both fists.

"Why'd you come up the back?"

"The front stairs are out. They tore up the wood ones and they're putting in concrete."

"They weren't out last night."

"Yes they were. You left your footsteps in the wet cement on every one of the stairs. They'll probably have to tear them out and set them again and charge us for it."

He remembered now the unexpected weight on each foot and hopping, thinking he'd stepped in a dog shit as he'd raked his foot along each successive stair without managing to scrape the substance off.

"Don't you want to know where I've been?" she asked.

"I can see where you've been."

Flora walked to the table and fanned a stack of brochures across the table. They were from real estate agencies and looked familiar and alien at the same time—ubiquitous, but nothing he ever picked up or thought would be for him. Whether by his parents' design or by his own narrow view, Nix never knew anything of prosperity. He remembered, for instance, the Josten's brochure for class rings when he was a freshman in high school. He'd spent all of homeroom and the math class that followed selecting the right stone, design, and precious metal that he thought suited him, only to take the brochure home and have his mother snatch it from him, swat him with it, and tell him that $249 was more than she would pay for anything. "What makes them think they can ask people for that kind of money?" his mother had asked, angry, for some reason, at him.

"This is something we need to do," Flora said. "Think of it as a necessary investment."

"What are we investing in?" Nix asked.

"Good question. Either we move or I move out."

"Move where? Out of the city? Is that what you want?"

"Do you?"

"I don't want to move."

"It makes sense."

"We could buy a place on the block."

"Why would you want to do that?"

"I wouldn't. I want to know I can," he said.

Staring defeat in the face, Nix remembered a couple they knew who'd been looking for a house for as long as they'd known them. "We can look," he said. "It couldn't hurt to look."

"Of course," Flora said, "we'll want to find something before the baby gets here."

Nix, who was on his way to the toilet when Flora dropped that bit of news, stopped and glanced over his shoulder in the stylized fashion of a soap opera star, then sprinted into the bathroom to throw up.

He had his head in the bowl when he heard Flora behind him. "Well, that inspires confidence," she said. "Here, move." She knelt beside him and vomited as well.

She reached over and spun a couple of feet off the toilet paper dispenser and handed him half. "It's going to be a hell of an eight months," she said wiping her mouth.

"When did you find out?"

"Last night."

"I called. Where were you?"

"In here," she said, "squatting over a plastic stick."

She fell back against the wall.

He sat beside her. "You all right?"

"Yeah," she said sounding tired but not unwell. "I've got morning sickness. What's your excuse?"

"Scotch."

Flora rolled her eyes. "Flush that, or I'm going to puke again."

8.

By this, his third ride in the limousine, Nix had mastered the supercilious posture of the chauffeured—left ankle across right knee, shoulder bag upright and open beside him on the leather upholstery, hands folded on left thigh—but he couldn't keep his knees still and, despite the frigid conditions in the over-air-conditioned car, he couldn't stop sweating, and he felt light-headed. He tried reading the *Financial Times,* which he found folded as crisply as a linen handkerchief on the mini fridge, skimming the front page. His eye wouldn't focus on anything but the largest headlines, all of which concerned projections—earnings projections, climate projections, cost projections—when Nix was of a mind to stop the projecting that had been going on in his head almost uninterrupted for the past fourteen hours.

During his last ride Nix, as punishment for being ignored, had stopped speaking to Hector. By this strategy, Nix had hoped to drive Hector in a fit of remorse to talk weather, baseball, and gripes about his wife's family. None was forthcoming on this morning, though Nix was glad to be freed from the urge to talk and relieved not to be talked to. As the car reached the Fontaine drive, slowed, and rounded the curve, Nix tossed the paper onto the seat beside him with a particular flair and looked out the window in time to see Mrs. Fontaine standing on the broad lawn next to the woman whom he'd met at the door of the coach house. The elder woman was holding the little girl against her hip. Nix was surprised at the ease with which she held the child, and even more surprised when she spied the car, put the child on the ground, and, amazingly, began to run. Nix turned to watch out of the rear window as his subject chased the car down the drive. She ran with an earnest pumping of the arms, like a three-year-old struggling to keep up with her older brothers or like the bookish girl in second grade who, at the gruff exhortations of the gym teacher, struggles to match the pace of her more physically gifted classmates. Her teeth were gritted and her lips fixed in what was either a smile or a grimace of pain.

"Wow," Nix said.

"Chief?" said Hector, confirming Nix's suspicions that Hector longed to speak to him.

The car stopped. Anders was there to open the door, turning him, deliberately, Nix thought, away from Mrs. Fontaine, as she threw her hands to her knees, struggling to catch her breath in the unexpectedly warm morning air.

"This way, Mr. Walters," Anders said.

"Lovely," Mrs. Fontaine said.

"Yes," said Nix, thinking maybe she was talking about the weather.

"There was a dreadful, dreadful headache and a fever and a pain in my right arm. But even at a time when my father was worried about such things, about exactly such things for Victor, he did not worry about me. My mother was attentive. She had remedies for headaches, as she had remedies for everything, but she was not alarmed, not that I could tell, and I generally could tell such things. I don't mean to suggest that they did not concern themselves about my safety or health. They simply never worried about me because there was never anything wrong with me. Then one morning my fever spiked and the headache was much, much worse, and then of course everyone knew."

"You were how old?"

"Seventeen, just. It was summer. I was working in his offices. Something my father didn't want, but I insisted. It wasn't just sweeping and filing. I worked. I kept the books for the entire company. The responsibility normally fell to Mr. Pentmann, but there were problems that I wasn't sure of the nature of at the time. A drinking problem? Yes, thinking back that's what it was. My father went to him one day when I was in the office and he had run out of work for me, and he asked Pentmann if he had anything, and Pentmann put me at the job of tabulating a pile of receipts. I did that so well there was another pile and then bound books full of figures. Soon he was laying the work out for me in stacks without being there to set me to them. He didn't come in at all one week, and my father fired him and didn't tell any of the bosses he was gone. Then the job was mine, though Father was constantly saying, 'Don't spend the day indoors.' As I said, we weren't allowed to go anywhere that people congregated in large numbers, but my father was a believer in the medical properties of fresh air. I spent my days in pursuit of solitary outdoor places. He had also heard that people who worked hard were more vulnerable to contracting the virus, so you can imagine how he felt when this happened to me. Of course I thought it was my fault and was determined no matter what happened that I wouldn't show any pain or cry in front of others.

"In less than a week, I went from my own bed to an enclosed respirator."

"A respirator?"

"An iron lung," she snapped.

"Sorry." Nix had heard of iron lungs, though always in connection with cigarettes, the Old Gold's his mother smoked, which came with slippery green coupons that could be redeemed for gifts from a booklet. "Save enough of them," the joke went, "and you can buy an iron lung." And because it was one of those things he only heard evoked as a warning—like reform school—Nix was disinclined to believe in their actual existence.

"I remember being put in the machine for the first time, and I have never spoken of this to anyone. It took two orderlies to operate the handles to lower me in. Everyone was crying, my mother, my father, even the nurses. It's funny to think about that. The disease was something so common at the time, but perhaps it was my family's grief that affected them. They wouldn't let Victor come to the hospital for fear he might catch something. I felt it was up to me to be brave and so I was. I remember saying, 'It's not so bad in here,' even though I was terrified. I suffered from a phobia of confined spaces. Victor used to trick me into going into the closets at our house and close the door behind me until my mother forbade it because I used to carry on so much when he did. And here I was, locked in a case with a yoke around my neck.

"Have you seen one of these machines? No, well that's not surprising. They looked old-fashioned even at the time, like a horizontal water heater. There was a whole series of pulleys and winches to put somebody inside. The bellows were so loud that it was very difficult to carry on a conversation. You had to speak between strokes. Half of the time we didn't hear each other, my parents and me, but we'd pretend and smile and nod no matter what the question was, and I would laugh and be gay and long for the hour when they would leave so that I could cry. And when I did I couldn't so much as move my head. I'd lie there feeling the teardrops fill my ears. There were times when I honestly wondered whether I might drown in my own tears." She paused for moment and turned from whatever bloom in some far point the room she'd had her eyes trained on and looked at Nix. "I'm not sure I want to include that. It sounds melodramatic or self-pitying."

"Are you kidding?" Nix said. "It's pure gold."

"Crying was the only thing that gave me comfort. When I cried, I thought I could feel my lungs move on their own. So I cried as often as I could as hard as I felt like, whenever I was alone."

"Did you ever think you were going to die?"

Mrs. Fontaine's eyes flashed as she looked up from her tea. "I was certain of it.

"Father tried everything. I believe for a time he thought he could buy my health. He donated thousands to the March of Dimes. He hired three private nurses at a time, and if he even sensed that I was dissatisfied with one of them she would be gone and another would be there to take her shift the next day. It got to the point that I was afraid to even talk about the nurses in front of him for fear that they'd get the sack.

"If there was a clinic that was rumored to have a high success rate, I was admitted; if there was a new treatment program, my father saw to it that I was enrolled. I was first treated at the Catholic Hospital in Lorain and then transferred, in an Army ambulance, to the juvenile polio ward in Cleveland, and then to a Sister Kenny center in Toronto, Canada. Father chartered a plane and had most of the seats taken out to accommodate the iron lung and two portable generators."

"Two?"

"A second in reserve in case the first failed.

"The Kenny treatment was hot, hot towels and deep painful massage. Day after day. It worked to a point—enough to keep my spirits up. That was the trick, at the time. The specialists realized that the mind has as much to do with treating polio as the body and medicines and treatments. Sounds obvious now, but that was a novel idea. When no part of the body will obey the brain, but the mind can grasp the nature of the betrayal, one is confronted with two choices, to become bitter and spend your days complaining about one's bad luck, or to resolve to get better. Simple enough, yes, but the truth is if you become too optimistic your hope can be shattered if the progress is too slow. Once you give up hope it's hard to get it back. I saw that happen more than once, especially with the littler ones. I tried to keep their spirits up. I was one of the eldest on the ward, and a lot of the children looked up to me in a way Victor never did.

"One day I realized my left pinky hurt."

"Your pinky?"

"I hadn't felt my hands since the day I became ill."

"Then?"

"Then I got better—very quickly at first, and then little by little. That was the way it went with polio. First it hits you like a piano dropped from a roof and then you wait to see how much—if any— of your physical ability you regain. First I could breathe with a portable respirator, though if you saw one of those, you wouldn't have thought it very portable. Then I found I could hold my head up, then sit up on my own.

"I was lucky, very, very lucky. Some people never walked again, some people never breathed on their own again, some people died. Children died. It was a children's disease.

"That's how I learned the limits of money, though I don't believe my father ever did. He told me once when I was older. 'Money never let me down.' He could go to church every afternoon and pray to Saint Osmund, the patron saint of the paralyzed, to cure me, which he did. Yet he knew that even if his prayer was answered—which it was—he still had hospital bills to pay.

"We all should have been grateful to him, my mother, Victor, me. Without my father thinking of practical things where would any of us have been?"

"Where indeed," Nix said, and caught himself. But Mrs. Fontaine proved inured to irony. Indeed, she came from a class of people, a generation where people said things like that.

On the way home Nix told Hector to turn up the air conditioning. "Crank the AC wouldja, Hector," he'd said and watched the cocktail napkins ripple in their rack above the fridge. Beyond the tinted windows the dirty streets shimmered from the heat, the opulence of the limousine making that which was not squalid seem squalid and that which was seem abject. The hydrants were open all along his block, and yet even this urban pastoral was marred by the Styrofoam fast food containers that glided down the gutter like paper ships. Kids darted in and out of the water blast, their sodden shorts and T-shirts hung loose and heavy from their skinny arms and legs.

It had occurred to Nix after the fact that Flora had held the announcement of her pregnancy in reserve during the argument of the day before. She had just waited for the right moment, which meant every word out of his mouth had been a waste of breath. He resented her for this, of course, and consequently resolved that he wouldn't have one word to say on the subject of her pregnancy until she apologized for the way she'd told him. Flora had said that she'd learned from Marcia about a good ob/gyn group that she thought she could get a midwife from. Nix had said, "Fine." After all, what was there for him to say? She would have a midwife and not a doctor, a decision Flora felt strongly enough about to have made without consulting him, not that Nix, under the circumstances, would have had an opinion about, much less objected to—even had he understood what a doula did. Flora said she would take three months of leave at half pay allotted through her benefit package and another three months unpaid, which she thought they could now afford given Nix's arrangement with Mrs. Fontaine. Nix listened to each point and responded when queried while assiduously avoiding a tint of bitterness or sarcasm, but, as a matter of spite, never asked any question of his own or offered any ideas or reflections on how marvelous the news was. They hadn't hugged or kissed because, although the announcement had ended the argument, it had not ended the argument with the exhaustion or conciliation that usually led to a hug and then sex, so neither of them was in what the therapists of the time would have called, a "hugging place."

With this mote of discord Flora and Nix had begun their journey toward parenthood. Destructive? Sure, somewhat, though perhaps not fatal to the relationship and certainly not to the child because, in that moment, Nix had resolved to be the best father ever, if only to teach Flora a lesson. He would attend every office visit, read the books, browse the magazines, including *NPP,* which in the five years she had written for them, he had never once opened. He had meant to, but something had always stopped him (that something being a complete and total lack of interest). He would haunt the antique shops in Andersonville for juvenile furniture or build his own. He would attend childbirth classes and learn—sitting patiently as minutes, even hours, of class passed without his having heard anything he did not already know—he would don the prosthetic pregnancy appliance that each of the prospective fathers would be asked to try on and even make a show of struggling more under the burden than he, Nix, tall and strong in the legs, would have.

"See you in the morning Hector," Nix said and slammed the door without—as he had, fruitlessly at the end of their first rides—tottering, with one foot on the pavement, waiting for Hector to reply.

9.

Up and down the block his neighbors lolled over their porch railings, fanning themselves with copies of *La Raza!* or sat in windows with ashtrays on their knees. The air on the landing was as hot and dry as an attic. It was no cooler inside, as Nix opened the door to a row of bags lined up across the dining room floor. They were acetate bags, metal-flake bags, and bags of deliberately rough-hewn unbleached paper, bags of spiraling psychedelic hues, and bags with twine handles.

Flora came out of the bathroom wearing one of Nix's T-shirts and a pair of his boxers, and started when she saw him. "You scared me," she said. "Aren't you early?"

"A little."

She looked at him for a minute, as she always did when she was trying to gauge his mood. "Want to see what I bought?"

"No."

She gathered bags in both hands and still had a couple she couldn't carry. "Are you mad?"

"No," he said, picking up the remaining bags and following her into the bedroom.

"You know," she said. "You haven't said how you feel."

"About what?"

"See."

"Yes, I have."

"No, you haven't."

Nix sat on the edge of the futon as she shuttled back and forth between the bags and her dresser drawers and closet. Mostly it was maternity clothes she had bought and, every few items, she couldn't resist the urge to hold it in front of her small body and say, "See? Cute."

"You know how I feel," Nix said.

"No, I don't. How?"

"I don't know," Nix said, fully aware that most women would have stabbed him in the neck already.

"You're excited?" Flora said the word rising at the end with an inflection of hope or doubt.

"Of course I'm excited"

"And you're worried."

"Yeah, I'm worried. No more than you'd expect. I mean you'd be worried if I wasn't worried."

Flora's eyes narrowed. "I could get used to it."

"Someone should worry."

"You've been unhappy."

"I guess I feel caught out a little bit. I'm not sure I'm up to this. The baby's not coming for another six months, and already I feel like you're a better parent than me."

"It's not a competition. I'm not out to make points," she said. "I'm out to make you a better person."

Nix smiled and she smiled back. "And it's my job to fight you every step of the way," he said and left her to her new clothes and went in the living room to watch TV.

When he had lived in Arkansas Nix didn't own a television. In the wooded corner of town known to the townsfolk as the Hollow, he owned little of anything. He kept a fork and a spoon and a single plate and a bowl and a pot he cooked everything that he ate hot in. He drank tea and ate the vegetables brought in by the truck farmers to the town square. In the spring, summer, and fall, he sat on his porch overlooking a half-dry creek and read the novels and books of poetry he had been assigned to read for his exams, and played three-handed poker by himself on a barrel top. During the short winters, when the wind found its way through cracks in the windowsills, he sat by the fire with a quilt over his legs and wrote in longhand on a composition tablet. This monastic life imbued Nix with a sense of piety and contrition. It made him feel whole and comfortable, alone and in his own skin, and he vowed he would live this way for the rest of his life.

Nowadays, Nix lay on the couch and watched whatever came on the television. And nowadays what came on mostly was the local news. Beneath the hairspray and the shoulder pads lurked the spectacularly talentless, young, and gorgeous anchors who dwelt in realms untrammeled by irony. Whether reporting a triple homicide or treed kitten, they read the words that scrolled by on the Tele-PrompTer with equal warmth and woe. Nix hit the power button on the remote, and the iridescent dot in the middle of the screen expanded, revealing the image of a Chevy van jutting from the shattered window of a muebleria in Pilsen. Car-through-storefront was the signature story of Channel Six, which was the station he watched most of the time. To Nix this was both natural and understandable: the footage dramatic, the politics neutral. Nix watched the unending lurid pageant with a leaden inertia that filled him with self-hatred. Weather was next—but first a commercial: A man in an office pleads soundlessly with another, who, unmoved, stamps the words Chapter 11 across a document in oversized red letters. As the first man puts his hands to his face, the set around him falls away, and he is left standing beside a foreboding precipice. Cut to a teenage girl in her room, putting a needle in her arm. A woman, her mother Nix assumes, breaks through the door and, as the girl pushes her away, raises a lamp as a weapon. Again darkness and they are standing next to the man at the same precipice. He clings to her as she stares with horror into the abyss, and Nix realizes they are meant to be the same family. It's been a bad day for all of them. A voice, the first sound of the commercial, says, "There is another way, another truth, another light." The words "The way, The truth, The light" appear in white across a black screen. They fade as a single large V with a cross in the middle of it appears.

$$\mathbb{V}$$

Something religious, Nix thought, as stultifying air humored the dusty ceiling fan, waiting for the halting Technicolor Doppler radar crawl across the digital map to tell him that it was hot out, as it often was in the summer, and would be tomorrow as well.

As Nix hovered between irritation and sleep, he heard a voice, somehow new and familiar at the same time, a voice that spoke of a shift in ocean currents in the central Pacific and their improbable effect on a stalled cold front organizing over the Canadian Rockies.

This convergence had trapped the air between them. This meant unsafe ozone levels throughout the Chicagoland area. The words cascaded with an automated grace, a sound poem of barometric phras-emes. How far from dangerous is unsafe? he wondered, although it's the voice that perplexed Nix. He opened an eye to see that friendly old Bass Wilkes was not at his customary mark in front of the mural-sized green screen. In his place a woman, Asian, with straight bangs, and shoulder-length hair in pleasingly prim navy skirt and blazer, gestured enticingly along the edge of a scythe-shaped front menacing the city.

"And this mass here, guys, in the Pacific will mean temperatures above normal this summer. Make sure you stock up on sun block because you'll want to spend a lot of time at the beach."

Across the studio, at the gaudy anchor desk—half Ghery, half Dr. Seuss—her colleagues grinned approval. They liked what they saw, or perhaps it's simply the hope that she may prove herself worthy enough to deliver them from the prattling gin hound Wilkes. "Toni Tann will fill in while Bass and Tiffany care for their new addition." Ordinarily, the projected photo of a newborn sporting his father's pompadour would catch Nix's attention, at least as much as the news that Bass was a first-time father at sixty, but Nix didn't even hear the news, eager as he was for Toni to rejoin the anchor team for the peppy banter that signaled the end of the broadcast and the beginning of the next broadcast, as the news stretched across the afternoon. He noted with admiration the practiced lean against the desk, betrayed by the rocking of her left ankle on the axis of a pointed toe, saying "Frank, I never *prom*ised you it wouldn't rain this weekend."

Nix flicked the snap open and slid his hand into his underwear.

"I had a terrific visit to Mrs. Hinckley's third grade class at Bollingbrook Elementary this morning," Toni continued. "They made some pictures that they wanted me to bring back. This one's of you Frank."

"What's that coming out of my mouth that looks like a cucumber?" Frank asked holding the drawing up the camera. "Can we get a close-up."

"It's a speech bubble. It says, 'Thank you, Toni.'"

Nix sighed, realizing that as long as Toni was on for Wilkes, his days were no longer his own. Hearing Flora's footfalls in the hall, he reached for the remote and tripped over his shorts.

"Porn again?" Flora said. It was a joke they shared. Neither of them felt they were watching enough pornography. They enjoyed the kind of nonadventurous sex that artists of every medium and genre held up to ridicule. They didn't have bad sex. In many ways bad would have been better than what they had, because bad leads to the kind of desperation that drives couples to risk and to potentially vast humiliation of experimentation and tests of trust and boundaries. In reality Flora was more of a sexual creature than April ever was. It was Flora who would draw up her knee and bury her fingers in her thick black hair as she lay naked on the bed, whereas April in her athleticism seemed to be unaware, even while naked, of the sexual function of her body, unless reminded in the most direct of ways. Yet he commonly thought about April when having sex with his wife, whereas he had never while fucking April conjured in his mind the contours of a hypothetical Flora.

"Yeah, porn," Nix said, flushed with arousal and shame.

"I talked to Veronika today."

"Uh oh," Nix said about some subjects he could not pretend indifference.

"Her aunt is moving into a retirement home in Nevada, which means her bungalow is coming up for sale, and Veronika told her about us and about how we're having a baby, and she said she wants to sell the house to us."

Nix winced. "How do we know we can afford it?"

"That's just the thing. She says she'd sell for what we could afford. She paid the thing off long ago and the money from the sale will just go to the nursing home anyway."

"Can she do that? Aren't there laws, redlining rules? What if one of Nestor's relatives wanted to buy it—would she sell to them? I doubt it."

"Why are you being ridiculous? I'm sure she loves Nestor."

"This might be very good news. We don't know it, yet."

"Well, we're going to look and we can see."

"When?"

"This afternoon."

"This afternoon?" Nix said, his voice virtually cracking.

"Yes, this afternoon. Time is a factor here." Nix followed her into the kitchen and stood behind her as she opened the fridge. "Who drank the tea?"

Nix carried the sturdy expensive teakettle she'd bought the day before to replace their sturdy inexpensive teakettle to the sink. "I'll make more." He turned the knob but the faucet released only a rusty trickle. "Shit."

"The hydrants are open," Flora said.

"Should you be drinking caffeine anyway?" Nix said, knowing even before he'd finished that he'd made a mistake. She stared up at him from under the locks of hair that the humidity had turned loose from her barrette, as she walked past him to the door, lifting her purse from the doorknob and opening the door in a single motion. Rather than try to stop her, Nix walked to the window and watched her emerge from beneath the eave, walk down the sidewalk, open the passenger door of the Honda, and get into the car. Nix watched for several minutes, as his wife sat in what had to be sweltering car, while behind her an aquatic ballet of prancing children and shirtless hoods played itself out in the plumes of water that roared from the hydrant.

Nix gathered his keys and shades and marched sullenly down the stairs and climbed in the driver's seat. "Where is it?"

"Sunnyside and Pulaski."

"Where?"

"West of California."

Nix whistled through his teeth. "I don't think I've ever been west of California."

Of course Mrs. Alvarez liked them as soon as she peered through the door hole. Charming the elderly was a skill each of them possessed independently. As a duo, they were irresistible. Stooped and hoarse, the woman led them on a tour of the house by way of clusters of black-and-white photographs in ornate oval frames. Nix was left with the impression that she had decided they would be buying the house and that they were not buying the shell of the house but the entire history that the house had contained, and that she was going alone and without memories of the past into her nursing home. She spoke of her parents (deceased), her sisters (likewise), her children, also gone. He and Flora drank her awful instant coffee, smiled, and nodded. I should listen to old folks go on about their lives for a living, Nix thought, then remembered that he did.

After coffee they backed their way to the door. "You have a wonderful family," Flora said, leaving Nix, given the rate of attrition, to marvel at her use of the present tense, "and, certainly, a beautiful home. You will be sorry to leave it."

"Yes," Mrs. Alvarez said, "call my lawyer."

"Well," Nix said, once they were back in the car. "That was weird."

"Weird how? She was adorable." Flora was driving, which should have been a red flag to Nix, who knew full well that she only drove when she was in a particularly good mood. "You're out of your mind. How often do people have this kind of house luck?"

"That's exactly my point. Why do you think it doesn't happen? There's something not on the level."

"You picked a strange moment to become suspicious."

"I'm always suspicious."

"You're always bitter. There's a difference. Besides she told us to talk to her lawyer. It's not like she's some kind of wood fairy living in an old mill."

"I'm not saying no or anything. I'm just saying be careful—an old mill?"

"That's where they live. Really."

It was dark by the time they pulled up in front of their building. The front door was still blocked off, and Flora shot Nix a look as they walked around to the alley.

"Shit," Flora said, "I hate it when the light is out."

Later Nix would remember, while talking to the police, that he had seen the two young men turn onto their block ahead of them but didn't think anything about it, nor was he particularly worried at the sight of them leaning against the phone pole behind Wede's back porch, despite the facts that the only light came from a half a block away and that there was no one in sight in either direction.

The taller of the two stepped forward and put his hand on Flora's shoulder as she walked ahead of Nix to unlock the gate. Nix thought they were drunk or playing around and gave him his most stern look, the one he reserved for profane challenges to his authority in his classroom, and said, "Cut it out, guys." At which point the second of the perpetrators lifted his arm almost shyly to reveal a gun and said, "Stick 'em up," leaving Nix, despite the immediate danger, to think, Are people still saying that?

Officer Mayne of the Gang Tactical Unit was friendly enough and cut a dashing figure in his flack vest and Airborne beret, and with a mustache that would've looked melodramatic on a white man. He asked Nix to describe the weapon.

"It was an automatic," Nix said, "not a revolver," hoping his ability to distinguish between the two counted for something.

Maynes nodded, reached to the holster on his belt, and produced his sidearm. "Like this?"

"Sort of," Nix said. "Only it had a sight on the barrel."

Again Maynes nodded. Reaching this time for his ankle he pulled up the cuff of his pants and drew a second pistol.

"Yeah, that's it."

"Baretta," Maynes said and holstered the weapon with a subtle variation on a gunslinger flourish that made Nix fall in love with him.

"Well, I'm sorry this happened to you, but"—he put his hand on each of their shoulders and drew them in as though in prayer—"we'll catch 'em."

They were eager to believe. So much so that when Officer Maynes returned, breathless, minutes later with a tale of stalking, cornering, and capture, led them to the back porch where they looked out over the scene of a young man shoved against their back fence by two officers, who, with a nod from Maynes, shined a flashlight into the boy's face, and Maynes smiled, a gold tooth gleaming, and said "There," Flora and Nix looked at each other sadly, as much because it was not one of their assailants as because they didn't want to let Sgt. Maynes down. For a moment Nix, and he imagined Flora, too, wanted to simply say "Yeah, that's one of them," and let Maynes have the glory, because as was clear from the kid held against the chain link fence, like a scene out of Soweto, that they had, in describing their muggers, described the dress and appearance of every gang member in the neighborhood, and for the rest of the night, at intervals of about a half hour, Flora and Nix were summoned to their back window to watch as suspects after suspects were dragged in front of the fence to have a light shined in their faces, their eyes revealing, in each case, a degree of resignation that indicated beyond a doubt that they had been through this before. In the weeks to come Nix and Flora were called down to the police station to page through the yearbooks of neighborhood high schools (since it was illegal to take mug shots of minors) and to attend line-ups, which were not the orderly affairs of cop shows with the room and the two-way picture window and the wall with the height lines etched upon it. Instead they were led one at a time into a darkened room at which point a piece of copy-machine paper was lifted from the window of a brightly-lit, closet-sized holding room to reveal a man standing inches from their noses. After a few trips to the station, they came to recognize from the way the police chuckled among suspects as they came and went ("Luis, I hope you beat the crap out of whoever gave you that haircut") that, as victims, they fell below the lawmen and lawbreakers alike on the pecking order. The pathetic parade of putative perpetrators continued until Flora turned from the window and told Nix, "This is your fault."

Part 2

The Loop (July)

10.

Even the neighbors who'd become jaded by the sight of Nix's morning lift must have been impressed on this day to see the usual limousine joined by a stout, imposing black SUV with tinted windows idling one in front of the other in an offset formation. Nix, vaguely unsettled at the appearance of this mystery car, opened the limo door.

"Not in here, chief" Hector said. "You're in the Ford with Mrs. Fontaine."

"No kidding?" He started to shut the door but stopped long enough to ask, "Why are you here then?"

"I'm your ride home," Hector mumbled.

Nix approached the second car feeling sorry for Hector but not knowing exactly why. He reached for the handle of the passenger side door but glimpsed a white cuff pointing him to the back seat. He opened the second door where Mrs. Fontaine sat with a handbag on her lap and Anders opposite her in an upholstered jump seat.

"Get in," said Mrs. Fontaine in a voice that struck Nix as festive.

"Wow," Nix said.

"Surprised?" asked Mrs. Fontaine, with a smile for Anders. He smiled back, though only, Nix sensed, out of professional obligation.

"Surprised. Yes."

"It's a change of circumstances. Something I thought up myself. Save you the time out of your day, and Hector, all the shuttling back and forth is making him unhappy."

"He *is* the driver," Anders said, roused from his customary officiousness into the tone of an overindulged eleven-year-old by forces Nix had yet to comprehend. They were both dressed extravagantly well, she in a black suit over a ruffled blouse, Anders in a gray suit and azure tie.

"All the more reason. We thought you'd like to see the offices."

"Which offices?"

"The corporate offices," Anders said.

"I've made a telephone call. It stuck me that our arrangement might appear more professional if you were to have an office of your own and our conversations were to be conducted there. Is that suitable?"

"An office for me?"

"That's right," she said.

"A small room," Anders said. He crossed his leg, revealing a sheer sock of fire-engine red. "Manage your expectations."

Mrs. Fontaine agreed. "Wise advice. We'll all be seeing it for the first time."

Lacking only the martial bleat of a snare drum, the two-vehicle convoy charged down the left lane of the Kennedy expressway, exited at Congress, and advanced upon the center of the city. After rounding a dark curve on lower Wacker, the vehicle veered into a narrow garage door whose portal was flanked by yellow revolving lights on stanchions, down an abrupt dip into darkness, and though a vortex of curves into the sudden glare of an underground garage.

The vehicles stopped beside a glassed-in plaza at the center of the garage where there was a thrum of activity. Cars, all of them dark and expensive, with their hazard lights flashing, disgorged suited men and women in groups of three and five, who passed quickly through the doors flanked by men wearing cheaper suits and earpieces.

"Here we are," Mrs. Fontaine said, cheerfully.

Nix was first out the car and found himself facing the men posted at the glass doors.

"What's your affiliation?" the one on his right asked.

Nix pointed over his shoulder with his thumb, "I'm with—"

"Mrs. Fontaine," said the one on Nix's left. "Good morning. Are you to be addressing the board?"

"No, she will not," said Anders.

"Perhaps in passing," said Mrs. Fontaine.

"She's joking," Anders shouted over his shoulder, as he hurried through the doors.

"Yes, I am," said Mrs. Fontaine to no one in particular.

Inside an oak-paneled elevator, a man in maroon livery pressed a gold button on a panel of gold buttons, and Nix felt his insides drawn floorward with the spike in G-force. The doors opened on a low-ceiling reception area where a single woman sat behind a low desk built into a white wall, bearing a flying F in gold relief.

The woman looked up from her phone bank, then down, and then looked up again. "Good morning Mrs. Fontaine. Should I ring him?"

"No need. If you see him, tell him I'm in my offices." She said *aww*-fices elongating the first syllable long enough so that it sounded pretentious but, to Nix at least, deliberately so. To which the receptionist looked to Anders for either guidance or pity, it wasn't entirely clear. In any case, she got neither from Anders who was determined to remain as close to his boss as a mother to a toddler in a crystal shop. Nix followed, realizing full well that if he ever found himself alone on the floor he'd be taken for a trespasser in a high security zone.

Beyond the sloping white wall lay a short hallway of glass-walled offices, which then opened on a large cantilevered room filled with cubicles, stretching from window to window in each direction. As they walked, men and women peered over the tops of cubicle walls and from behind half-open doors. Nix imagined they were awestruck at catching a rare glance of their president, but realized, studying the glances more carefully, what most of them were expressing was something closer to panic. Mrs. Fontaine seemed to be oblivious to the nature of the stares, only of the fact of the presence (if only the tops of their heads) of her employees, and she smiled and said, "Good morning" to each she encountered.

They turned left at the end of the hall and walked along a row of windows that offered a vertiginous view of the neighboring buildings, the sun projecting the swift flight of clouds against mirrored windows. Along the interior wall was a row of black-and-white photographs, all of them headshots, nearly all of them of men. "This is the executive wing," Mrs. Fontaine said. "These are portraits of our distinguished executives over the last forty years. And here," she as she reached the end of the vertical rows of frames to a last row arranged horizontally, "is our current brain trust—such as it is." Nix glanced at the pictures of these last, which made no impression except to note that each of them would have looked at home among their predecessors in any of the previous eras. Fontaine slowed to allow Anders ahead of her. He unlocked the brass door handle. Beyond that door lay a cherry-wood-paneled room with a smart, unoccupied desk, a modern couch of black leather and steel, and yet another door. Again Anders stepped to the front with a ring of keys, and Nix followed behind them to find himself in a corner office furnished in the same style as the ante room, not out of any nod to egalitarianism, Nix suspected, but out of an awareness that any appointment, no matter how elegant, would be rendered shabby by the view, as the offices faced northward and to the east, looking out over the river to the lake beyond.

"Sit," Mrs. Fontaine said, as she settled behind her desk. Nix obeyed, pulling up a chair from the wall and sitting facing the desk in the center of the room. Anders sat on a couch identical to the one in the front office, in a pose identical to that he had assumed in the car. "We'll discuss our schedule for the next week. Then Larson will show you to your office and get you processed."

"Processed?"

"We felt naturally that if you were to be working for us you should have a desk."

"I have a desk I work at," Nix said, "at home."

"This is a matter of convenience. What we hope in the future is that we will meet here. You can come to the offices at times we decide upon, and we can continue the process of interview."

Her use of the first person plural made his head hurt. He noticed its use in the royal sense in referring to herself alone, and yet had a hard time untangling those instances from those in which she referred to Nix and herself or to herself and Anders.

The phone on her desk rang. Mrs. Fontaine smiled at Anders, as though a point of disagreement between them had been settled by the fact of the ring. "Look at this. I'm not here five minutes and the phone rings. Yes," she said into the receiver. "Yes, do come up."

"Otto will be joining us," she said for Anders's benefit, Nix assumed, since he didn't know who Otto was. Anders nodded with what looked to Nix like a stoic reticence and then they sat in silence for moment. There was a pause that didn't last long enough to become uncomfortable before there was a knock on the door.

"Come in," Mrs. Fontaine said gaily. The door opened and a stout but muscular looking bald man of perhaps fifty came through the door wearing a suit of a fabric that looked, in the indirect sunlight filtering through the window, to be iridescent.

"Otto Joff," Mrs. Fontaine said, standing and extending her hand, "you know Larson, and this is Nix Walters, my biographer."

"Can I have a word with you?" Joff asked her, ignoring the other two men in the room.

"Speak."

"Zira," Joff said, with an imploring tone, "there's a board meeting this afternoon."

"Mrs. Fontaine is aware of that," Anders said. Joff's expression soured slightly as Anders spoke, but he didn't look in his direction.

"Really, Otto, I don't intend to attend." Her eyebrows lifted and she smiled at the poetry of her own sentence.

"Of course, you don't. It's just that if you are here."

"I am president of the company, am I not? It's on the stationery"

"Of course."

"Then why shouldn't I occupy my offices during business hours or at any other time?"

"If you *occupied* your offices during business hours with any frequency or even at all, then your presence would be unremarkable. As it is—"

"What are you saying? Were there duties that I've neglected? Have I shirked my responsibilities?"

"Not at all. But you've fulfilled your responsibilities from— elsewhere."

"That was by agreement, Otto. You know that."

"I do know that, Zira. But that begs the question, does it not?"

"The fact that I hardly keep offices on the premises makes my being here on this day awkward."

"As you say."

"No, Otto, as I surmise it is as *you* say, for all practical purposes."

"Nevertheless."

"Are you suggesting that I leave the building?"

"Don't be ridiculous. Wouldn't it have been rude of me to not pay you the courtesy of a visit?"

"Certainly, Otto," she said, standing and walking to the door, "though I'm going to be here a lot more regularly, and I don't want you to think you're going to need to drop by every day." She turned the knob and stood beside the open door. Joff obliged the gesture by walking through it. "No one notified me of a change in your circumstances," he said.

"That's because there was none," she said.

"Would you like Stonebridge to come down?"

"If I say no, does that mean he won't."

"Why would you say no?"

Again they sat waiting, neither she nor Anders saying much of anything. It was as though they conducted themselves this way every day. As far as Nix knew, they did.

There was a knock on the door and in came a man in his middle fifties, Nix guessed, like Joff, but having height and hair where Otto did not, as well as an elegant bearing and a tan.

Mrs. Fontaine stood and walked around the desk. "Phillip, what a surprise."

"Zira. It's been ages." He took her hand and kissed her cheek.

"I thought you'd be Konrad Voigt," she said.

"Really?" Stonebridge said, surprised. "Should I send him down?"

"Would you?"

"Of course."

"How's Gloria?"

Stonebridge, retreating behind the door, smile still plastered to his face, gave her the thumbs up.

It seemed like only seconds later that the phone rang again. She held up a hand as if to say observe.

"Yes? Who? Yes, hello. Who? Yes, thank you. Hello? Hello, Konrad. Yes, Yes, I did. Of course, I understand," she said. "I'll be around more, now it should be as before, talk face to face."

She hung up the phone and said, "Well, that was fun. Now, Larson will show us your office."

Expecting a room of the same style and appointment of the one they'd just occupied, Nix encountered instead a minimalism of straight lines, white walls, and gray carpeting, the smell of industrial epoxy that Nix found appealing, and a bare modular desk with nothing on it.

He may have looked disappointed because Mrs. Fontaine said, "Whatever you need, Anders can requisition: pencils, coffee cups, a computer, art for the walls, and the electric mail. Tomorrow at ten a.m. I will be here and we can begin again.

"Hector has expressed the opinion that you should be able to get down here on your own. Is he correct in that?"

"Yes," said Nix, though with mixed feelings because, though grateful to be free of the churlish Hector, the otherwise posh treatment was growing on him.

A half an hour later Nix sat on a tall stool in front of a backdrop of artificial sky, while Anders stood beside him, arms folded. They spoke without facing each other, both looking at the camera on the tripod with a plastic frog taped to the top.

"What do you think that's there for?"

"The toad?"

"Isn't it a frog?"

"To focus the eye."

"How long have you been working for her?"

"Five years."

"How did you get the job?"

"Why would you ask that?"

"Curious."

"Oh, I don't remember, particularly. A peer mentor at Kellogg mentioned the possibility. I was looking to make a change."

"So it was like it was for me."

Anders thought about this a long time. Staring at the camera's eye as though he were waiting for it to trigger automatically. "In effect."

"The cereal business?"

The question roused Anders from his daydream. "What?"

"Kellogg."

"The business school," Anders said with no small measure of disgust. And Nix felt the pinch of humiliation, for if he had known that he might have pretended to misunderstand for the opportunity of playing the fool, for the sake of the gag. But because he didn't know he was a fool for not knowing.

"No kidding? So you dropped out?"

"Really there's only so much I'm willing to talk about. You'll be this." He handed over a business card, stark white with the VoicPro logo embossed in silver.

"VoicPro?"

"They are an information services company Fontaine contracts with for all our communications. Mrs. Fontaine was adamant you should have benefits, health insurance, dental. It's an area of concern for her."

The news was more than Nix could fathom in the dry tones of the moment, and he felt he should thank Anders. Instead he asked, "What's everyone so worked up about?"

"There's general concern that Zira would come down to the offices on the day of a board meeting."

"How come?"

"There's a perception that such an act is meant to intimidate."

"Is that what she had in mind?"

"Yes."

"Why does she do it?"

"Zira's presidency, while real in any legal or fiduciary sense, is largely ceremonial. It was conferred on her in part when she ceded majority control. Lately, she has been making public statements about pending business. Ohio Steel, a subsidiary of FFS, is in Chapter Eleven. A condition of its restructuring is that it must divest itself of its pension fund. You can imagine what that would mean. Mrs. Fontaine feels that the parent corporation should assume that fund. A majority of the board of directors contend, correctly, that the corporation is not obligated to do so. They leaked Zira's plan to the press. A number of the shareholders demanded this vote on the Ohio Steel package."

"She's hoping by being here she can buck up her side?"

"Just say that is the fear of Otto and others."

"Do you think it will work?"

"That remains to be seen."

"Do *you* want it to work?"

"Why would you ask that?"

"I don't know. People don't always agree with their bosses."

"True. And if you're not the boss nobody cares."

Anders made no secret of the fact that he was uncomfortable with the line of questioning, which was sufficient impetus for Nix to continue grilling him. Though if Anders were impatient, he was seriously less agitated than he had been all morning. Nix found himself wondering if he had underestimated Anders, having thought of him as little more than a fawning Osric, until seeing him in action that morning. Even the bad novelist fancies himself a student of human behavior, and Nix had no doubt that Anders was against this excursion but had followed loyally and protected his boss and had done so without disturbing his tie. Yes, Nix concluded, there was more to Anders than met the eye, and Nix would have been happy to go on making him pay for it, had the woman not come into the room and begun preparing the camera without acknowledging their presence until she said. "Up here, look at the frog."

"Allow me to get out of the shot," Anders said.

11.

Nix pressed his fingertips along a wall of oak panels trying to divine the concealed handle of the FFS executive dining room door. As he did, he cursed Mrs. Fontaine for sending him downstairs with no guidance about where to go or what to do once he got there, and with an inflated sense of the privileges that being the corporate biographer might bring. "Why don't you go downstairs for lunch," she'd said. "They're having the goulash." Not entirely sure he hadn't been given an order and in any case happy to hear Mrs. Fontaine talk for the first time in his hearing about a food that didn't have its crust cut off, Nix obliged.

Heads turned as he pushed the door open too hard and stumbled across the threshold with the inertia. Those who turned to look, stared, and continued to stare until Nix found an empty table in the corner. He sat with his hands folded, wishing he'd brought a magazine or a newspaper, and studied the room, hoping as he did to exude a kind of a watchful authority that they might associate with some sort of systems professional, a man detailed to observe the workings of the lunch room, with an eye toward streamlining the food-to-mouth interface.

Having been built in the early sixties in the international style, the building's interiors were square and spare, though it seemed in the years since then attempts had been made to overlay some measure of class. Still, the oil portrait on the wall glowered pretentious and over-dressed above the diners. The subject of the painting—Nix guessed from the air of stern prosperity, to say nothing of family resemblance—was Zira Fontaine's father. Nix wished he could think of a way to convey to those in the room who stared and ignored him in seemingly equal parts that he'd spent the morning listening to Valdis Nagy's daughter, the president of their company, talk about her love life, such as it was.

After several minutes of watching cheery women in green smocks shuttle back and forth from tables to a pair of swinging doors without looking once in his direction, Nix noticed a small man of indeterminate age, with a short-sleeved business shirt and tie and deluxe, blue-tinted pocket protector, detach himself from a table of like-looking compatriots and walk over to where Nix sat. "You're going to be waiting a long time."

"I'm sorry?" Nix said, taking stock of the man's comb-over.

"They won't wait on you. They don't come to your table unless you've submitted a menu request for the day via inter-office mail or online via electronic mail. Mel Lazar." He extended his hand but was standing on the far side of the table so that Nix had to get up and walk around to shake it before retreating to the relative security of his chair. "I'm glad to know you."

"Walter," Nix said. For Mel Lazar he would be Walter Nixon.

"I know who you are," Mel said. "Mind if I join you?"

Facing either the prospect of talking to Lazar for the length of a lunch or leaving the dining room in humiliation, Nix debated for a second before gesturing to the chair opposite him.

Rather than sit, Lazar returned to his original table, said something to the others that Nix couldn't hear, picked up his tray, and returned to Nix's table as his former dining mates watched with expressions of what looked to Nix to be malicious expectation.

Once he'd sat down, Lazar went busily about the business of preparing to eat, pushing his chair in, unwrapping his silverware, spreading the napkin on his lap and was about to carve into the expansive potato pancake draped over the steaming bowl of goulash when he stopped. "Do you mind if I pray?" he said,

"Pardon me?"

"Do you mind if I say grace?"

"Not at all," Nix said, though he felt deeply uncomfortable.

As Lazar bowed his head, a couple of loose strands of hair fell forward, leaving two furrows of bald scalp unconcealed. He folded his hands in his lap and moved his lips soundlessly. "Thank you," he said. Nix dismissed him with a wave, and again Lazar lifted his knife and fork and was about to start cutting when he stopped again. "Would you like some?"

"Of what you're having? That's okay.—But maybe you could order something for me."

"Sorry, impossible. The system denies multiple orders from the same employee during the same meal period. That was one of my projects actually."

"You run the computers around here?"

"Part of it. I cal-calibrate the server," he said so rapidly and uncertainly that Nix wondered if he were lying and wondering what servers were. Did they need calibrating? If they do, did they need it so often that there's a guy whose sole job is to do it?

"I'll take some of that bread if you don't mind."

"Not at all," Lazar said and handed over a slice of rye bread as dense as a hockey puck. "You're VoicPro?"

"I guess. Butter?" Lazar slid a foil-wrapped patty across the table but not his knife.

"VoicPro people usually sit over there." He nodded in the direction of a pair of tables in the corner. Nix looked that way and saw a half a dozen people, mostly women younger than the others in the room scattered around the two tables. "Over there is TechPro, over there is Tech Solutions, there TechCom, over there is GlobalCom, and over there is Excellence Incorporated."

"Nobody's FFS?"

"FFS is everyone else. There are not many of them in the dining room this early. Over there's the executive table. They come down later. If they come at all." He looked around conspiratorially, lowered his voice, asked, "What's she like?"

"Who?" Nix asked, as he struggled to spread butter directly from the container onto his slice of bread.

"You know."

"Mrs. Fontaine?"

Lazar held his finger to his lips and nodded.

"She's given me permission to speak her name." Nix bit into the bread.

"So?"

"What? What's she like? I don't know. She's okay."

"You have to understand that few of us have ever seen her in person."

"You must be happy then that's she's spending so much time around here."

"Me? Not that much, to tell the truth. I'm something of a Voigt adherent. Konrad Voigt, FFS's board chair."

"I've met him," Nix said, though that wasn't technically true.

"You've met him?"

"Haven't you?"

"Sure," Lazar said with enough hesitation as to make Nix think he hadn't.

Nix realized that the less Lazar talked the quicker he would finish and the quicker Nix could get something to eat, yet he couldn't resist the urge to ask. "When you say adherent, do you mean employee? Is he your supervisor?"

"As the Chairman of the Board, Voigt does not maintain a staff here, but *supervisor* would be an apt term. When I say *adherent,* I mean I am conversant in his writings."

"On what?" Nix asked.

"On a broad range of subjects. He's very prolific, so much so that he's underwritten his own publishing operation. In general—and by that I mean philosophically—he writes on the subjects of theology and ethics. He proves by the use of charts and color-coded maps the existence of good."

"Don't you mean *God*?"

"No *good* is correct."

"Who would doubt the existence of *good?*" Nix asked. "Good is everywhere. No one would dispute that, even if there's not enough. It stills exists."

"Mr. Voigt's definition of *good* might vary from your own. He believes people you would usually think of as good are essentially parasites—nuns, social workers. What Voigt advocates is a way of knowing God through doing, gathering."

"Money?"

"Pardon me?"

"Gathering money?"

"Money, information."

"I got mugged last night, we did. We got mugged," Nix said, with no idea why, except maybe that the man said he wanted information.

"Really, last night? I'm sorry. Well, Voigt has plenty to say about that."

"About mugging?"

"About fighting back, about reclaiming our country one act at a time. Voigt says we could end violent crime in a generation but that we lack the courage to commit to the challenge. To make mistakes if need be to get it right. That's a Voigt Tenet, 'To do right you can't be afraid to be wrong.'"

"Sounds reasonable," Nix said.

"It is. It is," Mel Lazar said, pleased beyond proportion to find a sympathetic ear. "I could give you some of his books."

"I'd like that," Nix said, thinking he could always use them for background, might be interesting in a slow minute in one of his session with Mrs. Fontaine to see what she had to say about them. Though with the arrival of Charlie Fontaine on the scene there had been fewer and fewer slow minutes.

"I met him on the Queen Mary," she'd said. "It sounds funny to say that, now, but it's true. This was in a day when it was common for families of means to take their eligible daughters on cruises in hopes of paring them with wealthy young men, though in my case my father suggested this trip for my health and our doctor agreed, and for all I know that was all they had in mind. I believe he was happy that I was merely alive. My recovery had been something of a medical miracle. There was a photograph of me in *Life* magazine and a medical journal out East. But still, I was weak and emotionally uncertain. You can guess a young girl with a limp does not hold many illusions for her chances of romance."

"You were walking again."

"I was walking again—with a cane, which was a humiliating thing. It's hard to find one of a style that suits a teenager. But I was happy to be going somewhere and to be outside after so much time indoors and in bed. That is what I believe I was thinking about: days and days of ocean air and sun.

"Uncle Stanni came along. Mother stayed home with Victor. He cried all day before we left. You can imagine what kind of trouble he could have gotten into on a ship. Uncle Mike wasn't at liberty to travel at the time. Charlie was there with a man he'd said was his uncle but who was actually his father, Raymond. I never understood the reason for the lie. Stanni confided to me years later that he'd met the two of them in a dice game. This of course I was not told at the time.

"Have you seen a picture?" she asked.

It had been no small thing to find a picture of Charles Fontaine as a young man. Certainly there were dozens from the eighties in *Vanity Fair* and the *Enquirer.* But in the fifties, wealth had needed to be escorted with flair or panache to attract the kind of attention that it did these days, and no one was much interested in the crippled daughter of an up-and-coming steel-rod wholesaler. After the better part of an afternoon, at the Harold Washington Library, buried in the pages of the old green-covered *Readers' Guide to Periodical Literature,* Nix had found the photo not in *Business Week* or *Time,* but in a table tennis quarterly. Charlie stood, paddle pressed to chest of his white shirt, flanked by the scowling first and second runners-up of the Monaco Invitational. He looked, with his heavily lidded eyes and seemingly permanent smirk, like—adjusting for changes in style and the shifting cultural perceptions of the pencil mustache—a degenerate.

"Charlie was fond of ping pong and good at it," Mrs. Fontaine would confide in Nix later.

"He did this thing with his hat. I imagine that sounds as queer an observation as the Queen Mary, but men wore hats, everyone wore hats. Do you like the movies?"

Nix, caught off guard by the question, managed a noncommittal hand swipe before saying, "Some, if it's a good one."

"I used to love the movies. We'd go, my mother and I. They were something my father never had time for." She had paused, long enough to prompt Nix to look up from his notebook. "I'm sure there's nothing in the world so dull as listening to someone of my generation talk about old movies."

"Not at all," Nix said. "I like old movies more than the new ones." He worried that she might ask which was his favorite because in reality Nix had little interest in movies at all, but he realized quickly that she wasn't listening to him and was instead studying the picture on his desk—he and Flora at their wedding. It was the one personal touch he'd added to his office.

He watched her face as she struggled to reclaim the sensation of the memories of her first meeting with Charles Marie Rochefort de la Fontaine, or—as he had been known to the boys of the Seaman's Home of Hoboken, New Jersey—Charlie Fontana. His family was

originally from France, Forteleau, Fontana being one of those El-
lis Island constructions. So the fact that he reclaimed the ethnicity
might not have been as dishonest as other acts of his career, though
the fact that he'd awarded himself an aristocratic title was not unlike
the sort of thing he might be expected to do.

"He would grip the hat by the brim, between his fingers and
thumb, and twirl it as he put it on his head." That should've been
a clue, Nix thought. "I should have known then," she said so
quickly upon his thought that Nix wondered if he had spoken
out loud. "Stanni introduced him to my father and myself. My
father and his went to the bar for a drink, and Stanni went with
them and then it was just the two of us and Charlie looked down
at me where I sat on the deck chair—I had been careful to not to
let them see me stand up—and he asked me, 'Would you like to
stretch your legs?'

"You can't imagine what kind of thoughts that set off in my mind
because of course I wanted to walk with him but didn't know if he
knew I walked with a cane. I was self-conscious. My legs were still
weak, and it hurt tremendously for me to walk any distance at all.

"I took his hand and stood up from the desk chair, and we
walked from the chair to the railing. I remember trying not to
clutch his arm too tightly and at the same time not to lean too
heavily on my cane and wondering how I was going to manage
for any distance. 'Here we are,' he said and took my cane from
me and hung it on a rail as though it was something he did three
times a day.

"Thinking back now I can't remember what we talked about.
That's not uncommon, I suppose. It was a long time ago and I
imagine we talked just to talk. He told me he was French, which
of course he was by heritage, so not a lie, strictly speaking. He had,
nonetheless, been born in this country and yet still spoke with an
accent. No one who heard him speak thought his accent inauthen-
tic, and obviously he had learned to speak that way by imitating
his father, but many children of immigrants try hard to sound like
an American, I can tell you speaking from experience. So while
it wasn't something I thought about at that time when I had no
reason to believe him to be anyone other than who I thought him

to be, I came to believe after years married to the man that he had learned at a very early age that such an accent would take him far, even if he was too young to have understood why or where it was he might be going. But he was a delight to listen to, so I choose to recall, even if I can't remember clearly, that he did most of the talking and I listened.

"That night Charlie and his father joined us for dinner. We dined with the ship's first officer. There was a lot of importance placed on sitting with the captain, and Charlie's father was quite irate that his request to do so had been turned down. He made his disappointment clear to the first officer, a kind and somewhat shy Norwegian who explained that there were a great many passengers but, for reasons of efficient seamanship, only one captain.

"Because Charlie and I were seated together I was preoccupied, and I didn't understand the importance of the matter, given the fact that the Captain was a fat man with a tobacco-stained beard, who I presumed was unlikely to have anything interesting to say beyond the particulars of driving an ocean liner.

"After dinner Charlie took me up on deck to watch the sun set and then walked me back to my cabin. There were railings in all of the gangways, and I was grateful because I could let Charlie carry my cane, which he twirled like a comedian in a vaudeville show, while I concentrated on walking like a regular girl."

The phrase struck Nix as sad and strange at the same time. "Then what?"

"Then we fade to black. As I said, I liked the older movies."

"It'll be different in the new building," Lazar said suddenly. Nix had read in the papers talk of new FFS headquarters on the river, the tallest in the world, reclaiming the title from—whichever country had it now—but hadn't heard Mrs. Fontaine, Anders or anyone else talk about it.

"The executive dining room?"

"Pardon me?"

"What will be different?"

"Oh, I don't know. Everything will be different."

"This building seems good enough."

"Sure, but a growing company that doesn't increase the size of its headquarters isn't perceived to be a growing corporation."

"Is that a Voigt Tenet?"

"No," Lazar said proudly. "That was one of mine."

"I guess we'll adjust."

"Adjust? We? Just hope you're still here. People come and go. Voigt talks about that. There was time when corporations would talk about themselves as a family. These days the family is the corporation, private retirement accounts, health insurance, work out of the home, office equipment and supplies. One of the great joys of corporate life used to be stealing a stapler when you were fired. 'These days,' Voigt likes to joke, 'you'd be stealing from yourself.'"

"So you don't like this idea of a new building?"

"Nonsense, it will be a great thing—if Voigt is CEO."

Nix was distracted by a drop of goulash that had fallen from Mel Lazar's fork and landed miraculously on his shirt, on the third button from the top. Lazar had the foresight of draping his tie over his shoulder, thus sparing the orange- and brown-checked polyester a direct hit. Nix thought the tie was a clip-on, but saw close up that it wasn't. "Why are you telling me this? If I'm working for her that might not be a good thing."

Again Lazar looked left and right. "I had a feeling about you. That's why I came over. Voigt talks a lot about taking risks. I said to my buddies over there," he gestured without turning around, so was therefore unable to see that his friends, having given up the hope that anything dramatic would happen, had left, "'I bet this guy's all right.'"

"Now that I possess this information, what am I expected to do with it?"

"Nothing if you don't want. Or you could help us out."

"What would that entail?" Nix surprised himself by asking. Listening to Lazar on risk had inspired Nix to recklessness.

"Nothing, necessarily. Think of it like a political party, or a church. How much you become involved is entirely up to you. There are those people who do nothing, more identify themselves as members of the movement, and there are those, such as myself, I like to think, who are very involved. Of course if you take that route there is no end to the opportunities you have."

Lazar got up from the table. Nix stood to shake his hand. "You've given me a lot to think about," he said, incontrovertibly convinced that this man was unstable.

Nix returned to his office and dialed Mrs. Fontaine's extension. She didn't answer. He went looking for her and found her office dark and that she and Anders gone. Back in his office, Nix put his feet up on his desk and tried to recall his last conversation with Mrs. Fontaine. Why don't you go to lunch? she'd said. Nix took that sentence to mean something on the order of "take five," since it was the middle of the workday. She could have meant, and apparently did mean, "Let's call it a day." They'd never discussed how long these sessions were to last. They stopped when Mrs. Fontaine wished to stop, usually after five or six hours.

Nix didn't worry long before deciding he had little to worry about. There had been an abrupt shift (or was it a steady evolution?) in their relationship. She'd become more tolerant of his questions, and he'd become more confident about speaking up when he felt the need. Now that they were both going to be coming into the office, Nix felt he could be more at ease in her presence and felt certain she'd say the same about her feelings toward him. Consequently, Nix also found it possible to be more professional than deferential and, in being so, had come to recognize that the book they were writing together was going nowhere. Both from his position and hers. It lacked both form and focus. If Mrs. Fontaine merely meant him to transcribe their conversations, spell check, and shift the manuscript off to a vanity publisher, there was no reason for concern. If, however, she hoped to produce a book to be published by an actual book publisher with an eye toward actual sales, then they—and by *they*, Nix recognized he mostly meant *he*—had work to do. What Nix was less sure about was whether this was work that she and, more importantly he, was ready to undertake.

The new house was in chaos and promised to be so for some time. This was all that Nix, alone in his office, could make himself think about. It had been the first move for which they could afford to hire movers, and while Nix had been happy to be freed from

imposing upon friends, he had been unprepared for how useless
he'd felt as wiry, plucky men bounded down the stairs with dress-
ers on their backs. He hovered, waiting to be asked to help, endur-
ing their exasperated stares as they waited—hands on hips—for
him to get out of the way.

And then once the J. & B. Movers' van had rattled away with a check
for three hundred dollars more than the estimate (owing to a magi-
cal line on the invoice for something called "transfer costs." Nix and
Flora argued with them (Nix: "Isn't moving by definition a transfer?") and lost (Flora: "Next time we'll hire somebody who won't
screw us." Mover #3: "Yeah, next time"). Flora's family had rolled up
in her father's white Econline with aluminum ladders strapped to
the roof racks. Not all the nine other members of her family, actually just her mother, Rose, father, Armando, and her three brothers, Vincent, Tito, and Lou. With the exception of Lou, the oldest
of the DiCicco children, whose belly curled over his belt buckle,
the DiCicco men were small, able workers, who shuttled about the
bungalow with metal toolboxes and the digital efficiency of video
game heroes.

The brothers called Nix Wally. He'd once asked Tito to do so as a
joke, and the name had stuck with the tenaciousness of a rash. Rose
was not quite five feet tall and always spoke to him with her head
thrown back, so she could see him though the lower lens of her
glasses. The DiCiccos had never been able to find a reason to dislike
Nix, instead they all regarded him with what he took as a certainty
that one day he would let Flora down.

Nix couldn't have imagined them thinking otherwise about the
mumbling bookworm and his sullen mother. For the traditional
first meeting of families upon their engagement, the ten DiCiccos
had taken the two surviving Nixons to a restaurant in their red-
bricked neighborhood. While the DiCiccos slapped backs and nee-
dled the waiter, and ordered appetizers by the tray, in their native
tongue, Myrna sat with her elbows drawn and her coat on, picking
disconsolately at her risotto.

Everywhere he went in the house he saw DiCicco legs pro-
truding from beneath sink or behind the refrigerator, while Nix
milled dismally looking for a role to play in his own life. Now

Flora was at home stenciling a menagerie on the walls of the nursery. There had been talk in the literature about a nesting impulse, but Nix had assumed Flora would be immune. As it turned out she possessed such an instinct in steel-alloy Smith & Hawken garden spades.

After two weeks of habitation, Nix's office at FFS was unfinished around the edges. Tangles of gray nylon spiraled out from where the carpet had been cut. On the shelf above the coat hooks, a stir stick lay across the lid of a paint can. A promised computer had yet to be delivered and the narrow windows on each side of the door still bore the decals of their manufacturer. The framed wedding picture was the only sign of habitation in the office. It had been taken, as had all the pictures at the wedding, by Klaus Dunlop, a Tony-award-winning set designer Flora knew. Rather than the stock poses that populate most wedding albums, Klaus had a vision. He constructed a postmodern study of black and white candids. Both Nix and Flora had been proud of the images, dazzled, and felt Klaus had captured, as well as anyone could have, what they had hoped the day would convey. The pink dress set off more of a scandal than Flora had intended, with the DiCiccos complaining about the color it wasn't and Flora's feminist friends incensed about the color it was. In the end all found common ground on the fact that, whatever her motivation, Flora looked great in pink. And yet looking at the photo now and remembering how Mrs. Fontaine had turned the picture in her hand, after her talk of ocean liners and debutante tradition, with an absolute lack of irony and humor, the very image seemed trite and shabby.

It was this mood that Mel Lazar interrupted, tapping on the closed door and looking first through one window and then the other to catch Nix's eye. Nix startled, careened forward in his chair, setting both feet on the floor and both hands on the desk, before recognizing Lazar and waving him into the office.

Mel carried an overstuffed brown paper bag in both hands. "I brought these for you," Lazar said.

"I'm sorry," Nix said.

"In the cafeteria," Lazar said, gesturing over his shoulder, to remind Nix of the direction of the room.

"I know, I know," Nix said. "I remember."

"I said I'd bring some of Voigt's writings up for you, and here, I have." From the bag he produced a pile of books and held them forward with both hands, as if to set them at the feet of an idol. "You actually can keep these. I have other copies and am able to get more for free as part of my membership."

"Wow," Nix said. "There are—several."

"Yes, I said he's prolific." Lazar placed the books on the desk and pushed them within Nix's reach. The spines were brightly colored, with gold-lettered titles. Nix picked up the first. There was an unsettling lavishness to the cover, which was embossed and inlaid with a three-dimensional image of a diminutive bald man wearing dark glasses and a loose-sleeved white robe with a gold-embroidered collar. He stood in the standard pose of a prophet—his arms were outstretched, and he was surrounded by some foliage of fantastic, alien appearance. The book bore the title in a lurid script *Know by Doing: An Introduction to Practical Extremism* and beneath the title was the logo of a cross inside a V, so that the arm bars of the cross stretched to the tops of each arm of the V.

$$\mathbb{V}$$

Nix recognized this as the sort of thing employed by religious groups awash in cash and published for an audience that was uncomfortable with books—a lot of ornamentation, and a shimmering, holographic (literally) gilded lily.

"Which one is the first?" Nix asked. "Would I need to read them in order?"

"Yes, you should read them in order—I went ahead and arranged them that way for you. Start with *Know by Doing*, then read *Know by Being*, then *Do What You Are*, and then *Be What You Do*, and then *Principles of Practical Extremism*. *Principles* is mostly excerpts from the other books. You could read that if you just wanted to get an idea, but I thought from what I think I know about you that you'd want to start at the beginning."

"No doubt," Nix said. He noticed that Mel had tried to clean the spot of goulash off of his shirt. A wet circle radiated from an epicenter beneath his tie. "*Practical Extremism.* That's kind of an oxymoron, isn't it?"

"We say *contradiction.* But, yes, you're exactly right. The Central Tenet of Practical Extremism is that the pairing of opposites creates equilibrium."

"Well, thank you, Mel," Nix said, lifting his heels to the desk and opening to the first page of the book, he read,

> To act is better than to know. To know without acting is a crime of faith. To act without knowing is proof of faith.

"What are you doing?"

"I thought," Nix said, "I'd take a little time this afternoon to catch up on your man Voigt," thinking if he pretended to read Lazar would leave.

"I wouldn't recommend you read those in the office."

"Really? Why not?"

"There are unclear matters of alignment," he said. "Particularly in VoicPro, particularly on this floor. The scenario of succession that I described at lunch is one in the future. The current circumstances remain unevolved."

Nix was going to ask why, when a small, dark girl in an unusual flowered dress appeared in the doorway. He recognized the long black hair and tired eyes and was trying to place them when a woman appeared behind her. It was the woman Nix had seen at the coach house on the grounds of the Fontaine estate.

"Have you seen my mother?" the woman snapped, as though she blamed them for concealing her.

"Your mother?"

"Zira. Mrs. Fontaine."

12.

Frank was fucking Toni. Nix was sure of it. A man would have to be blind or a fool not to see—even if he didn't watch the two of them carry on five days a week, at 4, 5, 6, and again at 10. In just two weeks, a gut-sick Nix had watched their relationship degenerate from a producer-conceived, cue-card-generated, ratings-boosting, on-air flirtation into something sordid and sad.

"During the break, Toni was telling us about her trough."

"Fra-*ank*." Nix could only guess at what hard traveling had brought her so low.

"Well, something's going on down there in the tropics, Toni."

"More like a depression than a trough, Frank. If we pan out to the central Pacific. This swirling bank of clouds is forming over a warm current. Believe it or not, you guys, this is going to push the jet stream north, which is going to mean warmer temperatures for us all summer, 9,000 miles away, if you can get your mind around that, so Dorothy's going to want to make sure you drag the air conditioners upstairs."

"We've got central air, Toni," Frank says, eyes planted on the camera lens. "You know that."

Toni's teeth locked in a smile asks, "How would I know that, Frank?"

"She's kidding folks. Toni remembers the Memorial Day barbeque. I showed you my unit."

Jesus. Cue the laughing trombones.

Nix forgave Toni nonetheless. To not would have been uncharitable in the extreme. After all, she was, he assumed, a marionette of whatever divine hand of fate lowered her onto this stage in that blazer.

Nix assumed alcohol is banned in the dressing rooms before broadcasts hours. Thus there'd be precious little to ease the ache beside the kind of zipless encounter featured in bus station men's rooms and after-midnight cable: Carlos, the sports guy, walks in to find Patty Pilgrim, consumer reporter weeping into her make-up mirror. Passions flare like a California brushfire and no sooner are they getting busy on the vanity than Carlos is taken by surprise by restaurant critic Fenton James, the smell of affordable yet ultimately disappointing maki from Hasigumi's still on his breath. All this passionate commotion summons Gary the Gadget Guy with his solar-powered vibrating showerhead, new this fall from the Sharper Image. And, before long, the ineluctable cacophony of group grope rouses Frank who's in the hallway, pantomiming a chip shot from the morning's round to Toni, who finds herself presumptuously hoisted buccaneer-style over Frank's shoulder and cast into the heart of an epic slithering orgy, as Lottie Your Lottery Lady piles on for the afternoon Quik-Pick. God, if there were only something Nix could do.

"Coming next," Frank said, "how horny is your teenager?"

Nix heard Flora drop something in the kitchen and cuss. When she was working and he wasn't, she worked louder, so that the very sound of industry and effort might remind him of what he wasn't doing around the bungalow.

Nix had discovered that he had little more interest in renovating a house than he had in buying one. At first he'd enjoyed the trips to the massive home improvement center—which occupied an entire city block on which people once lived—to study the color swatch cards that Flora fanned out in front of his eyes. But when the time came for work, particularly painting (which Nix discovered to his dismay, involves hours of invisible preparatory work) his enthusiasm waned. It wasn't that Nix was lazy. Nothing could have been further from the truth (actually, some things could have been further from the truth, but Flora wouldn't have described him that way, and her judgment was the standard in this case). It was merely that the bullet train that was the Homeowner Express had left the station without him, and he could never catch up, no matter how fast he ran. Nix might have described what he felt as a selective depression, where the thought of home improvement—and nothing else—wounded his heart with a monotonous languor.

Marcia, Flora's boss, had come bearing a gift-wrapped, four-pound sledge and a zeal for destruction that made her valuable in all tasks requiring demolition. The collisions of style, period, and color in the house were spectacular, while somehow failing—with a consistency that defied all probability—to work together in any room, on even an ironic level. All one could do was marvel. Flora had made three lists, one of necessary repairs, one of necessary re-decorating, and one of a sort of if-money-wasn't-an-issue wish list. In fact, for Flora and Nix money was still more of an issue than for the average American, and whatever mark Flora had once used to separate the lists had somehow been erased or obscured, and she bought without heed to cost.

Flora argued that she had handled most of the details of securing a mortgage and therefore had the authority to oversee the renovation. Nix conceded that position but suggested that her role had been more a matter of evolution than design. She'd initiated the calls to the banks and mortgage brokers, so it was only natural that she call whenever a question or problem arose.

By the time they signed a contract, Flora had experted herself on all aspects of home financing, while Nix somehow knew less than he had before they started looking for a mortgage. He'd sat hazily at the closing, as document after document was passed from hand to hand with a bucket brigade rhythm that bypassed only Nix as Trudy, their owl-eyed, sleepy lawyer, leaned across his lap to pass each form to Flora, who in turn handed them to the sallow title clerk with the cigarette behind his ear who steadily sank behind an igloo of paper. Not sure how much of the process he should be letting flow by him, Nix did a credible (he thought) job of pretending to wonder what he was signing, asking about the importance of every third or fourth document, but not such a good job listening to the answers.

A commercial came on—local, from the looks of the production values. A man is rolling dice at a craps table. He is sweating, his tie loosened, collar unbuttoned. His expectant look turns to anguish as the croupier scoops up the last of his chips. Cut to scene of the same man tip-toeing into the room of a sleeping young girl. He snatches a piggy bank from a shelf, shakes the contents into his palm, and runs. Cut to a woman in a clothing store. She gazes in admiration at the dress worn by another customer, then notices the same dress on a mannequin. Cut to this same woman trying on the same dress in a dressing room. She registers pleasure at her reflection in the mirror, but her look turns to despair as she looks at the price tag. Then an idea seems to occur to her. She puts her overcoat on over the dress and hurries toward the exit. A saleswoman grabs the woman by the wrist but she is able to break free and runs. She reaches a street corner and collides with the gambler from the first part of the commercial and then the two of them somehow tumble off a cliff in the middle of the city. Super-imposed against a racing cliff-face with high-school-AV-club-quality special effects the two of them flail and scream as they fall and fall and fall. White letters rose from below the screen to ask "Who will catch you?"

Nix was thinking, given the plot of the vignettes, that that question could be taken more than one way, when he notices something in the fine print at the bottom of the screen. Was it a crest? Nix squinted at the familiar shape and realized it was a cross embedded in a capital V. It may have been that distraction or the banality and ubiquity of the commercials that kept him from making the connection. But now that he had the thought that he had been unconsciously processing this sordid evangelism provoked him in a passive way.

Next to the television was a box of CDs and tapes Flora had asked him to shelve more than a week earlier. Though Mrs. Alvarez was very much alive and now residing in Vegas, they'd hired a cleaning crew that specialized in sanitizing crime scenes to scrub away five decades of accumulated grime along the moldings and a sort of anthropological electrician who specialized in rewiring the ancient make-do circuitry. The painting and papering they were handling themselves, or Flora was mostly, with Nix available for high walls and ceilings. And, to Nix's surprise, an undeniable charm was being extracted from the structure.

To anyone not living in Chicago, the word *bungalow* conjures an image of a thatched dwelling in sunny climes. To a Chicagoan, the word describes a brick shithouse. The tropical bungalow features thin walls that swell and ripple in the trade winds; the Chicago bungalow is fabricated of bulkheads that can absorb a howitzer round. Theirs featured a wide living room, laid out perpendicular to the rest of the house, ingeniously conveying size. Beyond that was a narrow but spacious dining area, and beyond that a kitchen that made up for in cabinet space what it lacked in square feet. These houses were built for a generation determined to make do rather than to dream of unlikely wealth.

After Marcia had been round to glare at Nix and to tear out the stationary sink in the utility room, Nestor had arrived in old-school overalls, carrying a tin toolbox to install a new one. Nix had been surprised and, in the end humiliated, to learn that Nestor actually could plumb. He passed the afternoon flat on his back, head unseen beneath the sink, while Flora handed him wrenches from her perch on a folding stool beside him, somehow not hearing Nix even when he spoke inches from her ear.

All of which was not to say that Nix didn't appreciate the help. Indeed, all the work that had been done had made a dramatic effect. Things in his house he didn't even know he had—soffits, wainscoting, and plate rails—had been replaced, refurbished, or removed as was appropriate. Borders had been stenciled, drains cleared, ivy pruned, floors polyurethaned. And Nix had replaced, refurbished, stenciled, pruned, or polyurethaned virtually none of it.

He, taking the long view, believed there would be time in the life of the mortgage for him to pitch in. If nothing else he could repair the work done today when the time came years from now. He hoped that Flora would be as visionary on this subject. Though, as far he could tell, she was not. In his defense, Nix had not allowed her to carry anything heavy or climb anything high. Nonetheless in the great cause of home rehabilitation, Nix was not holding up his end, and Flora resented him for that.

The screen returned to the News Set of the Future and Toni was sitting behind the desk. This was a privilege granted only at the end of the program. "So the hot muggy air is back tomorrow but tonight is good sleeping weather."

"Thank you, Toni" Frank said. "Not that any of us is going to be doing much sleeping."

Nix swore at the screen and rocked himself into a seated position. He'd reached a turning point. There was absolutely nothing else for him to do at this precise moment other than go and help his wife. He could transcribe one of the hours of Mrs. Fontaine interviews left on tape but had developed an aversion to the task as keen as his hatred of plastering. To say nothing of the fact that, at that moment, Mrs. Fontaine wasn't standing on a stool in the next room, cussing loud enough for him to hear.

He'd begun drawing a salary at FFS, above and beyond the second payment pending for the completion of the book, and been hiding behind this increase in his arguments with Flora to an ever-decreasing degree of success. Nix reasoned that, once they stopped worrying about money, they would stop worrying altogether, yet he had the tension that was now coursing through the house with greater dependability than the electricity to show how wrong he was.

He stubbed his toe on a can of floor sealant and yelped, but Flora didn't turn around.

"How can I help?"

"Just keep doing what you've been doing."

Nix didn't know what she meant by that, but couldn't very well say, "You mean sitting on my ass?"

This room was to be the nursery. It was—fittingly—the smallest room in the house, a ten by ten square adjacent to their bedroom with a small window and a warped floor that was covered at the moment with scraps of discarded wallpaper and chips of paint.

"I can tear paper down. I'd bet I'm good at that. Not Marcia good but—"

"Sure," Flora said unconvincingly. She had not started to show yet. If Nix noticed a change at all in her appearance, it was in her eyes, which looked tired, but that could have come from working her usual heavy load at her job, managing a pregnancy, and rehabbing a bungalow without any significant help from her husband. The dust and paint shavings in her hair reflected the afternoon sun through the window like Mylar confetti on New Year's Eve, and she had a positively erotic strand of a spider web plastered to her cheek.

"What am I doing here?"

"You're using this," she said, handing him a round device the size of his palm. "It's a paper tiger. It scores the old wallpaper so it comes off easier."

"I tear it?"

"No, you use this—glop."

"Is it toxic?"

"It's got to be."

"Paper tiger. Mao said it."

"What?"

"America is a paper tiger."

"Was he wrong?"

Nix slathered the blue paper-remover with a thick brush, expecting the paper to fall away, but it simply got wet and refused to yield to Nix's tugging. "That remains to be seen. This room needs a train."

"A train?"

"I had a train."

"You didn't have a train. Your father did."

"Not true. It was mine. In name."

"You held the deed?"

"So my father always told me. 'Son, this is yours.'"

"'Just don't touch it.'"

"Exactly."

"Where is it?"

"I gave it away. We could start our own."

"Where would one go?"

"Along the walls. It could make stops at the dresser and the crib."

Already there was a crib, from Marcia, stowed in the corner beneath a tarp. Its arrival had struck Nix as premature, given the amount of work that needed to be done and the fact that each day's work on the nursery began with Flora wrestling it into a neutral corner before she started in on the walls or the closets.

"I suck at this."

Flora smiled. "You have to really, really, want the paper gone."

13.

One sustained ring meant an intra-office call. "Mr. Walters are you in for Mr. Mel Lazar?" a woman asked.

"Sure," Nix said. "Where is he?"

"On his way."

"From where?" Nix asked, but she'd hung up.

Determined to look busy when Lazar showed, Nix riffled through all five desk drawers before finding a blank notepad and set about filling lines with faux script. He'd managed to counterfeit two thought bubbles and connect them with an emphatic two-way arrow when Lazar knocked.

"—in," Nix said, and didn't stop pretend writing until he heard Lazar's rear end depress the pleather of his visitor chair's cushion. "You have a secretary, Mel?"

"Partially."

"Partially?" Nix asked—as much out of curiosity as spite. After the humiliation in the executive dining room Nix had been summoned to a screening room large enough to seat fifty and sat alone watching the video ballad of John and Joe, a kind of Goofus and Gallant pair of new employees, in which John impresses his superiors with his grasp of etiquette and table manners, while Joe commits every faux pas Nix had, and a few Nix hadn't dreamed of. The film ends with John moving up to the boardroom while Joe is escorted to the door by security.

"So you've got them there, I see," Lazar said. "The books, good. You read them?"

Nix looked up, as if realizing for the first time that Lazar was in the room. Desks are funny things, Nix thought—sit behind one and you start to feel like you're somebody worth knowing.

"I looked at them, yeah," Nix said. And he had, or Flora had, when he left them on the kitchen table. She'd been intrigued by the lurid cover designs on the book, then made the mistake of opening one.

"Wait a minute. Let me stop you there before you answer and tell you I understand that Voigt isn't for everyone."

Nix noticed a blue stain in the corner of Lazar's shirt pocket. Somehow ink from a leaking pen had outflanked the Maginot Line of his pocket protector.

"To be open to his ideas you have to have a certain—generosity."

"Since you say so, I've got to tell you it stopped me cold. His positions on women—gender, you would say."

"Understand most of Voigt's reflections on marriage are Contemplations not Tenets?"

"I have to say I *didn't* understand. Flora didn't." Actually, Flora had only looked into the books long enough to pronounce them "creepy" and to suggest, after being told who Voigt was, they were proof of the degraded state of global capitalism.

"Flora?"

"My wife," Nix said. He didn't use the word often and it sounded strange to him, though not as strange as *partner,* which Flora insisted on using, leading to endless surprise first meetings as Flora's associates were perpetually expecting Nix to be a lesbian.

"You're married."

"Is it a problem?"

"Of course not, marriage is the Fulcrum of the Voigt Societal Pattern. As such, there is a Tenet discouraging married men from discussing matters of the Philosophy with unmarried men."

"You're not married, Mel?"

"No," said Lazar sadly.

Nix found his tone arresting. From the looks of Lazar, Nix made him at least on the forty side of thirty. Nix wasn't the type to believe that happiness resided in marriage but he did worry about the Lazars of the world—worries that conjured up images of hot plates and holidays spent alone in front the television.

"You can't talk about anything Voigt says that's got to do with women?"

"I can talk about it. With other singles, in study groups."

"I'm sure he'd understand."

"I'm not," Lazar said, checking his watch, "but these are Tenets, not laws or commandments."

"In the first book. This stopped Flora, I can tell you, this about the Feminine Vessel. This is a *vessel* Voigt talks about, as in receptacle, not ship. Flora thought it was *vassal*. She said, 'Same thing.' I said, 'Not so,' right?"

Lazar shifted in his seat. "A vessel. Like a vase. It has been explained to me as a vase. The vessel is barren, cold, and dry, until it is filled—"

"With what? sperm?"

Lazar winced. "Yes," he said, "though not necessarily. They may, Voigt reflects, already hold … there is more to women than bearing children or being objects of sexual desire. Voigt is quite clear about that—though not until the later books." As Lazar spoke Nix realized with a small measure of urgency that the ink stain on his pocket was spreading.

"And the chapter on Corporate Responsibility?"

"That's a play on words."

"No shit?"

Lazar shifted in his chair. "Voigt discourages the use of profanity in conversation, particularly between married and single men. It's one of his Tenets of Discourse. Those are reproduced in the appendixes of all of the volumes." Nix wondered whether he should warn Lazar about the ink stain. "*Corporate Responsibility* means responsibility to the Body, meaning the human body, to the body politic—*politic* in this case meaning more a lot of people than politics as we understand them." Lazar's eyes darted around the room. The writer in Nix searched for the word—*furtively*, that was it, the word sounded cliché, but what other word was there for such furtiveness? "Is this your office?" he asked Nix.

"Yes."

"Really?"

"By *really*, do you mean am I lying? Well, when I leave here, I'm not free to detach it from the building and take it with me, no, but as long as I am here, yes it's mine and mine alone."

Lazar nodded at the door behind Nix's chair. "Is that her office?"

"Down the hall."

"What does she do in there?"

"I couldn't tell you what happens when the door is closed."

The phone rang. It was Hector. "Ten minutes," Hector said. Each day Mrs. Fontaine came in to the office, Hector called ahead to give him a ten-minute warning. Nix wasn't sure whose idea this was, whether Mrs. Fontaine wanted him to be prepared for her arrival—though there was absolutely nothing Nix would need to do in preparation—or if it was merely a courtesy call from Hector so Nix could stash the bong before his boss got there.

"Now, I hate to cut you short just when we got rolling, but Mrs. Fontaine will be here in a couple."

"She's coming here?" Lazar said, looking this way and that as if he'd dropped something. "Well. What did I come in here with? Nothing. Good afternoon. We'll talk again," and left before Nix could alert him to the spreading blue stain on his shirt.

Minutes later, the latch turned and Hector stuck his head in the door, looked in Nix's general direction without actually looking at Nix, and then receded before Mrs. Fontaine strode in wearing a white linen dress, the first time her clothing reflected the physical reality of the climate, as it was a hot day. She was followed as always by Anders, also dressed for the weather in seersucker.

"Where is your couch?" Mrs. Fontaine asked, in lieu of her customary greeting of "Good morning, Mr. Walters."

"Right behind you."

"Forgive me," she said one hand to her eyes and a second flailing for Anders's arm, who took her hand. "I have a blinding headache." She lay flat on her back with her arms to her side and closed her eyes, as Nix looked on, utterly at odds about what to do.

"Should I call a doctor?" he asked, finally.

A quick laugh burst from her lips. "It's a *mi*-grane. Larson will get us a damp washcloth and some ice, and we shall begin."

"Of course," Anders said.

Once he and Mrs. Fontaine were alone, Nix wasn't sure what he should do. Never having had a migraine himself he didn't know whether even the sound of his voice might make the pain worse as she lay on his couch in the posture of a corpse. So, he sat with his arms folded on his desk in what he hoped was a professional pose. He thought with more people coming into his office he should have some art on his walls but didn't know how to acquire it. The training video had not been explicit on this point, though the narrator had made clear that one was not free to hang one's own art, as the tasteless Joe had found out when he'd hung an airbrushed portrait of a swimsuit model reclining on a Harley Davidson.

After what seemed like several hours of silence but in reality may have been no more than two minutes, Mrs. Fontaine turned her head in his direction and opened her right eye. "What are those?" she asked.

"Sorry?"

"On your desk?"

Nix felt a cold sweat on the back of his neck. "Books," he croaked.

"Whose books?"

"They belong to someone in IT, in information technology. He lent them to me."

"Let me see." As she craned her neck, Nix lifted the top volume. He could only imagine what effect the iridescent and shifting image would have on her headache.

Mrs. Fontaine squinted. "What is it? Who is its author?"

"Konrad Voigt," Nix said, warily.

"Voigt, our board chair?"

"Yes," Nix said.

She looked for a moment longer, then lay her head down. "What are the other ones?"

"They're by him, too."

"Really? How many are there?"

"Lazar gave me four. I don't know how many others there are. Much of the material is repeated."

"Lazar?"

"The employee I mentioned who lent me these books."

"What are the subjects of these books?" Mrs. Fontaine said, measuring the word *subjects* as though it held more importance than any in the language.

"They largely pertain to his—personal philosophy," said Nix.

"And what is his personal philosophy?" Mrs. Fontaine asked, aping—Nix would've sworn—his tone.

"That is hard to tell from what I've read."

"On what pretense were these books given to you?" she asked, but before Nix was able to ask what she meant by that, Anders returned with a washcloth and an ice pack.

She took first the ice pack and placed that at the base of her neck, then folded the washcloth and laid it across her eyes and then lay flat again, now with her fingers interlocked on her stomach. "Where were we?"

"You were on the Queen Mary."

"Yes, well we were through with that. Shortly after we returned to the States, Charlie came to Ohio. His father was the only member of the family to attend the wedding, which should have told me something, except that Charlie told me that he had lost family members to U-boat attacks in both world wars, and the survivors were reluctant to travel by sea. I know that sounds ridiculous, but such things did happen. Stan and Mike did not believe him but thought rather that his family were snobs and believed themselves too good to come to Cleveland, Ohio, for a wedding to an American.

"We went on a honeymoon to Warm Springs, Georgia, to the spa that President Roosevelt had built. I thought Charlie was a wonderful sport, a young and handsome man, to be spending his honeymoon among invalids. There may be some personal information I would like to add to this section, but I'm not comfortable doing so in this method of dictation.

Nix looked at Anders, who raised an eyebrow. "Of course," Nix said, relieved.

"When we returned from that trip we moved to Chicago."

"That was when?"

"Nineteen-fifty. The move was Stan's idea. He had been in the Air Corps during the war and came home from the Pacific convinced that, in ten year's time, everything that had been made out of iron and steel would be made from aluminum. The days of steel were over, he said, but we knew nothing of aluminum. Stan said that the overhead involved in building processing or manufacturing facilities was too high to bother with and suggested we get into warehousing and shipping. If anything the demand for metals was greater than it was before the war. We were brokering sales all over the world, taking commissions on exchanges of materials we never laid eyes on, from Japan to Cairo. We'd become accustomed to trading and were trading in commodities, whenever someone passed along a tip. Then in 1971, the country went off the gold standard, and it was Mike who came up with the idea of money as the medium. 'People would always want money,' he said. We had been selling steel to make money. Why not eliminate steel from the transaction and sell money? 'Eliminate the middle man,' Stan said. No more unions, no more supply worries, no overhead."

"Still that must have been a difficult adjustment."

"It was. Our first house on Logan Boulevard had been very small. For all of us—Charlie, myself, Stan and Mike, Victor, and Father. Mother moved in the eyes of the post office only. We kept the house in Lorain, and she spent most of her time there, except the winters, when she'd join my father in Miami Beach.

"We opened a small office off of LaSalle Street on Madison. You have to understand that in those days currency trading had none of the caché it enjoys today or the stigma. It wasn't like you see in the movies where men talk on telephones in their cars. We made money gradually with small purchases and sales of currency. And as I might have said of my illness, we got well gradually. There was almost no vulnerability, no chance of exposure. We bought the building we had been renting and rented out the spaces we weren't using and in short order we bought a second and rented that, and then with the money being made from renting out one building and most of a second, we bought a third building and moved into that. Shortly afterward we sold the first two for large profits. With the profits we made from that sale, we began making much larger trades. This was a turning point for the company. What we considered to be conservative trades were five times greater than our previous positions. We found we had reached a point where our sales activity was beginning to attract attention, so we had to—reevaluate our standing. And we were careful. We learned early that success was largely a matter of paying attention. If we were properly positioned we couldn't lose. Make gains in small increments."

"What was Charlie doing at the time?"

"I had insisted he be made vice president."

Nix looked at Anders, and they shared forlorn smiles.

"I can imagine what you're thinking," Mrs. Fontaine said and Nix looked quickly to see if she'd removed the washcloth from her eyes. "The fact was Charlie really was very good with business matters, as long as he was paid enough to keep him from stealing. Of course, I didn't know that at the time. Largely because, I imagine, he was being paid enough. He traveled a great deal, representing our interests abroad."

"You trusted him."

"Did I? *Trust's* an old word with a modern meaning. I didn't trust him in the way people trust today. There was also in those days a sense of forgiveness. I was not naïve about Charlie and his interests. Men who didn't carry on in such a way were rare, to say the least. And I didn't believe I could expect any better for myself. I don't wish to make myself an object of pity, but I walked with difficulty, I tired easily, and I was not beautiful."

Again Nix and Anders exchanged glances. Nix felt at this moment he should offer reassurance and believed Anders was thinking the same thing, but what to say? How do you tell a woman forty years your senior and your employer that you believe her to be attractive?

Before either he or Anders could interject, she swung her legs swiftly to the floor and sat up, and Nix watched with unexpected admiration as she struggled to overcome what was clearly a severe bout of light-headedness. "Perhaps," she said, "we are going in the wrong direction."

"In what way?"

"This is cold," she said, offering the washcloth to Anders who held it with two fingers like a soiled diaper.

"Would you like another?"

"No. I shall sit." She also lifted the ice bag and held it by two fingers until Anders relieved her of that, as well. Then she retrieved a handkerchief from her purse and wiped off the wet spot the melting ice had left on the couch. "I'm not entirely sure I know at this point where this is leading," she said.

"We're proceeding chronologically," Nix said.

Zira Fontaine looked at him sharply.

She fixed her gray eyes upon him. "Is it your feeling that readers will find what I am offering of interest?"

This was the first time she had asked such a thing, and Nix had to think about it. "There will have to be some shaping, you're right about that. But, yes, I don't see why not, depending on what direction you want to go."

"What are my options?"

"Well, it's not clear that you have a menu of options, exactly. More likely you make choices along the way about what to include and what not to, what to make of what you use. As a professional matter it is understood that while no one would want to actually tell anything that isn't true in an autobiography, details and events may be arranged to, say, bolster a theme."

Mrs. Fontaine glanced at the pile of Voigt books on Nix's desk. "What considerations might go into shaping the book, as you say, in such a way that a great number of people may wish to buy it?"

"That depends on you. Largely, the basic memoir market is worse than glutted. You being who you are, we can probably find a publisher who will buy it. How much the book sells will be a separate question. You might find a significant interest if you are willing to divulge the secrets of your success."

"What is your advice?" Mrs. Fontaine asked, in a tone that suggested to Nix that she was doing him a favor by asking.

"I think it would be a mistake to change what we're doing right now. Most importantly any autobiography that is going to be successful on its own terms, not to mention commercially, is that you must confront and reveal even those aspects of your life you may have kept people from knowing about when they occurred."

"What do you mean?"

"For example, we could talk about your daughter."

Anders looked up from his notebook and glanced at Nix and then at Mrs. Fontaine and then back at the notebook.

"Claire? Why would you mention her?" Mrs. Fontaine asked.

"No reason. She stopped by the office yesterday. It occurred to me you haven't talked about her."

"The little girl had a dentist appointment. I haven't mentioned Claire because we haven't reached that stage of my life in my telling of it." Her tone stiffened. "Are there other considerations you believe we should be discussing now but are not?"

"That would depend on you. The works that are most successful from writers in financial fields often provide advice on financial matters, on the reasoning that readers would like to think they could learn from you."

"You mean a book on how to make money?"

"Basically."

"Do you think that would be of genuine interest?"

"I don't have to think. There's evidence to prove it. Go to the bookstore and look on the money shelves."

"It's vulgar, though, isn't it, voyeuristic? To spend one's time reading how others acquired wealth."

"One could argue that that's easy for you to say."

"Perhaps so, but it seems unlikely that I would be able to deliver on the promise. I mean it's not possible to become rich by reading an instruction manual."

"Who knows? The important thing is there are plenty out there willing to try."

"The secret to my success is that there is no secret to my success, except hard work and caution."

"But you weren't cautious," Nix said, with smile, knowing that she would not like what he was about to say. "You married Charlie Fontaine."

She stared at him the way she did whenever she wished to convey the impression that he had forgotten his place. "Anders, would you go get Hector?"

Anders, whose position it appeared to Nix, depended solely on his ability to mask his exasperation at his boss's blurted commands, flipped his notebook shut and left.

The moment he was gone, Nix started to speak but Mrs. Fontaine held up a hand to silence him, then reached into her purse and retrieved an envelope, which she handed to him. Thinking it was a check, Nix thanked her and put it on the desk. "Open it" she said. Nix obeyed and withdrew a garish rectangle of vellum.

"What is it?"

"An invitation. Each year the Center for the Ambulatory Disabled, of which I am board chairman, holds a black-tie gala. The event is to be held at the Museum of Surgical Science, and you are to be my guest."

"Well," Nix said, "great. Flora's going to flip."

"The invitation is for you alone."

"I have to go by myself?"

"You will not be by yourself. You will be going as my guest."

"Wow, okay. But why not Anders?"

"I could ask Larson to come. He's done this for me in the past. However, I am asking you. We will arrange transportation on the day of the event," she said, prompting Nix to look at the invitation and see that the ball was in three days. Presumptuous, he thought, for her to assume that he would not have made other plans, though he hadn't.

"What—" he began but then the door opened and Anders appeared followed by Hector, who, with an air of abject humiliation, carried before him a gift wrapped in silver paper of such splendid grade that Nix could see his bewildered expression in the reflection, and trussed with a white-trimmed blue bow of fantastic proportions. Hector waited anxiously for Nix to take the package from him, and Nix hesitated, wishing to exact the full measure of psychological torture from Hector.

"It's a housewarming gift," Mrs. Fontaine said, "—for your house."

14.

Flora looked in sorrow upon the crystal nut dish and with even greater sorrow into the box in which it came, for there was no gift receipt. With her head in her hands and her elbows on the table, she studied the object and the way the light passing through the glass prismed pleasingly on the white canvas drop cloth she'd put down before she'd ripped the chandelier out of the ceiling.

"It's pretty," Nix said.

"Yes," Flora said.

"And expensive, I'll bet."

"Oh," Flora said, "it's expensive."

Nix picked the bowl up rotated it ninety degrees so that winged handles were visible and set it down again on the table. "You hate it."

Flora shrugged. "I don't hate it. Not the style I would have chosen."

"Where should we put it?"

"In the box. We can't leave this out. It'll get broken."

"How's it going to look if she comes over and the bowl's not out?"

"Do you really expect that Zira Fontaine will come to our house? Do you really *want* Zira Fontaine to come to our house?" Flora asked and that ended the argument, because Nix could not deny that he neither expected nor wished Mrs. Fontaine to visit, and as he realized this, the dining room seemed dingy in contrast to the shining bowl. The house of which they had both felt so proud now looked to him like one of those backyard dollhouses that kids decorate with shabby cast-offs from their real house.

"Can we just leave it here for now? While we're on the subject, I've got a thing with Mrs. Fontaine on Saturday. I've got to rent a tux," Nix said, though this was only marginally on the subject because he was angry with Flora and wanted to hurt her feelings

"What thing?"

"It's a ball for her charity."

"*Saturday?* I'm not going to have enough time to shop."

"Sorry, honey, just me," Nix said. "It's a work deal." If Flora was disappointed, she didn't show it. God, she's good, Nix thought. "I'm going to take a shower."

"Water's turned off. Nestor's replacing the drum trap."

"What's a drum trap?"

"I don't know if that's what you call it. The pipe that goes to the overflow drain in the bathtub. I took a bath last night and water dripped into the basement."

"When's he coming?"

"I don't know. He said today, but now I don't know when. You know Nestor."

Nix did and saw that as a problem. "He could take days to getting around to it. In the meantime we've got no water."

"We've got water. I can turn the valve back on, if Nestor doesn't show up. Just stay out of the tub."

Nix, never one to kick and scream, felt a serious tantrum coming on. He had refused to take a ride home with Mrs. Fontaine, something he'd never have done if he had actually been listening to Toni Tann's forecast because it was—as they said in Arkansas—hotter than nine kinds of hell. He'd left the FFS building to hot soupy air and had trod the sweltering city streets to the subway to find it inexplicably closed. Thinking *This is the way the world ends,* Nix had settled for the lakeshore express bus and a transfer to the Wilson, neither of which were air conditioned. On the second bus, he sat behind the rear door, where the heat of the engine battled the heat in the air, while the sight of the women up and down the aisle fanning themselves gave him motion sickness, and the hoodlums on the back bench sneered at the package on his lap, and he was able to remain composed only by telling himself that when he got home he would be able to take a shower. This she had denied him and it wasn't just that—though that was a lot of it. Nix further had the feeling that all this work around the house represented more than a grotesque manifestation of the nesting instinct. There also seemed to be a desire on her part to disappear into her nest. It was as though she'd erected a sheet of drywall between them and the only way of breaching it would be for her to bore a hole and snake a voice tube through. And perhaps it was that sense above all others that impelled him to calm. "Where is the valve?" he asked. "I can turn it on myself." He found the knob from her directions, turned it on and then ran the water in the basement sink, washed his hands and splashed his face. That felt so good he splashed his face a second time and then he was stripping off his clothes, filling his hands with cold water, pouring them over his head, and watching the water swirl down the sump. When this proved insufficiently satisfying, he pulled a clean towel off the dryer, saturated it under the faucet wrung some of it out over his head, and finally wrapped the sopping terry cloth around him and felt better.

"Hey," he heard Flora say behind him and he turned to see her standing naked among her clothes, looking, with her hair up and her dark prominent nipples and new pooch to her stomach, a little like an Incan fetish. "Splash me."

Nix held the sodden towel above her head and twisted. Water cascaded upon her head and struck the concrete floor with a satisfying splat.

Nix wrapped his arms around her, but she slipped away and leaned on the sink. "I've got to go to a demo tomorrow downtown," she said. She was a bar of soap, this one.

"What's it against?"

"You know, free trade. What do you want, hot or cold?"

"Give me cold," he said, as Flora pressed her thumb to the faucet stream, sending a violent cone of water toward all corners of the room.

"Do you think that's a good idea?"

Flora stood on her tiptoes shaking drops from her hands. "Marcia does."

"Why doesn't she go?"

"I've been begging her to let me. But she doesn't think there's much to worry about. Everyone's committed to nonviolent action"

"I'm not worried about the cops. I'm worried about the heat."

"I'm okay as long as I drink water. Marcia climbed Machu Picchu when she was seven months pregnant."

Nix wiped water from his eyes with the wet towel. "Why?"

"Because it was there."

He drew her close and the erotic possibilities of the moment seemed to occur to both of them simultaneously. As they dropped the towels and embraced, though, they heard the sound of booted footfalls on the basement stair and Nestor call, "Someone call a plumber?"

The Viceroy was the Highlander without the tartan cummerbund, and the Marquis without the French cuffs. Nix suspected that Seth had sized him up and steered him to Puttin' on the Tux's discount rack. No matter. The Viceroy appealed to Nix's minimalist tastes in formal wear, and he wasn't bothered that the jacket and pants were not actually wool but Ewex, the most convincing of synthetic wool substitutes, because, after all, with all the garters, false shirt fronts, and reusable pumps, artifice was the operant mode of rentable clothing—though, just the same, he couldn't keep his eye from drifting in the direction of the Regent, which glowered over the narrow showroom with an aristocratic bearing that bordered on the aggressive.

Seth, at Nix's feet with a tape measure, looked up from beneath his hair. "What're you looking at?"

"Nothing."

"You're checking out the Regent, aren't you?" he said.

"I noticed it, yeah."

"It's funny, you went for the Viceroy but I could tell from the way you browsed the rack that you had taste, more than taste because if you're looking at the Regent, then you have an eye for value, too. Who's getting married?"

"Huh?"

"No school dances this time of year."

"It's a charity event."

"Oh yeah, which one?" Nix told him and thought Seth would fall over backwards. "Dude, no way can you wear this."

Nix—having grown up in a nuclear family so committed to shabbiness that when he was once required to wear a suit for a grade school pageant, he had to be sent next door to their church-going neighbors to have his tie tied—had always harbored a fascination for elegant dress. His own father had been so constitutionally opposed to the principle of what he called the "class deceit of the electric loom" that he had appeared at the Art Institute to receive an award for Achievement in Animation wearing a tuxedo T-shirt beneath a blue velveteen sport coat gone threadbare at the elbows. Nix shuddered as he remembered the Gothic tableau of his father and mother posed in front of the hallway mirror on their way out the door. He in his Wavy Gravy get-up, she in her K-mart floral print and draped with the shawl, which Nix guessed she felt made her looked elegant but instead looked like something she had knitted for the couch. He felt even deeper sorrow when he recalled their return: staring down from his bedroom window with the babysitter as his mother struggled for purchase on the rickety porch rails, fighting to hoist his father, who was plastered to the stairs like a dehydrated sea lion, to the door.

All the while his father was singing a song heard many times but never the same way again,

> Old Bill Jones had a daughter and a son
> Son went to college and the daughter went wrong

while Myrna tugged at his sleeve, imploring over and over again, "Floog, Floog, Floog," in endless combination of tones, as though hoping to strike the proper chord to rouse him.

> Whoopie ty-yi-yeh, get along little doggies.

Not long after *Life During Wartime* appeared, Nix's publicist had agreed to a photo shoot for *Esquire* for which Nix posed at a table containing the ruins of a wedding feast. Wearing an Armani tux with the tie loosened he sat with his elbows on his knees as if he had survived a cataclysm. It was this notion of private event as national disaster that struck a tone with his generation. Initially, Nix had balked at the idea of a tuxedo, but the photographer had insisted and his publicist concurred. In the end, Nix couldn't keep his eye off the mirror, to the point that the photographer demanded it be covered with a sheet of paper for the duration of the shoot.

All of which, in the way of back story, went farther than Seth's limited (though not inconsiderable) sales skills to explain how Nix found himself walking out of Puttin' on the Tux's door, index finger looped around a tuxedo hanger, hoping that Flora didn't know what tuxedo rentals normally ran.

15.

At that same moment Flora was across town, wearing a black sleeveless T, khaki cargo Capris, and sandals made of real leather she had bought at a stall in Cozumel. She'd tied a red bandanna around her neck and cuffed a surgical mask to her bicep. On her forearm, she had written the telephone number of the National Lawyers Guild in green ballpoint. In her pocket she carried a wedge of lemon in a baggie, four packets of Saltines, and three packets of travel wipes. She was going to protest.

It was a glorious morning and Flora climbed the stairs to the Western stop on the Brown Line, which had a distinctly boutique feel in comparison to their old Blue Line. She sought out the one bench on the platform that was not covered in morning shadow. As the stop filled up she looked for others who shared her destination. It was ten o'clock on a Friday. The commuters were gone and most of those waiting for the train were dressed for a ballgame. There was one woman with flowing gray hair and an ankle-length embroidered denim skirt whom Flora made for a sympathetic soul but wouldn't dream of asking. Instead she closed her eyes and let the sun warm her face. She was concentrating on not thinking about anything when she became aware of an unpleasant odor.

It took her a moment to identify the smell as one of rotting fruit and opened one eye to see a nearby garbage can. Faced with the choice of moving into the shade or tolerating the smell, Flora decided that the smell was not strong and stayed where she was. But when she closed her eyes again she found that she could think about nothing else and suddenly felt nauseated. She looked left and then right to see if anyone would notice if she threw up. There were three teenaged girls huddled nearby, one of whom was stealing a glance at her, and beyond them a man gazing in her direction over the top of his newspaper.

Flora saw a discarded waxed bag on the platform nearby and picked it up, thinking if she needed to throw up she could throw up in that, but the bag had once held donuts and the lingering smell of powdered sugar made her even sicker. So, she did what she had been doing earlier during these bouts of nausea, which was to flex her toes and pinch the bridge of her nose with her fingertips, and by the time the train squealed to a halt, the churning in her stomach had stilled.

Just the same, when Flora stepped on the car, she looked for a forward-facing seat—anything else and she most certainly will be sick—and found the last one, having to step swiftly in front of a baggy teenager. The gray-haired woman from the platform was not in her car, but she saw here and there people young and old wearing sun hats and tie-dyed tank tops, balancing furled banners between their knees, and she felt cheered by the private sense of shared undertaking. Mingled in with shoppers dangling bags from each finger, and ball fans with their ball caps on their way to the ballpark, she and her fellow activists were anonymous in their disparate commitments. When they came together for the march, they would be the expression of a single ideal.

The train jerked to a stop. Flora's stomach roiled. Her sense of well-being left her again, and she found herself wondering if she would be able to transfer to a careening #55 bus. She had yet to be sick in public, but worried about it a lot. She was one who, despite the day's destination, did not like to call attention to herself, did not like to give the impression that she might need help from anyone. Thankfully, the rest of her ride was free of sudden stops or reckless acceleration and Flora felt the cold sweat on the back of her neck dry away and, with it, the persistent sense of doubt she'd felt all morning. After leaving the damp subway and a short wait on a sunny corner, she boarded an agreeably empty bus, feeling as though she had overcome an obstacle she would not have to face again.

The address on a flyer lead her to a block of warehouses west of the Loop. Flora didn't know the neighborhood but located the convergence center by the unmarked squad car across the street. Flora walked through the battered door of what had once been an industrial laundry to find a room clamoring with brash activity.

Already, there was a problem. The SWAT team had surrounded a building four blocks away, in which the giant paper-maché puppets that were to be carried along above the heads of the marchers were being constructed. The police had quarantined them, saying they could be used as weapons. "Weapons of truth," replied a negotiator from the Wildlife Defense Fund, which struck Flora as a tad glib, but what the hell. Negotiations were continuing to secure their release. The archbishop had been summoned.

Signs and posters clustered like bark on the walls, all of them torn so consistently ragged that Flora thought it intentional, a dash of constructivist theater: "Comrades, witness this scrawled message that I have torn from a larger piece of paper and taped to a wall!"

Here, garment workers from inland Carolina towns huddled with clergy from Calcutta slums to talk cotton. Over there, ragged guitarists from Oregon suburbs distributed tracts, warm from the photocopier, among student officers of the Ivy League. Amid this polyglot of grievance, pledged association, and promised response, Flora was looking for the representatives of the Women's Reproductive Consortium, who, according to their mission statement, was "an ad hoc group of health, social, and political professionals dedicated to issues of women's personal social and political wellness," and of whom Flora, before receiving an action alert less than a week earlier, had not heard.

But then, Flora heard of new groups nearly every day. This movement, like the others here, was a movement among many movements. Most related to the others only vaguely. Some even opposed each other in their goals, and it was only at times like these that they were all united. Like the chromosomes on the flipchart in the office of the geneticist that Flora and Nix had consulted because Flora was getting to the age where she had to worry.

She thought it impossible, as they watched their teenaged-looking genetic counselor Kimberley—who wore a retro cowl-neck, a mini the width of a ski band pulled on over black tights and canvas slip-ons—lay one transparency on top of the other, for all these variously twisted threads to converge without distraction or incident.

It was a young profession, Flora reasoned, as she considered Kimberley's age, or lack thereof. Nevertheless, the woman's youth didn't make Flora feel any better about the fact that even though she was young by any reasonable standard, she was already risking a child to have Down syndrome or worse simply by conceiving. "We don't think there's any reason to worry," Flora said, "but ..."

"You're knowledge seekers," Kimberley replied with tilt of her head that indicated that she found this particular species adorable.

What draws together such elements as are inclined to repel? Flora wondered of the people in the room. Tyranny? Too strong? No, not if the word was directed at a condition and not a person: the tyranny of strength over weakness, of selfishness and ignorance over basic human rights. Yes, that sounded right.

It's immodest, Flora felt, to think oneself right about everything, but there are some things she just knew: the rich will do just fine without anybody's help; war begets war; Jesus was with the poor, not the priests in the temple. These things are truths, beyond dispute. She and her compatriots are mocked as naïve for their optimism and dedication to justice, sure, because if they *are* sincere, then everybody else would have to admit their own greed and apathy. Listen to yourself, she said, hormones. But, no, she hated it when people said that, even other women, especially other women, especially other pregnant women. Don't listen to me. It's just the hormones talking. Flora thought, there is truth in hormones.

She found her group sitting beneath the international woman symbol, splashed on butcher paper in green poster paint. Among the women gathered there was a reliable mix of pant-suited, middle-aged NFP program directors sitting on folding chairs, Central American agricultural dissidents in native costume standing along the wall, and queer rights agitators seated cross-legged on the floor, each with silver rings looping through her lips like a spiral-bindered notebook. To enter this circle one has to bring something. And mostly what people want people to bring these days is more people. "How many people can you bring?" always the question. How many bodies? It is a numbers reality as crude as medieval warfare. What Flora brought was the sanction of the Progressive Parent Union, 501(c)3, the political action arm of CENPO. She knew that PPU like all NFPs were both hated for their mainstream instincts and necessary for the legitimacy they lent to the cause. No matter how much anybody there might admire the anarchists for their willingness to get their skulls cracked, nobody wanted one standing in front of a camera with a microphone.

The hypocrisy was truly annoying, but Flora was in their shoes when she was younger, so she understood. She knew some of the circle by sight, others by their nametags, and still others not at all. The talk was about past actions, panels, symposia, and plans for future meetings. There was little talk of the coming march because everyone knew her role. They were there to be seen, to be photographed and filmed by a hostile and dismissive media. They were there, above all, to be there, to be a number—each three would be counted as two by the police, as four by the organizers, and as one by the television news. Officially, the foundation Flora represented had not issued a position in support or in opposition to the day's action. Flora was there merely to provide a presence, in the language of the movement. To be one of thousands in opposition to what? Flora forgot. No, it was the FTAA, she remembered, though was not sure what those letters stood for, just another miniature alphabet in the acronymic drift that marked the evolution of regulatory bodies for global trade. It was a war of acronyms: ATTAC against GATT, the concrete potential for violence lying in the initials while the rest of the world became obscure and abstract.

Nedra of the Chicago Global Project, a dependably familiar face, stood and, after failing in two attempts to silence a dozen conversations, shouted, "If you can hear me clap once." A spatter of claps drifted though the room, the last from the back insincere, people clapping because others have clapped. "If you can hear me clap twice," Nedra called louder. The response of double claps was quicker and more robust than the singles had been. "If you're FBI clap three times." This time one person clapped, a bitter boy in his late teens in black T-shirt and black jeans. "What's the name and affiliation?" Nedra asked.

"Kenny," the boy said.

Flora rolled her eyes so keenly she got dizzy. Anarchists only ever gave their first names and never those of their groups. Kenny was skinny, with a yellowed complexion that Flora guessed came from months of living like a raccoon in abandoned buildings and eating out of dumpsters.

"Does everyone have the number of a contact person in case of arrest?" Arms were raised to show that all had done as Flora had done. "Does everyone have a copy of the action statement?"

A hand rose in the back to indicate a question. "Were those points adopted at the plenary? I thought there was some dispute about one and three."

Nedra stood on her toes to address the questioner. "What I understand is that we are not describing this document as an adopted platform. We are presenting these points as opportunities to address the media on topics of concerns to the global community, particularly those of the Global South."

The Global South—from Nedra's verbal wallpaper, Flora snatched another phrase that comforted her, the Global South. The words gave her a sense that the objectives of social justice were clear and contained.

"We are getting word," Nedra says, "that the police will not allow us to continue the march beyond Michigan Avenue. As we've agreed, those planning direct action may want to move to the front by around State Street."

As Nedra said this, Flora glances at Kenny. Direct action is a metaphor for acting sufficiently violent to get oneself beaten by the police. But Kenny betrayed no reaction. Likely he and his friends already knew when their time would come.

"All right," Nedra said. "Let's go."

A south side Methodist minister called for a prayer. This was another thing Flora loved, the prayer. As a good lapsed Catholic she had no desire to pray, and there were many in the crowd who were Muslims or Jews or more avid atheists than she. Yet they all bowed their heads and clasped hands and didn't expel so much as a chuckle, as the voice boomed, "Oh heavenly Father."

As they emerged from the convergence center, Flora squinted at the police vans parked across the street that had joined the one car she saw on her way in. The officers, in riot gear, stood arms folded in front of their vehicles and watched as the building emptied. Even a couple of years ago, such a show of force would have been unthinkable. Now they were commonplace. What was worse, it seemed to Flora, no citizen—outside of her marches—thought such police actions troublesome or even a bad thing. No laws had been broken, they were blocks from the parade route, and yet the police had come solely as a way of announcing to those assembled, "We are here."

The afternoon was sunny and dry, and Flora allowed herself to be carried away by sensation. The fear that she'd throw up had left her. She fell in among three young women in a sort of uniform of bright skirts and white kerchiefs. Each of them carried a white lacquer box and wore a white armband with a cross drawn on it in red magic marker. Flora smiled at them and nodded and thought she detected a nod in reply from the nearest girl, but couldn't be sure, and in any case it was nothing more than that.

At the end of the block, she looked to her right and then her left and saw crowds of a like size to the one she was in, moving eastward on the parallel streets, north and south. Banners reflected off the glass of the office buildings making the windows glitter like modern French sculpture. The medic girls were silent, unsmiling, walking it seemed to Flora with their noses in the air. How old were they? She wasn't a good judge, anymore. Twenty, maybe a little older. Perhaps ten years younger than Flora. Had she been like these girls? Perhaps exactly so, though with no such seriousness of purpose.

Her family had not been political, unless you count her father, who—her mother claimed—wept only twice in his life, once when Kennedy was shot and once when Nixon flashed his last V from the step of the helicopter. Otherwise the more pressing matters of a household of eight children getting by on a laborer's salary elbowed out more distant matters of politics and the general predicaments of the world, as far as Flora remembered. Yet from her first dem-onstration (in solidarity with undocumented cleaning staff at her university) she had felt a sense of comfort and elation such as she imagined must come to natural musicians the first time they pick up the instrument that has been intended for them by some mirac-ulous accident of genetics. She loved the banners and the songs and she loved the chant: "The people, united, will never be defeated." The sentiment to her was beautiful and, she thought, impossible to argue with. And yet most people did argue with it. To speak up for the rights of the majority against the rich and the powerful seemed to be despised by the majority and by the rich alike. This realization came to Flora quickly, as she found the indifference with which the plight of the campus workers was met among her peers. The dis-dain those same peers seemed to have for those who would stand beside the poor filled her with a mix of confusion, regret, and self satisfaction.

Whatever Flora was asked to bring, she brought. What she brought above all was working-class street credibility, something she understood right away was a kind of currency, something that secured for her a graduate student for a boyfriend when she was only a sophomore. She lived with him, breaking her mother's heart, in a farmhouse, miles from campus. In the evenings, she cooked dinner, and they sat by the fire and read from his philosophy books and drank the sour wine he'd made in the bathtub. At the end of the night, he'd fall asleep on the couch and she'd do the dishes. Eventually, she had realized—not too late—that she was living her mother's life for college credit.

Down Randolph Street they marched toward the Haymarket, the obligatory step-off for any march worth its convictions. She had walked these streets before—for reproductive rights, against the Contras, for Mandela, against Grenada, for gun control, and now, in darkening days, against global corporate greed.

Out of the corner of her eye, Flora glimpsed one of the puppets, free of bondage, bobbing eastward on a parallel course and was thrilled at the sight. At the next intersection, she watched as it executed an awkward, slapstick change of course, wheeling left and heading straight for her. She looked to the south and saw a third cohort of marchers join the possession. Those who saw the puppets first begin to cheer, a cheer that grew as the great lumbering heads became visible to more and more of the marchers, until the point at which they executed a second bumbling turn in the direction of march.

The possession contracted like an accordion as they reached Haymarket Square, marked now by a memorial to the policemen killed— no mention of the liberty that died on this spot. Flora was grateful for its existence, for the sense of the struggle against the demoralizing indifference of the powerful. There were speeches. There are always speeches and then the march would begin. She didn't like this part. It was hot and her back hurt. Even under the best of circumstances she felt they went on too long. Sub-Commandante Marcos said this was the battle of the punch-clock versus the hourglass, and Flora found herself smack-dab in the middle of the hourglass faction and caught herself looking over her shoulder at the fringes of the crowd, watching the less committed drift away and wishing she could herd them back in place and tell them to be patient, that the talkers would stop talking soon and then we would march.

All the different groups—dolphin protectors, labor unions, women's groups, peace groups, pro-tariff groups, immigrants' rights groups, East Indian dam-resisters, lettuce pickers, peach pickers, salmon fisherman, third world debt campaigners—wave their placards and banners each time their particular cause was addressed from the rostrum. Dozens, scores, of non-governmental entities each its own agenda, all of them singing together, just as those swimming cosmonauts of human code *had* come together inside her. There had been an ultrasound, confirming the good news, a slim, vain doctor lubricating the nurse with praise and approbation, narrating every narrow step. Nix had sat quietly beside her, a nonentity, a germ in a sterile room. The nurse manipulated a toggle on the console and the curser darted across the black and gray screen stopping at a peninsula of blue amid the black, "There," he said, "a fist. It's moving."

Moving. They were walking again, as they got closer to the lake, Flora felt a breeze drying the sweat under her arms and on the back of her neck, and did not feel sick to her stomach, could not remember, even, what it was like to feel sick. Someone started to sing "We Shall Not Be Moved," and Flora sang along, the words coming to her lips by habit, her mind somewhere else. She was thinking about a baby girl she had yet to meet but already knew. The marchers sang a new verse, one she'd never heard before.

> North and south together
> we shall not be moved.
> Just like a tree that's standing by the water
> we shall not be moved

And now Flora was thinking of an actual tree, beside an actual river and she was sitting on the grass beneath its leaves with a baby. She did not see Nix, but she knew he was not far away.

She was jolted from this reverie by a sharp wolf-whistle from a man standing at the curb. Though a goal of any march is to draw a crowd, Flora dreaded bystanders because people, especially men in suits, can be rude and yell things that hurt, even if she knew that they are small-minded and wrong. But on this day, perhaps because of the nice weather and the color of the banners and puppets, those who bothered to look their way seem to appreciate what they see. Here and there the Teamsters got honks and fist pumps from idle construction workers.

As they approached Michigan Avenue on Randolph, they passed in front of the FFS building, where her husband worked. As it happens, she didn't know he worked there, nor would she ever imagine that he was watching the march from the window nearest his cubical on the twenty-seventh floor. Nix had mentioned the building but Flora in her mind had never distinguished that particular structure from any of the other bland, gleaming headquarters along the river.

Like an Eisenstein montage, police in Star Wars storm-trooper dress drew their batons with robotic precision and began march- ing toward the head of the procession. As Nedra had predicted at the morning meeting, the police meant to bar them from marching further along the route. It as a tactic they were using these days to force a response. Flora had heard of this happening in Madrid and Genoa and in Kuala Lumpur. The police chiefs of the world's great cities attend seminars at which such measures are dreamed up to control and demoralize their citizens.

It was this arbitrary application of force that Flora saw as injus- tice, because these men—and women—in their armor don't know and don't care why they march. All that mattered was that they made certain that the freedom to dissent, for which the marchers are chanting, remains—in any real sense—an illusion.

A disturbance Flora couldn't see, a roiling in the crowd, erupted just in front of the people in front of her. They were hitting people. The boy who identified himself as Kenny and two other of his com- rades in black cargo pants, pushed past her, as beside her the girl medics quickened their pace, their fingers moving to unsnap their first-aid kits.

Then there was what sounded like gunfire, and Flora's heart leapt. "Rubber bullets," someone says. The crowd in front of her that had been growing denser as the marchers' progress had slowed, turned solid. Then came the gas, first a canister directly in front of her, then one to her right and a third to her left. Her skin turned cold with panic, and she yanked the surgical mask off of her arm, noticing as she does the phone number written above her wrist, appearing somehow permanent, the sight of which filled her with a dread worse than the gas and the gathering clubs.

Now the direction of the crowd reversed as people in front of her begin to retreat from the violence ahead. First she saw the frightened, then the injured, a man limping, clutching his thigh, a woman holding her stomach. Many people came covering their faces with rags, with them came the smell of gas, which Flora had first found merely unpleasant. Now it was oppressive. She had to fight to keep her eyes open. The running figures around her dissolve into a blur. Then her breath is nearly knocked out of her by human collision, someone rushing to get to the rear of the possession has run into her. Flora saw a man through the tears and the thickening cloud of gas. When he removed his hand from his bloody face to push her out of the way and she saw that it was Kenny. His expression is twisted in pain, and she realized in horror that his right eye was either gone or so covered in blood as to be invisible. Before she could say anything to him, he pushed his way by and was gone, leaving a bloody handprint on her shoulder. And no sooner was Kenny gone than Flora felt impelled forward by some mass of bodies behind her. She couldn't guess what had possessed this movement in the direction of danger any more than she could resist it. She didn't try. She pressed forward fast enough to stay ahead of those coming up from behind, moving as one toward the helmeted police and their weapons.

Carrying the tuxedo over his shoulder and with his nose pressed to the glass of the twenty-third floor of the FFS building, Nix watched the gray of the street disappear beneath the advancing kaleidoscope of color. From this height he could make out the presence of banners but not the words, the presence of the massive puppets but not the likenesses of whom they were depicting. He didn't know that his wife was among the crowd, although she'd told him more than once she would be. He didn't remember her saying it—there are so many of them, these marches, more and more these days. He wouldn't have been surprised to hear that she was down there, but didn't worry as the first explosions of gas began flowering upward toward him.

A two-toned chime indicated an announcement was coming over the intercom. In the moment between the chime and the announcement Nix wondered what it will be, surrender? evacuation? "Attention," a woman's voice gently insists, "Locks are being changed on all doors to the twelfth- and eighteenth-floor health clubs. Those wishing new keys must return new key vouchers, signed by your supervisor, to Human Resources by 12:00 Friday. This announcement will not be repeated."

As a contract employee, Nix was not eligible for a key to the gym, and so stopped listening as soon as he heard what the announcement was about. Instead, he pressed closer to the glass to watch the ragged black line of police swell and contract against the onslaught of humanity amid the gas that settled along the ground like morning fog. From a height of twenty-seven floors, he couldn't tell who held the upper hand, but knew it was only a matter of time before one of the people who occupied cubicles nearby would ask him what he was doing at their window. In the meantime, he watched the struggle below, already a fact of the landscape.

16.

"One hundred and eighty dollars. Are you out of your mind?" Flora poked her head out from behind the shower curtain to deliver the second sentence, underscoring the rhetorical nature of the question.

This was her third shower since she had gotten home from the police station. She had been steaming for almost an hour to rid herself of the smell of pepper spray. Her skin was red, from the hot water and the scrubbing, but the cayenne odor still tweaked Nix's nostrils as he wrangled his bowtie. "Why?" Nix said. "Is that a lot?"

"Yes, it's a lot. Did you notice when you were in the store any other suits that were less than that one?"

The room was stifling and Nix was concentrating on moving slowly to stave sweat. "You'd have to have been there. It's not as though they had price tags on everything. It was more a matter of matching the right tux with the man."

"Did they actually say that?"

It may have been wishful thinking, but Nix wanted to think that her anger over the cost of the tuxedo proved that Flora hadn't been scarred outside or in by being gassed, shoved, trussed with dozens of others into vast orange netting, handcuffed with a plastic zip-ties, and held in jail for sixteen hours. He stepped in a puddle of water, soaking one of the shear socks he'd purchased to wear in the buttery shoes that paired with the Regent. "Not in so many words."

"Can you return it?"

"I've got to return it. That's the point of a rental."

"I meant before you wear it, for a cheaper one."

"She'll be here in ten minutes. Besides I think it's necessary for somebody like me who makes less money than anyone there to look my best. It's like a statement on behalf of our class that we know how to dress," Nix said, hoping to appeal to her political sensibilities.

"Did the salesman tell you that, too?"

Nix peeled off the wet sock and dangled it in front of Flora's blow-dryer. "He didn't tell me anything. I made my own choice. I think it looks good," and when he said that it made him sad because as he looked into the porthole of mirror he'd squeegeed out of the steam and saw that he did in fact look good, there was no way Flora was going to tell him so.

Once the sock was dry, he looked for a place to sit to put it back on; as he did he stepped the other sock into the same puddle.

It happens that the one-phone-call rule in jail was a myth, as evidenced by the three messages Flora had left on their voice mail in ten minutes. Sadly, other guarantees to the rights to the detained that formed the foundation of the American Judiciary System that Nix had learned from *Dragnet* reruns, such as right to counsel and habeas corpus, turned out to be illusion. "Marcia thinks I should go on TV," Flora called from the shower. "She thinks a pregnant woman brutalized by the police is a powerful image.

"I told her it's not so visually powerful if I'm not showing yet. She said, 'That's the point. You can't go around gassing people indiscriminately.' What are you doing?"

"Looking for socks," Nix called back.

"Didn't they give you some?"

"They're wet."

She stuck her head out of the shower again. "You can't wear any of yours. You'll look ridiculous. Get a pair out of my top drawer. It's funny, one day I'm getting cracked over the head in front of the Fontaine Building and the next day you're having dinner with them."

"It's a charity ball," Nix protested. "It's for charity."

"Oh, come on, Nix," Flora said. "That's a lie they tell themselves."

Dressed with only five minutes to spare, Nix paced the living room, glancing out the window for Mrs. Fontaine's arrival. When the car did come, forgetting to kiss his pregnant wife goodbye, he ran out the door the way he used to flee from a drunken Floog when the neighborhood kids called from the street.

Hector waited at the open door. "Special treatment?" Nix asked.

"Fuck you," Hector spat under his breath.

In the car, Mrs. Fontaine was on the phone. The yellowy shimmering fabric of her dress billowed in the draft of the open door.

She held up a preemptive finger to silence him, and, once Nix had settled in the jump seat opposite her, handed him a clear plastic box. Thinking this was some essential artifact she wanted him to keep his eyes on, Nix placed the box in his lap keeping it secure between his palms the way a nine-year-old girl might hold a box full of new-born kittens in a veterinarian's waiting room.

"You must put that on," she said, once she'd hung up the phone. "There's an orchid theme."

Inside the cardboard box he held was a second box, this one plastic that came apart in his hands as he tried to open it without damaging the boutonniere inside. It was purple and alien-looking and went so well with his suit that Nix flushed with embarrassment.

Affixing the blossom to his label meant having to skewer a loose straight pin though a strip of ribbon, through the fabric of the jacket, and again through the ribbon on the other end, and Nix couldn't manage it.

Mrs. Fontaine patted the seat beside her. "Sit here," she said with such certainty and familiarity that Nix instantly complied.

She put the pin in her mouth like a tailor and smoothed the fabric of his jacket. "This is not difficult, unless you are a man and have to do it by yourself." As she leaned closer to insert the pin, Nix caught a full whiff of her perfume, which was different from the one she usually wore and smelled somehow wealthier. "You have a lovely home from the looks of it." She glanced up at him as if to measure his reaction. Her gray eyes studying him seriously. "There is no reason why you shouldn't be happy there."

Having run with a delinquent high school crowd, Nix had rejected prom as an establishment plot to coerce young Americans into social conformity with the bludgeon of sexual acceptance. Somehow, however, the girls in his circle of friends found dates, leaving Nix and his buddies to spend a depressing evening in the back of somebody's van, drinking wine, rolling joints, and trying to convince themselves how lucky they were to not be dancing, laughing, and getting laid. Looking back on that night from the distance of adulthood, Nix pitied the young Walter, wished he could offer him the comfort of knowledge that his life would turn out well enough. On the other hand, the moment that Hector pulled the car up to the museum entrance, the grown, tuxedoed, and corsaged Nix would have gladly changed places with young dateless Walter, as he realized just how desperately he had underestimated the vast scope of the evening.

A tangle of reporters huddled at the start of a red carpet, crowding the arriving guests into a shining, wealthy mob. The glare of lights reminded Nix of his season of celebrity. Nonetheless, he was thoroughly unprepared for the attention Mrs. Fontaine would draw—he watched the television cameramen snub out their cigarettes and hoist their cameras to their shoulders.

Hector opened the car door. Nix stepped out first. "Thank you, Hector," he said, "that will be all," and heard Hector curse in Spanish, as Nix noticed Mrs. Fontaine groping vainly for his arm. He moved closer so that she could clutch it, which she did with a startling savagery, revealing to Nix for the first time not only the extremity of her impairment but also her skill at concealing it.

A corpulent man of florid complexion stepped forward with both arms extended as he closed on Mrs. Fontaine, introducing himself as George Jorgenson, the director of the museum, an introduction that must have been for the benefit of the media because it was obvious from the way that she said "Hello, Georgie" that they already knew each other. "Good to see you," she said and then stepped aside, introducing Nix as, "Nix Walters, the writer." She squared herself to the assembled reporters and spoke in an amplified stage aside, "We are grateful to you, Mr. Jorgenson, for the use of your wonderful facility and are certain that, while we all shall enjoy ourselves this evening, the true beneficiaries of this evening will be the children of Chicago."

"How much money do you hope to raise?" a reporter shouted

Mrs. Fontaine smiled and addressed the general direction of the questioner. "I would never presume to prejudge the generosity of our guests. We hope to do better than last year. That is all I will say."

"What is Konrad Voigt up to?" a second reporter yelled. Nix, startled, looked at Mrs. Fontaine. If she'd heard the question, she showed no indication. Nix didn't have long to wonder before another voice, invisible behind the glare of lights, called out, "Mr. Walters, is that the Regent?"

"It is," said Nix, dumbstruck and pleased to catch a glimpse of himself in the reflection of the museum's glass door and see that, in the persistent illumination of camera light, he looked fantastic. The contrast of his skin against the exaggerated white of his shirt collar conspired to make him appear more tan than he was, and the cut of the jacket gave his torso the virile line of a Cossack, the mere sight of himself causing him to straighten his posture as—Mrs. Fontaine's arm in his—he strode through the doors, held open by footmen as they approached.

Sadly, Nix's hopes of reclaiming even a flake of his brief gilded age grew dark nearly instantly, as he got a load of the crowd inside. They were ancient nearly to the man. They clogged the foyer, the women in no hurry to cast off their furs, the men fussing at their opera scarves. And Nix registered with sorrow that the ultra-rich were, mostly, ultra-aged, suggesting the acquisition of wealth was merely a matter of gathering what their contemporaries spilled as each in time keeled over dead. What Nix half-hoped, half-expected to be a Sodom of excess and license was nothing more than a way station on the turnpike to the hereafter.

Nor did the Museum of Surgical Science merit the esteem Nix had granted it in his imagination. The entire ghastly collection existed solely as a Tribute to the Misguided: cupping, trepanning tackle for the laying open of afflicted skulls, various splits and spine-straightening contraptions indistinguishable from the devises of the Inquisition. It appeared from the grim appearance of the devices, laid out beneath glass in orderly rows, that the first requirement of early medicine was that the cure be more excruciating than the symptom, and Nix wondered whether this location was a wise choice for a benefit on behalf of the disabled.

They passed a display case that contained what looked to Nix like an unornamented sarcophagus of indeterminate materials and what he realized at once was an iron lung. "Is that the sort of thing they had you in?" Nix asked.

"Yes, exactly so," Mrs. Fontaine replied. She did so without a hint of emotion, though it struck Nix as strange that she'd answered without actually looking at the display, and he wondered if perhaps she'd been here before to look upon the instrument of her childhood confinement.

As a huddle of septuagenarians buttonholed Mrs. Fontaine, Nix noticed the bar nearby and, presuming he was free to go where he liked, decided upon a drink. As he neared the bar, he saw, at the end of the counter, a head of naturally blonde hair among the bleaches and tints, and the short dress of a young woman among the modest—though sometimes insufficiently so—gowns of the elderly. Had he been more familiar with the guest lists of Chicago's A-list charity affairs he might not have been surprised as the woman turned. As if aware that someone was staring at her, she looked in Nix's direction, her face registering surprise as well, though not one that shared his look of fulfilled expectation because she had not been thinking of him at all.

"Wow," April said, popping an olive in her mouth.

"Hi." He closed in for a hug as she held out her hand for him to shake and found himself taking her hand and crushing their arms between them, as he pulled her closer with his left. "Who are you here with?"

"No one," she said, "You?"

"The guest of honor."

"The host. Who's he?"

"She. Mrs. Fontaine. The hostess."

"Oh," she said, mulling his reply. "—Oh?"

"No—not oh—I work for her."

"Doing what?"

"I'm helping her with a book."

She gestured to the bartender, asking Nix, "Are you drinking?"

"Yes, I'm drinking," Nix said, loud enough to turn graying heads.

"Bourbon?" she asked, both an order for the bartender and a request for confirmation from Nix that her choice was acceptable "Same for you? If we have to come to these things we might as well take our revenge by drinking top shelf. How have you been? Congratulations on your book."

"Which book?"

April made a face of coquettish embarrassment. "I'm sorry, I don't remember the name. Did you write more than one?"

"You're kidding?"

"Why?"

"Forget it," he said, and they were quiet until the drinks came. They were heavily poured, and Nix started to sweat as he took a sip. April swallowed hers in a single swig, wiped her lower lip with the thumb of the hand that held the glass, set it down, and motioned to the bartender for a second.

Nix laughed. "Last time I asked Lenny where you were, he said NASA."

"I was."

"Really?" Nix said. "I thought he was putting me on."

"That might have been something I never told you. I hardly told anyone that I wanted to be in space. People think you're joking. But I washed out. Medical disqualification."

"You?" Nix asked, remembering her as a strong swimmer and effortless runner.

"A bad tooth. I told them my sister broke it with a field hockey stick."

"Seems a bit strict."

She smiled, a smile Nix remembered well, and it seemed for a moment that no time had passed. "I'm not in a way talking about the tooth. When girls make themselves throw up, the acids from the stomach eat away the teeth. It's common among overachieving girls. The number one cause for rejection among women applying for the program, I was told."

"I never would've guessed."

"Something else I never told you. Boys I saw longer than you never knew."

"No one did?"

"My girlfriends knew. All the girls in my sorority knew, but they were all in the same boat. We used to say about girls that we blackballed, 'She belongs somewhere else.' Horrible, isn't it? What's worse is that no one could ever say that about me. I belonged exactly where I was."

"I always thought you were unique."

She shrugged, as though the compliment annoyed her. "Shows how much you knew."

"Where are you now?" he asked. When she looked at him strangely, he said, "What are you doing?"

"Risk management," She said, "for an underwriting firm."

"I didn't know you could manage risk."

"You can. You just can't prevent it. Look," she said, "it's a term of art more than a metaphor, so don't get carried away."

Nix leaned his elbows on the bar. Talking to April felt easy and familiar, which was a relief—and odd because they had never felt easy and familiar with each other in the brief weeks they spent together on a beach, and he would've liked to have forgotten all about why they were there and stayed with April at the bar, but then a waiter tapped him on the shoulder. "Señor Walters? Mrs. Fontaine seeks you," he said.

"I'm being sought," Nix told April.

"So the man said." Nix couldn't tell from the smile on her face whether he was being pitied or mocked, but knew if he were to step away just then he could retain at least a semblance of the self-regard he'd reclaimed in their short conversation. This he knew, just as well as he knew that he wouldn't be able to resist asking: "Want to talk some more after dinner?" Which allowed her to say, "Sure, if I'm still around," and, in saying this, shrank Nix to a size that would allow him to pole vault into his drink on a cocktail straw.

17.

Like the loaf-wards of a Geatish mead hall, the eminences of the foundation sat along one side of a banquet table, on a dais, facing the elderly thanes at tables arranged before them. Nix sat between Mrs. Fontaine and Jorgenson, watching the guests eat, their elbows busy and insect-like, as they sawed at Tennessee rabbit and herded burgundy snails around their plates with the last rigor of a generation determined to achieve nothing but dying rich. All arms and hands and relative silence, men sitting with women they've slept beside for decades, having nothing left to say. Then again, Nix thought, at their ages, eating poses significantly more risk and must be undertaken with solemn concentration. He scanned the tables for April's blonde head rising above those of the women and many of the men's and spied her sitting at a table among uniformly tuxedoed, gray-haired men and women four decades older wearing gowns that revealed freckled, leathery cleavage, and it dawned on Nix that what was for a him a one-night descent into purgatory might be for April another day at the office. Her table was near the dais but in the wings, not directly in his line of sight but visible without turning his head perceptively. Still he had to make sure she never caught him looking at her, while he was keen to catch her looking at him.

Looking over the origami napkin and the array of multiple glasses, forks, and spoons, not knowing when they were to be used, he wished Flora were there. She would know which utensil was to be used for what, or she would laugh and say, "That's what I was about to ask you." He had been too busy dreading this event, hadn't been able to think about what long-term effects might come from the violence of the day. Now he was worried about her, and he felt that he had made a mistake by leaving her this evening, coming only out of a desire to strengthen his position with Mrs. Fontaine. Flora had broken him of the knack for isolation he had nurtured since college, had forced him to see that there were motives and anxieties that lay behind what he felt was an instinct for monastic self-reflection. Now he was dependent upon her in situations like these and was both grateful and resentful.

A squelch of feedback from the public address system wrenched him from this line of thought. He turned to see that Jorgenson had ascended to the podium and, after the necessary references to the wealth of the assembled and the decadent quality of the food, began: "When she was asked why she has never appeared on the cover of her own magazine, Zira Fontaine remarked, 'I thought I would reserve that honor for people our readers would actually like to see.'" He paused as laughter drifted up from among the groundlings. "This is the Zira we all know, a woman whose works speak loudly, but she is reluctant to speak for herself. A reporter once praised her for her insistence upon anonymity in her charity, and Zira shot back that we should not forget that those who call attention to themselves may be doing good as well and that we would all do well to pay less attention to motive and more to need. This evening I know you will join me in assuring her that she is the one person we wish to see."

As she prepared to stand, Mrs. Fontaine put her hand on Nix's forearm, he thought, at first, as an endearment but then felt her grip harden until her nails tore at his skin as she hauled herself up to her feet. Nix looked up to see her apparently smiling at him, then realized from the way her lips quivered with the exertion of being pressed against each other that she was in agony. By the time she made the three steps to her spot behind the microphone, however, any trace of pain or exertion was invisible in her regard. She adjusted the microphone height with the brisk efficiency of a sound engineer and shifted her stance forty-five degrees so that she could address Jorgenson without having to look over her shoulder.

"Thank you, George, for your generosity and kind words, though those that were directed toward my humility may ring a little hollow, considering I've brought my personal biographer with me today." She nodded at Nix, who gave a desultory wave, triggering a second crescendo of laughter among those who must've thought initially that she was joking.

"But I assure you that I stand humbled before you, as I ask you to reflect on the reason that one of our greatest presidents Franklin Delano Roosevelt should grace our most diminutive unit of currency. This was neither a slight nor an accident, and if FDR had been alive to see his profile in frieze upon a slender coin less than an inch in diameter, smaller even than a penny, he would have been delighted.

"As more than a few of us in this room will remember when the financial existence of the National Foundation of Infantile Paralysis was threatened by the Great Depression, the comedian Eddie Cantor called for a "march of dimes," knowing that while the good people of this nation lived in the shadow of a horrible epidemic, they had precious little to give. The result was the most successful fundraising effort in history, as millions of dimes were mailed, some singly in envelopes, some in greater numbers in jars of all sizes and descriptions—leading to the development of treatments, advancements in therapeutic equipment, and ultimately a vaccine less than twenty years later.

"Of course, you don't need a woman who has made a good living in currency valuation to tell you that a dime doesn't go as far as it used to."

As Nix, along with Mrs. Fontaine, waited for the laughter to die down, he reflected upon the timing, delivery, and structure of her speech, specifically on how all of these elements were missing from the way she related to him the events of her life, day after day, in her office.

"We must resist the new voices that mask determinism with a false piety, who claim that 'charity inspires envy among the wealthy and impoverished alike.'"

Although he had never heard Mrs. Fontaine express such sentiments during the natural course of their conversations, the quoted phrase sounded familiar to him. Among the faces turned toward the podium were looks of fond cohesion, and Nix had to concede that there was a necessary value in his having witnessed this. As much as he had—perhaps self-consciously, perhaps not—insisted on believing that this memoir of hers was an act of naked, pointless vanity, he had to admit that its subject was a woman of extraordinary accomplishment.

Under the dimmed lights of the hall, Nix detected the sheen of a bald skull beneath a comb-over and thought the man was Mel Lazar. Looking more closely, he saw that it wasn't. Though a number of FFS middle management had been acknowledged before the program, Lazar was not one of them, nor was Voigt, nor was Betty, the

administrative assistant for Lazar's division that McI tried to pass
off as his personal secretary, nor were any of the beige executives
that Lazar huddled with in the executive dining room. Of course,
Nix—being new to FFS and still untangling the cat's cradle of divi-
sions, contractors, sub-contractors, and sub-sub-contractors—didn't
know how unusual their collective absence was. Still their exclusion
seemed too pervasive to be coincidental. Then it struck Nix where
he had heard that critique of charity that Mrs. Fontaine had quoted.
It was a Voigt Tenet. At least as far as one might glean from his
recorded teachings, Voigt didn't hold charity in high regard, believing that giving to the less fortunate "however that may be defined"
instilled in the giver a false sense of virtue and was best displaced by
self-interested meditation. Again, perhaps a coincidence, one didn't
have to read the papers to know that voices of greed were afoot in
the land, but hard to ignore, one coincidence on top of another.

"I would like to conclude my remarks by remembering something my father told me. When I asked him why the classmates who
teased me for my limp were popular while the few who were kind to
me were the class outcasts, he said, 'Zira, you must remember, good
will prevail, but it will not prevail on its own.'"

She reclaimed her seat amidst a pounding ovation. No doubt there
were many here like Nix, whose presence was mandatory and who,
like Nix, had been surprised by the passion and breadth of goodwill
that Mrs. Fontaine had expressed, thus to that degree it was what a
crowd psychologist might characterize as a spontaneous expression of
relief. As she sat nodding curtly at intervals of ten or fifteen seconds
to the continuing applause, Nix leaned in and said, "Very nice." She
didn't reply. The Zira Fontaine he conversed with daily would be, for
as long as the clapping continued, concealed behind a public mask.

Once this oblivion had faded, Mrs. Fontaine leaned in and told
Nix, "I am expected at this point in the evening to receive all who
wish to speak to me. This is not something in which you are asked
to participate. When the line dwindles, please alert Hector to bring
the car to the door."

"Where is Hector?" Nix asked.

"I'm sure I don't know," she said. "Find the man who is in charge of
service personnel. It is they who always know where the drivers keep
themselves."

Having no other charge or recourse, Nix went looking for drink. The bar was closing up, but, with the twenty-dollar bill he'd tucked in his breast pocket, he persuaded the bartender to leave behind a half-drunk bottle of vodka, from which he poured himself a drink in a used glass and watched the guests hobble toward the exits. He saw April walking to the door. She turned and craned her head, as though looking for someone. Whether it was he or not, Nix would never know, though he easily could've snaked his way through the frail crowd, grabbed her by the arm, and said, "Let's get out of here." She could've said yes or no. If she said yes, Nix could spend a pleasant evening over drinks asking all the questions he'd been unable to answer for himself. If she said no, he would have his answers in a single word. One way or the other—validation or repudiation of the image Nix held of himself, at least with regard to his perceptions of how women felt about him, stood across the room in a blue organdy knee-length cocktail dress.

But he stayed where he was—only half aware of the odd stares he received from a passing couple, glancing at the unknown gentleman they'd seen on the dais who now slouched against the derelict bar with a bottle in his hand—and watched her leave. She looked once and, he hoped, before she disappeared she would look around again, but she didn't. If she had been looking for him, she was not curious enough to look a second time, and that was all he needed to know.

Once she disappeared from view, Nix collared the first waiter he could find, which happened to be the same man who'd relayed Mrs. Fontaine's message. "Could you find Mrs. Fontaine's driver and ask him to bring the car around front?"

"Yes, sir," the waiter said, leaving Nix to wonder again if this was the sort of command he was accustomed to receiving or if Nix had delivered the order with such authority that the poor man did not feel he could refuse and consequently spent the next twenty minutes desperately trying to track down anyone who knew where the drivers were.

When Mrs. Fontaine found Nix a half an hour later, he was feeling a flush of inebriation beyond what might have been required to dull the edge of an awkward evening. Mrs. Fontaine smiled warmly in recognition. The lights of the museum, which had been dimmed for the dinner, were restored to their standard magnitude. In the improved light, she looked damp-eyed and exhausted. She handed him a stack of envelopes. "Can I ask you to take these for me and bring them to the office? Really people should know better than to hand me things, but what can one do?"

She took his arm, as she had when they arrived, a gesture that felt on this occasion as familiar as it had felt uncomfortable on the first. As they walked out the door, Nix expected the damp chill of an August evening but felt instead a blast of insistent heat, so forceful and disorienting for this late in the night that he found himself looking for its source before he realized that it was in the very air.

"Goodness, it's hot," Mrs. Fontaine said.

"I was just thinking that," Nix said. Indeed everyone in the city must have been thinking the same thing. The car was at the curb. Hector stood by the open door, mopping his forehead with his sleeve. "Hector," Mrs. Fontaine said, "I don't think the world will come to an end if you take off your jacket."

"Thank you, Mrs. Fontaine," Hector said, with a knowing smirk for Nix once she had passed that Nix didn't have a chance to return before noticing that Mrs. Fontaine had disappeared from his peripheral vision, and he looked down to see her crumbled on the floor of the car.

Nix's first thought was that she had merely tripped and moved eagerly to help her up, thinking as he did of how he might minimize whatever embarrassment she would certainly feel at her clumsiness. However, the hand that Nix clasped to help her up was clammy and limp. Panicked, Nix called for Hector.

"What did you do?" Hector hissed.

"I didn't do anything," Nix said. "I think she fainted."

"I didn't *faint*," Mrs. Fontaine said from the floor. "Please help me to my seat."

Nix and Hector elbowed their way through the narrow doorway and into the chill of the air-conditioned rear compartment of the limousine. Hector got in first and Nix was ultimately glad he did as Hector, by virtue of a firm grasp on Mrs. Fontaine's elbows, was able to hoist her swiftly and gently into her seat, where she sat looking small and lost, until, as though a switch had been turned on in her head, she seemed to regain her senses and asked Nix, "Do you have the envelopes I gave you?"

"In my pocket," Nix said, and patted the commodious side pocket of the Regent to confirm.

"Do we go to the hospital?" Hector asked.

"No, not the hospital. I'm fine. Take Mr. Walters home."

They drove several blocks in silence, Nix understandably startled and Mrs. Fontaine likely embarrassed, until at last she said, "It is my fault. I can't allow myself to get overtired."

"But you're feeling better?" Nix asked, hoping she'd say yes whether she was or not.

"Yes, I am fine. Thank you," she said and they drove on for several more silent blocks before Mrs. Fontaine spoke again. "Here is where Anders would say, 'You had them eating out of your hand.'"

"Of course, you did"

"Do you think they were approving of myself or of the words I had written?"

"I'm not sure."

"There's a difference."

"Yes."

"This is something we can address—on Monday."

"I was thinking the same thing," Nix replied as the car slowed in front of his house. In spite of himself, Nix found he had opened the car door before the wheels had stopped turning.

"It really is adorable—your house. Tell Flora that I hope she is well," she said.

"Thank you, I will," Nix called over his shoulder, aware even as he did that this was the first time she had ever spoken the name of his wife, whose silhouette he saw withdrawing from the living room curtains into the darkness of the house.

18.

The summer after his first year of writing school, Nix spent two months of languid days on the second-hand couch on the porch of his shack in the hollow south of town reading *The Stories of John Cheever.* It was his Cheever summer, the summer he got wise, or wise, anyway, if not to the world, then to the way he was perceived within it. For sixty-two days, from early June until August, he read a story a day. In the mornings, barefoot, wearing his basketball shorts and T-shirt, though on the warmer mornings just the shorts, with a glass of iced tea and the book, though some mornings just the book, he sat and read, not entirely unaware of trucks on the gravel road cresting the hill beyond the stand of shortleaf pine on his neighbor's property.

He'd begun without the intention of beginning. The book was assigned reading for his written comprehensive exams, which were a year and some months away and as far out of his mind as Albania. Still, he'd bought a copy of the Cheever, along with one of *Tristram Shandy* for seventy-five cents apiece at a used bookstore on the rationale that he'd have to read them sooner or later, and they were never going to get any cheaper. He had set the two dog-eared paperbacks on top of the shelved books on his cinderblock and plank bookshelves, and for two months they had remained there unmoved, until the morning after the term had ended, and Nix was sitting at the card table he'd set up in the kitchen, eating granola out of the one bowl he owned. He noticed the books when he was looking for something to read while he ate and, having rejected the Sterne as unsuitable, snatched up the Cheever. On the first page in large, bold print was a quote pulled from the author's preface. "These stories seem at times to be stories of a long-lost world when the city of New York was still filled with a river light, when you heard Benny Goodman quartets from a radio in a corner stationery store, and when almost everyone wore a hat." Such a description captured Nix's attention, not only for the romance of the prose but for the homesickness he felt for no place in particular except that it be north. He turned to the read the entire introduction and had finished his cereal before he reached a line directed to the men and women of the author's generation "who were truly nostalgic for love and happiness and whose gods were as ancient as yours as mine, whoever you are." These last clauses stopped him, not so much for the part about ancient gods (which on first read he wasn't sure what that meant, beyond a sense that *gods* suggested secular myths and preoccupations), but rather for the final tacked-on element "whoever you are," which at once acknowledged the reader and held him insolently at arm's length, while conveying a sense of annoyance at the prospect of being judged by the faceless multitudes. Thus displaced and lonely, Nix read on, hoping to confirm what he wished to believe: that he was the sort of personage the author might recognize, whoever the author was.

A slow reader ever since he'd learned how, Nix wrestled with the densely printed, yellowed pages. The first story, "Farewell My Brother," had Nix's eyes wandering from the page toward no object in particular after almost every third sentence, as he contemplated the world suggested within the paragraph. Though his own family lacked even a faded elegance, Nix felt some association with the genial, threadbare pretensions of the Pommeroy's to the point of expelling a gasp of admiration when the narrator bashes Tifty over the head with a root.

By then Nix's coffee had gone cold, but rather than get up to pour another cup, he began the next story, "The Common Day," and had read the first pages before realizing that he could see no end to this and thought that if he was going to go for a run as he had planned, he had better go before it got too hot, which meant then or never, and so he left the book spine-open on the table and ran west across the highway and around campus and back across the lush grass of the cemetery of a town grown still with the summer heat and the absence of students.

Most of his classmates were gone. Nix himself had left and then returned. In May he'd gone to Chicago to attend his father's funeral. For Floog had died of heart failure, his death as a private man following that of a public one by more than a decade, prompting Allen Ginsberg—himself with a foot in the grave—to remark upon hearing of the elder Nixon's passing, "Again?"

The service was presided over by an officer of the Ethical Human-
ists Society, a man of an amazing age, who stood in front of the
limited gathering (his mother had kept secret the time and place of
the ceremony, if that's what it was, to guard against the presence of
gawkers or Stroonies) with the morning's newspaper jutting from
his jacket pocket, read from Voltaire and Kierkegaard, and afterward, a propos of nothing, had shown Nix his gnarled hands and
told him of a childhood lost sorting shale in the coal fields of Penn-
sylvania. Upon finding out that Nix was a student of writing, the
man wondered if Nix would be interested in reading a play he'd
written about Jesus, Buddha, and Muhammad.

"Is it set in a bar?" Nix had asked, joking.

The man had replied, "Why, how did you know?"

Myrna, who'd pulled a black-hooded sweatshirt on over her dress
to fend off a late spring chill, asked if he had to get back to his classes.
Nix was as relieved to say honestly that he did as she seemed relieved to hear it.

By the time his running route brought him back to the gravel hollow road, he'd decided to read a story a day from the Cheever, as a
way of providing direction and structure to a summer that would
have otherwise lacked any.

Nix was inclined to read the stories as an indictment of Cold War
suburban America, largely because the Heller and Roth novels that
lined two-deep his father's bookshelves read that way, and certainly
that was the mode Floog, knowing no others, chose. However, Nix
quickly came to understand that no revolutionary manifesto lurked
behind these stories, in fact the preface, read properly, was an apology, an apology in the ancient sense, a longing to justify, a longing
to belong to a society that the writer should know better than to
wish to be a part of. It was motivation Nix could well understand,
and, in the course of the summer, he came to understand a good
deal about place and circumstance. In the afternoons and evenings
he made his way more or less randomly around the Ozark hill town
with his mind on the upper east side of Manhattan of forty years before, avoiding conversation when he could, and when he could not,
engaging in the kind of genial, vacant drawl of a cultist in need of
deprogramming. The mornings he spent trying to catch the ghost

of the author lurking between the leading of the lines.

After his father's funeral, Nix had found, among his Floog's effects, hundreds of train cars and engines, thousands more partial train cars and parts, whole sets of minute, intricate tools for the repair of the trains, miles of track, and a small city's worth of miniature buildings, stacked in orderly rows on pine shelves his father had built in the basement at some point after Nix had moved out— such precise work as was remarkable from a man who couldn't shave himself, on the rare occasions he did, without letting whole ounces of blood. The spare parts Nix sold to a hobby store for forty dollars. Of the rest that was in one piece he donated to the hospital in which his father drew his final breath. The hospital saved one of the trains for its Christmas display and auctioned off the rest, for several thousand dollars. Also, Nix found, in one of his father's ancient filing cabinets, many dozen vintage sunbathing and nature magazines that could have fetched considerably more than the trains, had Nix not tripled-bagged them in plastic yard waste bags and waited until he saw the garbage truck down the alley before tossing them into the dumpster.

In addition to the trains and the nudie magazines, he found a third item of an even more indeterminate value. Among boxes stuffed with half-filled sketch pads, dried-out pens, and chewed pencil shafts, Nix found an accordion folder of the sort lawyers use, and in that wrapped in newspaper and bound with twine was a thick manuscript, containing hundreds of pages of inked panels.

Nix recognized the artist immediately as his father, though the work was unlike anything he had seen either from of his Earth-Hippie Faze or from the later Nekkid-Robot Faze. He turned page after page, with fingers becoming black with ink, without coming to the end of an episode. All the characters, mostly circus performers, and predominant among those, clowns, recurred from scene to scene, and he soon realized this was a graphic novel of a scope and depth he'd never seen from his father before. He returned to the cover and, separating the first two pages that had been stuck together from years of compression and moisture, read the title page: *Clown U.* Beneath the title was the seal of this educational institution, featuring a lion and, apparently, an ape standing on their hind legs, each sporting an outsized erection and holding an unfurled banner between them that bore the motto, "Only sadder than the tears of a clown are his departmental politics."

From what Nix saw while flipping more pages, most of the episodes pitted the central character—Nil, the Desolate Clown, whose face bore a thickly painted frown—against Perfidio—the Dean of Clown University. Nil wore a smock decorated with zeros, omegas, and question marks. Armed with a flower that squirted lemon juice and a vinegar-filled seltzer bottle, he spread a sorrow just shy of gloom wherever he went, while Perfidio, like all arch villains, had an origin story: he was once the Principal Harlequin of the Royal Vienna Circus until discovered practicing animal husbandry in the elephant cages. Because this was mature Floog work, but Floog work just the same, there was the usual assortment of slutty clowns and hillbilly clowns (largely members of the Clown U. varsity sawdust football team), there were also unusually complex, even thoughtful, clowns.

As near as Nix could guess from the references, the book had been created during the Reagan administration, and, like the earlier Floog oeurve, was largely apolitical, though no doubt anyone wishing to could have discerned echoes of the Iran-Contra hearings in the heroically mundane episodes of back-biting among the clown faculty and in the arcane unravelings of collegial sabotage. Most episodes ended with Nil, thwarted in even his aims of the day, retreating behind his Veil of Dolor that descended over our anti-hero like a bed sheet over a parrot cage. It was all so bleak as to be—intentionally or not—broadly hilarious, and Nix found himself laughing out loud at one of his father's comics as he hadn't done since he was ten, the last age at which he was too young to understand what they were about.

His mother had driven him to Midway Airport on the far fringe of the city, farther than she'd driven in her life, so that they could save twelve dollars on a plane ticket and had left him at the gate with ten dollars, just as his father had the day when Nix, at the age of twelve, had flown to New York for camp.

He returned to a ghost town. The semester had ended the week before. His professors had recorded incompletes. Department secretaries had proctored his exams to his students. He was supposed to—

he had planned to—devote that summer to writing. For someone who (regardless of what anyone thought of the quality of the work) had filled nearly three hundred pages in a weekend, Nix's output of a single short story over the course of two semesters represented something of a tapering off. "You can't twist the arm of the muse," Pettijean had told him in their first conference, and Nix had liked the expression so well that he had resolved to do the muse no injury at all. Although happy to wait for inspiration, Nix began to wonder if he would recognize so elusive a quantity when it showed. Easier just to read. If writing was a drawing out, an exhaustion, then reading was a taking in, virtually costless, an inexhaustible resource. Having been raised in a household whose failings were matter of public speculation, the private failings of the men of the "The Swimmer" and "The Seaside Houses" were a puzzle. Nix understood—indeed was almost addicted to—reticence as a defense mechanism, even as he remained largely ignorant of the power of external forces arrayed against him. At the time, fatherless and alone, and years away from his marriage to Flora, he had little to lose, but the one thing he had yet to learn about fate was its patience.

Part 3

Lake Forest (July)

19.

Nix was awakened the next morning by unexpected light. He freed the sheets from around his ankles where he'd kicked them during the night and pulled them over Flora's shoulders. Then he walked to the kitchen, which was warm at that hour but not unbearable. The living room, on the other hand, blazed with the morning sun and heat. Out of habit, he switched on the set, and there was Toni. The map behind her, color-coded to show temperature gradations, glowed red over Chicago. "Across northern Wisconsin we see a line of storms of violent intensity. Folks up there can expect high winds and flash flooding, but the real story for us will be the heat. This front will act as a barrier, blocking cooler air from coming down from Canada, while you have this front racing up from the Gulf of Mexico, bringing with it very hot air, possibly temperatures of a hundred degrees for the first time in a long time. So we're all going to want to do what we can to stay cool, Frank."

"Gosh, Toni, sounds like we're all going to strip down to next to nothing this week," Stuckey said, but Nix, aside from marveling that Toni should be dressed and made up and in front of a camera at this hour of the morning, felt nothing. Nothing that is except for some combination of anger and concern for Flora, whom he'd seen at the window when he came home but had gone to bed and pretended to sleep, leaving him to lie awake sweating vodka and feeling like shit. Now he couldn't be sure if she was really asleep—she *had* been sleeping a lot more—nor could he be sure if he wanted her to wake up before he left for the day. He took a short, cold shower, ducked his head in the bedroom to make sure Flora was still sleeping, threw on a short-sleeve shirt and his lightest-weight slacks, and was on his way out the door when the phone rang.

It was Lenny Spitz. "You rang," he said.

"This is weird," Nix said, "I just saw April last night."

"Who?"

"April March."

"No shit?" Lenny said. "How are you and—what is it—Flossy?"

"Flora. Fine. It's hot, real hot."

"Yes, well, summer, you know," Lenny said.

"Worse than that," Nix said, "I mean like over a hundred. Flora's pregnant and we just have the one air conditioner."

"Congratulations," Lenny said.

"What?"

"On the baby. What are you up to?" Lenny asked.

"What do you mean?" he asked.

"I am calling from the plush offices of Spitz and Cravett, LLC. What do you think I might mean?"

"Now that you mention it," Nix said.

"Run me the gist."

"You know Zira Fontaine?" Nix asked

"The publishing broad? You're writing a book on her."

"More like for her."

"Does she have representation?"

"No."

"Sure?"

"Pretty," Nix said. "She would tell me."

"If she's New York there's no problem, but she's Chicago, which means you can knock a zero off the advance. When people want to read about the sharp-clawed ladies of the glossy rags, they mean N-Y-C, Q-E-D."

"I never thought there'd be any commercial appeal, though I think she does, on some level," Nix said.

"I don't know," Lenny said. "There are a lot of ways you could go with that. You could write it straight the way she tells it, and you don't get as far as she's gotten by being dumb, so it's my bet there's a clause in your contract guaranteeing her final approval on all versions."

Nix had never bothered to read the contract and didn't answer.

"I'll take that as a yes. Or you write your own book, no law against that, as long as you toss in enough details that a defense lawyer can page to and say, 'Your honor, the plaintiff does not collect stamps.' The success of something like that would be difficult to guess sight un-seen and would of course depend on the skill of the author. Or—and now I'm thinking out loud—you could go with a behind the scenes at the writing of the memoir kind of thing. I mean, these things are spreading like weeds, and you might get some interest if you exposed what goes on in the trenches, is she a Nazi? Is she nuts? How much of this shit do you think she made up? The success of a project in a type of situation like that would depend entirely on the dirt."

"I don't know," Nix said.

"Got to go," Lenny said, "I'm going to be up your way next week. We'll have lunch"

Nix, hung up the phone, looked into the bedroom a last time, saw Flora stirring between the sheets, and virtually ran out the door, bracing himself for the blast of heat as one does for the shock of cold on frigid winter days. The air itself seemed to smell of heat. He walked by the small park at the end of their block. It was deserted except for a line of passers-by that had formed at the park's one water fountain, and Nix watched as each person in line turned the faucet handle and bent to drink, but no water bubbled forth from the fountain. Each person would curse, turn, say, "It's broken," to the next in line and leave. Then the ritual would repeat itself. Nix watched this happen three times in a row, all of them driven to desperate hope by thirst.

The train platform appeared to undulate in the heat, heat so extreme as to be a curiosity, at first. The sheer shock of such conditions as he'd never experienced before served to take his mind off of any discomfort he felt. A quick look around, however, that he may have been the only one who felt that way, as everyone else was dragging, limp and sullen, across the searing pavement.

Of course, Nix hadn't recognized Lenny's voice right away, though once he had, he also had to confess to a flush of anticipation and vanity before those sensations had given away to memory of the last time they spoke on the phone. *Foyl shmuck,* Lenny had called him. It took a rabbi to translate for him. "Lazy," Rabbi Fein said, "it means. It's a word you never hear," he said, "because there are no lazy Jews." Nix was supposed to have been working on *Bride of Illustrator,* a sequel, more or less, to *Life During Wartime.* At least, that had been the plan. At least that had been Lenny's plan. By the time of that final, clamorous conversation, Nix had the profound impression that Lenny didn't think he could sell a second book, and he was therefore surprised to find himself being hollered at by Lenny for not writing a book that Lenny didn't think he could sell in the first place.

Which made Nix part right and part wrong. There was nothing personal in the screaming. Lenny screamed, as a tool of the trade, to keep the other guy off his feet. Clichéd but effective, yell at somebody and you've got their attention. Let *them* stutter, tell you how you're wrong, tell you to calm down. It's all about you. Secondly, there was a time sensitivity angle. Lenny had thought he had a chance of selling a second book after *Life* on the blow-back alone, and thought that if Nix proved something to him by getting straight to work on it, then there was hope that he might have a career after all. Lenny didn't have much faith in the kid, but he'd had some, until, of course, he found out Nix hadn't written a word.

So Nix took the fact that Lenny had returned his call with no small sense of vindication, thinking that the stars were right for a comeback, that the great wheel of fate that had turned away so suddenly and unexpectedly, had rolled his way again, even as he admitted to himself that he hadn't begun writing anything new since Lenny had started the whole thing with that *foyl* business. The truth was that laziness was not the problem when it came to Nix and writing. It was simply that, at the time, Nix had decided that precocity was most of the point. Any fool could write a novel. The trick was writing one at twenty, when the very fact of such prodigy generated marketing copy. By the time Nix had come to believe that there was more to writing than fame, he was no longer famous and no longer writing.

Nix knew he was never going to write another novel. What he lacked in imagination, he didn't come close to making up for in talent. On the other hand, there might be something to be made of what Zira Fontaine had given him. She had shown no sense of what she would need to do to attract a readership, but then Nix, who truth be told was slow in taking his task seriously, had not encouraged her to do so. He also would not tell her about Lenny but he would make clear to her that she may have more of a future as an author than she might expect at the moment.

As the train raced between stops, he looked out his window at a city slowing down, brought to near stasis by a crippling, suffocating heat. The sidewalks were deserted; the cars, hot enough to burn flesh, rolled by slowly, radiators on the verge of erupting.

Nix liked his office on weekends. He liked the sleepy nod from the security guard at the desk, and using his key card on the main doors of his floor gave him a sense of ownership, while the walk past darkened cubicles full of untold caches of unguarded loot gave him a tingle of criminal opportunity. It had felt weird at first to come to a building that headquartered a company in which he had no stake. Men and women sprinted for elevators, slammed phones into their cradles, and shouted invectives of joy and victory, and none of it had anything to do with Nix. Fortunes were being made along these halls, but Nix could expect nothing from them. On the other hand, if the FFS stock price were to collapse on Monday, he could walk away as easily as a bystander whose back had been turned to a traffic accident. Still, among the others on his floor his regular presence around the elevators and halls had conferred a certain legitimacy upon Nix, even if they had no idea what he did. And he had been making friends: Lazar and Trina, the black receptionist at the end of the hall, who crinkled her nose and laughed at everything he said, even though he wasn't entirely sure she remembered his name. And, most importantly, he had a friend in Zira Fontaine.

In fact, he liked going in on weekends so much that he'd taken to going when he didn't have to. This day he had the excuse of meeting Mrs. Fontaine. The meeting wasn't for four hours, but no one had to know that, and by no one he meant Flora. At a newsstand on Wabash, he'd bought two papers from a fat man, who slouched on a stool, shirt open, trying vainly to cool his bare, sweating belly with a miniature fan. Nix stood at the elevator bank, grateful for real corporate air conditioning and looking forward to a quiet morning with his feet up.

That hope was dashed when he found Anders waiting at his office door, wearing an immaculate cream-colored silk suit, red tie, and, on his head, a straw boater.

"Morning, Anders," Nix said, laughing in spite of himself, "how'd you know I'd be in?"

Anders doffed the hat with a flourish. "I didn't," he said.

Nix shook his hand. It was cool and dry. Everything about the man was cool and dry. Without being asked, Anders followed Nix into his office and was seated with his legs crossed before Nix turned on the lights.

"Where's the boss?" Nix asked.

Anders hung his hat on the toe of his shoe, Nix noticed for the first time that the band matched Anders's tie. "Hector's bringing her down later. How was—the event?"

"Uneventful."

"That's not what I heard," Anders said, without smiling.

Nix respected Larson Anders. Normally he liked people he respected, but in Anders's case he made an exception, maybe because the things that Nix admired about Anders were the things that Nix found most annoying. He took care with his appearance in a way Nix never did, but, as the day's get-up demonstrated, he had a tendency to go overboard and was always worrying a loose strand of his fine blond hair back into position or, as he was doing now, arranging his hands on his crossed knees as he sat to provide a clear view of his manicure. "Is this what you came down here to ask?"

"Not at all. I had business down here. And, as I said, thought I'd drop by to see if you were in."

"And ask about the ball?"

"Just wondering if you had a good time," he said, straightening his cuffs. "We care about you here in the FFS family."

"It wasn't the sort of thing I'd want to make a habit of."

"Good idea," Anders said, standing up. Nix hoped for a moment that he was leaving, but instead Anders walked over to the one piece of office art he managed to get Facilities Management to install in the room, a faux-impressionist Venetian scene, and studied it. "Do you know how many attended?"

"A hundred."

"A hundred and twenty-six."

He turned from the picture to look Nix in the eye. "Do you know how much money was raised?"

Nix shrugged.

Anders sat down again with his elbows on his knees, holding his hat by the brim between his fingertips. "A million, two. Break that down, it comes out to be about nine thousand dollars a person."

"What's your point?"

"You're out of your depth."

"No shit? Look, Larson, I don't know what you're feeling and—don't take this the wrong way—I don't really care. All I want to do is finish the contract and get out of here."

"What if she wants you to stay on?"

"At FFS, why would she?"

"Why not? She likes you, and I don't know if you noticed it or not, but there's not exactly a surplus of loyal employees around here."

"Did she ask you to ask me?"

He laughed. "I'm just asking."

"So you made a special trip?"

"You know Aesop's fable about the bat?"

"No," Nix said. He did, actually, but wasn't about to do Anders's legwork for him.

"There once was a war between the birds and the mammals. The bats could not decide which side they were on. So, they were with the birds when the birds were ahead and with the mammals when the mammals were winning. In the end, when the birds and the mammals made peace, both sides scorned the bats, and condemned them to the night."

"I have no side to choose."

"There's more to know than you can see. As you say yourself, you are not part of this. You stand to lose very little. It's the rest of us who will have to decide when the flood comes which direction to swim in search of dry land."

"I'm telling you I don't even know what the sides are. What is it between Fontaine and this Voigt?"

"Don't get hung up on personality," Anders said.

Nix was going to ask Anders what exactly he should get hung up on, when there was another knock on the door and Mel Lazar's head floated into view sideways through the half-open door, like the head of a balding, middle-aged sex doll preceding its owner into a room. Seeing Nix, he said, "Eh, there's the big guy." This was the first time he'd addressed Nix in this fashion, who wished it hadn't

176 When Bad Things Happen to Rich People

happened in front of Anders. Seeing him, Lazar straightened himself up and entered the room straightening his tie. He'd sweated
through his short-sleeved dress shirt. A sleeveless T-shirt showed
clearly beneath. "Oh, hi, Larson."

"Mel."

"You two know each other?"

"We work for the same company, Nix."

"Walk far, Mel?" Nix asked.

"Just from the El. I'm a sweater," he added quickly, as if proving he
knew this about himself would mitigate the embarrassment. He sat
on the couch next to Anders who did little to conceal his discomfort.

"They have showers down in the gym," Anders said.

"There's a note in my personnel file," Lazar said. "I'm not allowed."

"Well, as much as I'm eager to hear more of this," Anders said,
standing again, "I must be going."

"Got work to do, huh?" Lazar said.

"No," Anders said and shut the door behind him.

Lazar pointed a thumb toward the door. "Is he a friend of yours?"

"He's Mrs. Fontaine's assistant."

"I know that. I was wondering how it stood with you two."

"Why would you wonder, Mel?" Nix said.

"After last night a lot of people are asking about you."

"What are they asking?"

"Did you notice there were no FFS vice-presidents present? Their
invitations got lost in the mail. That's never happened before. I'd
have to say the only thing worse than not getting invited to that ball
was being the one guy on the floor who was."

Nix heard the ventilators come on and the vinegar smell of Lazar's
sweat dissipated. "I never would've thought going to a charity ball
was a hostile act."

"Gosh, Walter," Lazar said, "how come you didn't know that?"

"What's going to happen to me, Mel? Am I going to get knifed in
the parking garage?"

"Aw, come on, Nix," Lazar said. "If anybody's going to get in trouble, it's me. I've spent a lot of effort convincing people that we can
trust you. Then they see you sitting next to Mrs. Fontaine in the
society pages, and they get nervous. And they—"

"I'm in the papers? Which one?"

"The *Tribune*."

"No kidding? What are they nervous about?"

The ventilator stopped, and Lazar, noticing that the room had grown silent, lowered his voice. "When we move we're going to need to know which side you're on. I've been more or less given the task. And when I say that I mean to know where you stand when we move."

"You mean move to the new building?"

"Figuratively. I'm going to tell you straight out. Voigt is calling for a vote of no confidence from the board. If that passes, Voigt thinks Fontaine will resign as president."

"Can he do that?"

"Yeah, he can do it. Why not? If he's got the votes."

"Does he?"

Lazar for the first time that Nix could remember reflected something other than charity. "*Now* you're interested. To tell you the truth, I don't know. These people don't talk to me. They talk to Voigt. I think he'd like to have more time but after last night he believes that Mrs. Fontaine is suspicious. He's worried about a counter operation, so he's pushed up the meeting."

"The shareholders have to vote."

"They'll go along with the board."

"Kind of ironic, isn't it?"

"What's that?"

Nix wondered if Lazar was being ironic himself though one look at his face assured Nix he wasn't. "Irony is a matter of philosophy. Ask Konrad Voigt."

"I've committed his Tenets to memory. I'd remember. What about the Contemplations?"

"Never mind."

"I'm trusting you by telling you this. But even if you were to warn Mrs. Fontaine, it wouldn't do any good. She knows by now about the meeting, and she knows who she's dealing with." Nix said nothing. Of course, he would tell her. "Look," Lazar went on, "This is nothing personal against your boss, except that she's the past. She's hampered by an old way of thinking, on logic, on drawing conclusions from observation. That's last-century thinking. We're talking about practical faith. That's what Voigt calls it, when faith is applied to real world problems then reality becomes whatever you believe it to be. If you think about it, Nix, the idea itself is irresistible."

The phone rang. Lazar looked at it nervously, as though he thought it could hear him. It rang again. "I'm not going to answer that," Nix said. "I don't have to. It's Hector calling to say that Mrs. Fontaine will be here in ten minutes. I told Anders already none of this makes any difference to me. I'm an independent contractor."

Lazar got up to leave as he always did when he knew Mrs. Fontaine would be coming. "Somebody's got to sign your checks."

"All right," Nix said. "You've got me there."

"Think it over, at least," Mel said, as he opened the door. "Ask yourself who is going to be signing checks around here a week from now."

20.

It's usually the other way around, isn't it? A man becomes successful and leaves the wife who sacrificed everything to get her there.
In the case of Charlie and myself, it was the opposite. I don't believe
the first caused the second, rather that the two events coincided. I
am not so naïve as to suggest that Charlie's departure coming when
it did was an entire coincidence because I have come to accept the
reasons why Charlie married me. For a while I was convinced there
was that but also this. I now realize that there was only that. Which
is not a happy thing to know, but once I learned the lesson, I never
had to learn it again. This is already more than I wished to say on
this. I am not writing a gossip book. My emotional misperceptions
are of no value, now that I know that I have been wrong. What good
is it to say, *This* is what I used to think but don't anymore?

The magazine was an accident. We had acquired a building from
a bankrupt printer, and the property on the premises, including
electric presses, was part of the deal. It was Charlie's idea to publish a newsletter for traders. That is how the *Chicago Currency Brief*
came to be. We charged a dollar, which was a lot of money in those
days for four pages of newsprint, but Stan said that we should remember our readers were not shoe clerks and would be more likely
to buy a newspaper that was overpriced, thinking that its publishers
must know something others don't. And as it turned out he was
right. Two factors contributed to our success. One was that FFS's
rapid growth and profitability had garnered us a better reputation
than even we realized. The second was timing. This was in the early
seventies, at a time when currency traders were becoming specula-
tors. The English Pound crisis and the possibility of making millions overnight has attracted recently, shall we say, a different type
of trader.

From the beginning there were fears of conflict of interest issues.
Our lawyers warned us that any currency, any trading strategy, discussed or promoted in the newsletter that resulted in a loss for an in-
dividual and a profit for FFS exposed us to litigation. So it was decided

that we would spin off the magazine into its own division. We hired Forrest Fremont away from the *U.S. News and World Report*, and he brought over some good magazine people. What happened then is what happens whenever you create a specialized division. You hire people with a particular expertise and the first thing they do, whether they are aware of what they are doing or not, is to create out of their task a rationale, justification for their continued existence. This is usually a good thing, because it suggests creativity and ambition, but at the time, I didn't look forward to the meetings with our publishers.

Nevertheless, the newsletter remained profitable and the publisher at the time, Ed Rowley, who was once at the old *Chicago Daily News*, and who had taken over for Fremont who went on to *Newsweek*, convinced us to go glossy, which we did in 1976, at which point there was the question of a new name and we had to come up with something of a more general appeal. Ed suggested *Fontaine's*, along the line of *Harper's* or *Forbes*. It was Charlie actually who suggested *Zira*. There are people who may be surprised by that, choosing my name over his, but the truth was Charlie could be very generous. He never raised his voice to me. Not once. Of course, by the end of our marriage, he could not say the same about me. But for a while everything was very nice, quiet and comforting. I would say domestic if I could be certain the term would not be misinterpreted or quoted in some way out of context. Making money was easy, and I felt we were going about it in the right way. Pardon? What happened then? Because, yes, you're right, when everything seems to be going well, something has to go wrong. What happened in my case was that people started to die. Mother first, of a stroke, a weakness in an artery running through the brain that had gone unnoticed and undiagnosed. Then my father, less than a year later. I never thought of him as the sort of man who relied heavily on his wife in the way that so many husbands of his generation did, but I don't doubt that her death was what ultimately caused his. Victor asked me at the funeral if I felt guilty that, despite my wealth, I was unable to help them. His grief had driven him to anger against me. I didn't answer. I forgave him. Nonetheless, that's not the sort of thing you want anyone asking you at a parent's funeral, least of all the brother you had kept out of harm and put through podiatry school.

Then Uncle Stan died. In many ways that was worse than losing my mother and father. To me, he represented everything about
this country that had been good to us. They had come over alone,
the brothers Stanislaw and Mikhail, found work, and made it possible for us to follow them. They fought in the war—which seemed
very dashing to me as a little girl—and had come home. When they
came home they set about making their lives better and threw their
lots in with us. That was what the company meant to us, the success
of my father and his uncles.

After Stan died, it was just Mike and me and Claire, of course,
and Charlie, who as I said, was often away. Mike had never been
involved in the business in the way that Stan was. As far back as I
can remember, Stan always found something for Mike to do, and as
far as I knew he did what he was told. Stan never once complained,
but after his brother's death Mike was more at a loss than I was. I
realized that I would have to rely on myself and on my staff and no
longer on my family.

In the end, I went short on Charlie, as the traders would say. I
set up a trust for Claire. In case anything should happen to Charlie
or I or our marriage, no one would be able to use her as leverage.
Yes, I was specifically thinking of Charlie when I took that step. So
you could take that as proof that I was not surprised that he would
leave. The real question is did I think he was going to leave because
of the sort of man he was or because I did not believe I could be
the woman he needed me to be. I don't know. Except to say that I
relied very strongly on my strength of will to do what came easily to
others. From those daily acts of will, I developed a self-confidence
that many other women of my generation lack, I believe, which may
explain why I've always distrusted women, which is why as well, I
believe, that I was always very stern with Claire—too much so. I
thought it was for her own good, but all parents say that, and most
of them believe themselves. Certainly I can say from the way Claire
has turned out that I was wrong. I will tell you all this now, though
I expect I will allow very little of it in the book.

Charlie loved Claire. Loved her more than I did. That is a ter-
rible thing to say about your family, particularly for a mother, but
it wasn't personal, really. I expected Claire to be strong and she

was not. It was not her fault. She had no reason to be strong. She was healthy and rich. And she was plain. I wasn't the only one who thought so, though not Charlie. He thought she was the most beautiful girl in the world. I'm convinced that is why she stayed with me when he left. She believed his leaving was wrong. I am sure she also believed that she would have been happier with him than with me. But she stayed with me, to punish him.

As you have likely guessed, I will not be talking about Mr. Swift. This is not because I am afraid to or am unwilling. This is because I believe there is little I can add to the record of an episode in my personal life that has been credited with initiating a golden age of tabloid journalism. You are surprised that I know that? Of course, I didn't watch television, but Claire did. She had a television set in her room. Charlie bought it for her. She had asked for one, told us that all her classmates had them…. It was a Catholic school that year, if I am remembering correctly … Charlie confirmed this. He was more aware of the trends and fads that bedeviled the psyche of teenagers. Claire said I was old-fashioned. I might have said I was uninterested. By the time I had reached sixteen, I was already preoccupied with work, of my own accord it is true, but nonetheless. I found it difficult to follow Claire's material obsessions as she grew older. Dolls from Holland were one thing, televisions and stereos were quite another. In any case, Charlie left shortly after the television arrived, and I know that Claire watched much of what was said and shown in her room, with the door shut and locked.

On the subject, I will say that I never believed that Charlie was homosexual, and who would know better than his wife. I believe that Charlie was far more compassionate and sensitive than people have given him credit for. I believe he wished to leave, and though I do not blame myself, the situation around the house was difficult. I compensated for the losses in my life by losing myself in work. He was accustomed to being off on his own, but he also had been accustomed to having me there when he needed me. And so he left. But he left knowing, because I often said—too often really—that I knew he would one day. When he decided to leave, I doubt anything troubled him more than the thought that he would be proving me right. That is why I believe he concocted this story of an affair with Wolfgang, who worked in our Miami office, doing what I was never entirely sure. Charlie had hired him and vouched for his qualifications, even after the relationship became public, and he must have thought he would spare my feelings if I could say that he left for reasons that were beyond my control.

In the years since this happened, I have been told by some women that they would prefer their men to leave them for a man rather than for a woman, and I have said at those times that I cannot imagine formulating an opinion one way or another. What Charlie understood— I told him the first night we walked together on the deck of the ship—was that I believed my disability made me undesirable.

It should go without saying that if I believed Charlie went to such lengths to protect my feelings over the nearly twenty years we were married, I am not likely to believe that he conspired to have me murdered. Of all the nonsense surrounding the entire matter, that was too much. Poisoned crab dip, ridiculous. I am allergic to shellfish. Charlie knew that. The dip itself, without the cyanide— or whatever it was supposed to be—would have been enough, but he would have known very well that I would never have touched it. Nor is it true that Charlie Fontaine embezzled from FFS. That I did say in the press, only because it was my fiduciary responsibility to discourage damaging rumors. I might from the distance of time agree that the compensation he received was excessive by the standards of the day, but that is a question of judgment and degree and not a matter of legality.

The rumors were repeated until they grew into myth. The fact that I flatly refused to talk to anyone from the press about a word of this did not help. On the contrary, there seemed to be a contest to print or broadcast lies so grand and salacious that I would be forced to respond to them. I became an object of suspicion and of ridicule. You have heard the jokes, I am sure. Yes, that one. Right, yes, *enough*. But I did not respond. Where would I have begun? You say, This is not true. Well, what about this. I am not going to comment on that. Then it is true? There would be no end. And after all, as I insisted again and again, I had more important matters to attend to. I might have been heartbroken, but I remained president of a company and a mother. I had no choice but to go on.

Claire chose to remain in the house with me because she knew that Charlie and I would have both preferred she live with him. She refused to see him for years and refused to listen to me for just as long. When I enrolled her in a boarding school in Maine, she refused to go. She said she would not be "interned in a gulag for rich snots." Her words. Then she turned around the next week and demanded we send her to a girl's school in Switzerland. That lasted four months. Apart from what we might think about the Swiss, their school headmistresses are strict. The charge that time, I believe, was a boy in the dormitory. She was sent home and was enrolled, at her request, at Lake Forest High School, a public school. There she thrived for what seemed like a long time but may have been closer to a semester. For the first time in as long as I could remember, we were on friendly, even affectionate, terms, and I was not worried about what she was doing when she was not in my sight.

What happened then was that the school and the houses of those few wealthy students who attended the school were struck by a crime wave. The police told us later that they knew immediately the criminals were students at the high school. Apparently detective work in real life resembles less Agatha Christie than market research. Professional criminals adhere to mundane, but apparently effective, habits of operation. Any pretty crime that does not fit those characteristics is blamed on teenagers. Obviously, once it is determined that teenagers are the culprits, the remaining task is to identify which teenagers.

Claire being one of the culprits disgusted me more than anything else. Claire being brought home in a police squad car, handcuffed and pregnant. No, that part was not apparent, but she told me soon enough, more out of spite than a Catholic girl's act of contrition. My concern was not for what the neighbors would think. Certainly our neighbors on either side can not see our drive through the fence and the pines, though it's likely they all knew everything about the entire affair before her foot touched the driveway. As you know from what I have told you I did not come from money, and the last thing I wanted to do was to raise Claire to behave as though she had. I took it personally that my daughter would flout the privilege her upbringing had given her. That was all right for old money. We, Stan and Mike and Victor, were a generation of immigrants' children. We knew what were up against and what people expected of us.

Claire, on the other hand, was a monster—thick-ankled and lazy. That was from my side I'm afraid. No, not I, somehow in my case, perhaps because of my affliction, I was spared the coarse eastern European features, some paradox. It is unnatural to hate your child, or should be. I am not proud that I did. I always blamed her for her circumstances. Of course I have come to see that I was also to blame. Mothers, we are to understand from the contemporary literature on the subject, are obligated to love their children, despite of their failures. We are to understand as well that this love should be, in some way, instructive, teaching both the parent and child the importance of compromise and compassion.

At the same time this was happening, women began to write to the magazine to express their support for my position and an admiration for me personally. Then or shortly thereafter, editors from other magazines, mostly women's magazines, began calling for interviews and asking me to contribute articles on the subject of the professional woman and the compromises she must make in her personal life. I had become, it seems, through no desire or fault of my own, a symbol for the circumstances more and more women were experiencing in their personal and professional lives.

Women began buying *Zira* under the mistaken impression that it was published for women investors. What they thought when they actually read the magazine, I don't know, but at the time women were becoming investors and so the timing was fortuitous. Initially, I wasn't eager to assume the persona, but I was, before anything else, a businesswoman, and our magazine division was wise enough to know a valuable thing when they saw it. We replaced Ed Rowley with a girl from New York, Dolores Nazaar, who was credited with transforming *Zira* into the lifestyle magazine that it is today, but the reality was that we hired her because we were going in that direction. Nevertheless, *Zira* became a resource for the thousands of women getting divorced and finding out for the first time that planning for the financial future of their families was another burden they were expected to bear. And I found my name, though it was one of a single mother with a daughter on the verge of being sent to reform school, had been branded—as our marketing division would have said—as the epitome of the single professional mother.

How was one to feel about that? I have forgiven myself for the errors I have made, most especially those that have hurt my family and have come to believe that I have dealt with the obstacles I have faced when they needed to be dealt with and have caught up with the rest when time allowed. My brother Victor likes to say, "If you could expect the unexpected they'd have to call it something else." That was meant for my father, but Victor never had the heart to say it to him. He knew what we had put Father through.

That's not entirely true. I have always known that wealth invites calamity. Greed is corrosive, or perhaps it is just that success abhors a vacuum. Ten years after *Zira*'s founding, an author we commissioned conducted a survey to determine the Best-Run Corporation in America. FFS was ranked first. We couldn't run the article obviously. How would that have looked? We paid a kill fee. The writer sued anyway. He offered the article to the other magazines. For reasons apparent to all but the author, none of them would run it. I never regretted not publishing the survey, which seemed to me an invitation to disaster. I am more superstitious than I care to admit. The truth remains. There are as many visionaries with MBAs in successful enterprises as there are in failed ones who believe they can do better than the current managers. Such thinking inevitably leads to ruin because departure from a profitable model must lead to bankruptcy almost by definition. The opposite of success is not more success; it is failure. The same is true of this company and it is possible, likely even, that those people will be in charge before long.

There is little I can add here that would not sound philosophical. The child? No, the one you have seen is not the one we are talking about. Claire had an abortion. Her idea, but I insisted, as well, and she thanked me afterward. No—the little girl here is Hector's. I should have fired him for that. Maria. I had asked that she be named Marie, Charlie's mother's name, but they named her Maria. I should have fired him for that, too.

—

21.

A *crock,* Nix thought, as he stepped over the squirrel sprawled on the pavement at his feet, inhaling in frantic shallow gulps and past the rows of elderly men and women seated on the concrete floor of the subway where they'd been driven, instinctively, like cattle, by the heat, or of the stench of sweat and desperation on the car itself, despite the steady thrum and blast of cool air from the vents. Just how much of a crock, Nix couldn't say. He knew little about the intimate details of Mrs. Fontaine's life beyond what she told him. He did know, however, that Charlie Fontaine lived in Miami with a man named Wolfgang Swift, described as his "life-partner of 13 years" in a profile of their Italianate villa with attached tiled piazza in *Miami Architecture.* Nix also knew that apart from what Mrs. Fontaine deemed reasonable compensation for Charlie's separation from the company, he had, in addition, shifted two million into a "travel account" he alone had controlled, and that twenty years after the events surrounding Charlie's departure Mrs. Fontaine's reluctance to have him prosecuted, or to at least sue him, was the chief charge critics like Voigt leveled against her. Above all, Nix knew what he knew because he had found all this information in an hour in the library. Mrs. Fontaine's book was in the end her own, and she was free to say what she wished no matter what Nix knew to be the truth. This was ghostwriting not method acting.

The note sat on the table, a 4" by 7" piece of ruled unbleached paper torn from her stationery pad. Nix found the mere sight of it—centered alone on a bare surface—something to worry about because Flora was not the sort to leave notes. They had always been too aware of where the other was to bother. So unsettling did he find the thought of the message that the note might possibly contain that he couldn't bring himself to read it. Rather he went into the living room and sat sweating through several minutes of Carlos, the sports guy, on the Five News at Noon. The Cubs were playing indoors in Houston this week, lucky for them. This theme of the team's good fortune was reprised in several variations, including those pointing out the "irony" that it should be cooler in Houston in July than in Chicago, before Toni came on with the end-of-show weather word. She wore a sleeveless white blouse and shorter than usual khaki skirt. A wisp of her hair had fallen loose and she looked too weary to push it back. "Don't go outside unless you have to, and when I say have to, I mean an honest to Christ emergency.

"The fact, Frank, is that the maps are decorative. The radar shows us where the weather is, and the computer models predict where it might go and why with dazzling accuracy. But none of that can change the fact that it's very, very, very hot. It's just going to get hotter. There is nothing we can do."

The camera switched to a wide shot of the anchor, open-mouthed, gaping though wide, tired eyes. Frank's lips appeared to move just as the screen went blue. Nix bounded down the long hallway to the kitchen to retrieve Flora's note.

> N.—
> Went to Veronika and Nestor's to cool off.
> Back in days.
> XO, F.

it said.

Okay—not as bad as Nix at first feared. Though there was an uncomfortable degree of ambiguity in the phrases "cool off"—was she pissed, or just hot?—and "Back in days." Had she left out a phrase, *a couple, a few*? The construct *days* suggested an event protracted beyond tolerance. Since they didn't leave notes for each other, Nix had no sense of her shorthand, if that's what it was.

He'd resolved neither quandary to any degree of satisfaction when the phone rang. Certain it was Flora, he snatched the receiver on the first ring.

"Buddy." It was Lenny. "I'm here. Meet me."

Nix stammered. "I can't get away right now. Flora's pregnant and—"

"Flora?"

"My wife?"

"Which reminds me to ask why I never went to that wedding."

"You weren't invited."

"Bud-dy."

"No one was. It was a civil ceremony," Nix lied.

"Does she know you changed your name? Put her on."

"She's not here," Nix said.

"Don't worry about it. I'll come up for lunch. Name the place."

Veronika sounded as though she'd dashed up a flight of stairs to answer the phone. "She's asleep," she said when Nix asked to talk to Flora.

"Then wake her up?" he said.

There was a silence before Veronika spoke again, during which Nix conjured in his head a conspiracy on the other end of the line. "Would you wake her up if you were here?" Veronika asked.

"I would if I told myself to do it."

"Don't you think we're better off facilitating healthy rest patterns?" Veronika said, with a clinical authority so convincing that Nix gave in.

"Tell her to call when she wakes up," Nix said.

Happy to throw on a pair of shorts and T-shirt after a morning of sweating in slacks, Nix was actually looking forward to a hot afternoon, as a reminder of his days in Dixie. On his way to the door, he noticed the manuscript of *Clown U* he had retrieved from his father's possessions and, remembering that Lenny had been a fan of Floog's work, decided to bring it along.

Nix had arranged to meet Lenny at a deli a few blocks from their house. He suggested the place because he and Flora hadn't had a chance to try it out, and he didn't want to be outdoors any longer than he had to. Though even this short walk was more than Nix had bargained for, as he found himself hugging the buildings he passed in search of shadow and thinking, *This is the way the world ends,* not with a bang, but with a swelter.

Nix had actually only seen Lenny in person on a handful of occasions and none of them fewer than ten years ago, but he recognized immediately the man in the white ball cap and vivid yellow cowboy shirt with brown-stitching at the pockets, sitting beneath the delicatessen's massive cool-air return, fanning himself with the laminated menu.

Lenny recognized Nix, as well, likely because he was the one person under sixty in the room. It appeared the only people ignoring the warnings to stay indoors were those the weather was most likely to kill. "Buddy, you weren't kidding about the heat. My cab driver, Pierre, from Haiti, no air conditioning, didn't break a sweat. I had to wring out my boxers, the bastard."

"I told you."

"You told me, you told me. You're writing a book with the magazine tycoon married to the gay French gigolo that robbed her blind?"

Nix noticed Lenny was wearing a golf cap, though the Lenny he remembered was not a golfer. Of course, the Lenny he remembered was not above dressing for golf, even if he had no plans to go. "It sounds bad when you say it that way."

"That's got to be gold, depending on what's come out already. Basically, as I might've said on the phone, these projects are priced by how bad she's willing to make herself look. Plain and simple. Readers don't respect writers who won't reveal humiliating details about themselves to sell books."

The man who came to take their order was as old as the patrons. Not seeing any other wait staff around, Nix thought he must be the owner, that he'd sent his staff home for their safety, but couldn't afford to close for as long as the heat wave lasted. Nix guessed that this kind of collision between safety and job security was going on all over the city. He ordered pastrami on rye, as he did whenever he went to a deli for the first time. Lenny ordered the same and a bowl of matzo ball soup. The waiter whistled and walked away.

"You've got to be out of your mind. Soup?"

"It smells good," Lenny said, setting the menu against the napkin holder. "We were talking dirt."

"She's given me some. I can't use much of it."

"Why not?"

"She won't let me."

Lenny took his cap off to mop his forehead with his napkin, revealing a comb-over that made Lazar's look good. Lenny had wound a long, yarn-like lock from one side of his head to the other, a single brocade stretched across his otherwise bald skull. This was a shock because Nix remembered Lenny as having thick, black hair. It was a reminder of how rapidly things can be lost.

Lenny caught him looking and said, "I think to publish this book would be a service to society."

"Are you putting me on?"

"Naw, because it'll suck and get shredded by any critic caught dead reviewing it, and if that keeps even one other rich bastard from writing his memoirs, it'll be worth it. Come on. Used to be just generals and writers who wrote down their life stories. Then it was movie actors, then the ballplayers, and now it's every flipping millionaire you meet at a silent auction. The problem is there's a good reason why they're rich, and it's the same reason why they're dull. Learning to act or throw a ball faster than anyone else or getting shot at are risky propositions. Anybody looking to get rich is going to eliminate the middleman, so to speak, and go right to where the money is."

Nix laughed. "Mrs. Fontaine said something along those lines."

"What'd I tell you."

"Course, she also had polio, so I doubt she was going to do anything like those things you're talking about."

Lenny looked up from his plate, a rivulet of coleslaw dripping from the edge of his mouth. "Polio?"

"Yeah," Nix said, pantomiming the application of a napkin to the side of his mouth. "Does that change anything?"

Lenny shrugged, dabbing at his face. "These days disease memoirs are better than money memoirs—provided the diseased memoirist in question has overcome her ... affliction."

"It's polio, Lenny. They now can prevent it, they can treat it, but I don't think they can cure it."

Lenny was distracted by something at the next table. "That would largely be the editor's call. I'm not sure how they'd go with that. Face it, polio hasn't been hot for what forty years." He signaled the waiter. "I'm going to get potato pancakes. Want some?"

Nix looked over at the pile of latkes on a platter flanked by paper cups of applesauce and sour cream. "Sure, why not."

"At this point," Nix said, "I can do what I'm contracted to do and be done with it. Why do I feel like a failure?"

"You *are* a failure." *Foyl shmuck.* "What do you have for me there?" He pointed at the folder with his fork.

"I found it with Floog's things. I know you were a fan and thought you'd want to see it."

"Yeah?" Lenny said as he dipped a napkin in a glass of water and washed and dried his hands. Then he turned back the title page and ran his fingers over the paper, as if the puckering were a kind of Braille, "I was sorry to hear." He turned the pages slowly, shaking his head, grunting at times, letting loose quick snorts of laughter. "It's not just the art," he said, "the structure, the use of the banners, this is friggin' amazin'," Lenny said, as might have Weevil. The waiter returned with a platter. Lenny slid the manuscript into the bag and speared at the pancakes and spooning out sour cream. "Can I have this?"

"You mean to keep?—no. Take it with you if you want. Just get it back to me."

"You're a prince. Eat these," he said.

Nix dug in, too. They were very good. The improbability of the situation struck him as the first bite cooled in his mouth.

The check came. Lenny picked it up without hesitating and studied it. "Cheap," he said, "and not half bad. I ought to move out here if I wasn't living so well out East. So, you saw April?"

"Yeah."

"Tell me."

"Nothing to tell," Nix said. "It was a big room."

"You owe her. More than you know."

"You're an asshole."

"Yeah," Lenny said, "but I have a career."

When Nix got back home, he saw Veronika's car idling out front and assumed Flora was back. He was glad to have been gone when she got home so it didn't look like he was waiting by the phone. He approached the car, only to be startled by the apparition of Nestor rising from the driver's side door. "Glad you showed, man," Nestor said, "I was low on gas and figured myself for goner if I lost the AC." He shook Nix's hand and put his left arm across Nix's shoulder, leading him up the walk, as though it was his house he was ushering Nix into. "I'll tell you straight out," Nestor said. "I'm here for her clothes." He was wearing a Panama hat, white tropical wear, and leather sandals.

"Her clothes?" Nix said. "Are you kidding?"

"I don't know," Nestor said. "Some of them. She's going to be buying some maternity things. In the meantime, she gave me a list."

"Why didn't she come herself?"

"Veronika didn't think it would be wise for her to drive, being as it's as hot as it is." Nestor said, a point Nix couldn't argue.

"The phones still work, don't they?"

"I can ask her to call. You know how she is."

"Yeah, I know how she is. How come you know how she is?"

Sweat gushed down Nestor's face. "Man, it's hot in here, too. You've got to go to one of those cooling off centers."

"There's an air conditioner in the bedroom."

"Then why aren't we in there?"

"Or we could just go over to your house, if that's the problem. If your place is that much cooler, I mean."

"It is but I got to be frank with you, I don't know how that would go over."

They went into the bedroom and sat side-by-side on the bed, their feet stretched out in front of them, their backs resting against the headboard. The room smelled of dirty laundry and dank air from the air conditioner, which hummed feebly in the window.

Nestor looked around the room. "Which dresser's hers?"

"The one with the candy dish full of earrings on top of the doily."

"Of course, I never pretended to have any skills of observation."

"What's that supposed to mean?"

"Did you ever think that the reason you're a lousy writer is that you don't see what's going on around you?"

"No, I never thought that."

"See."

"What should we do here?" Nix said. "It's funny you being over here now. You always seem to be around when I'm not."

"What's that supposed to mean?"

"I'm just saying you've been kind of handy around here," Nix said. "Do you want my advice?"

Nix looked at him and noticed they had their hands folded in front of them in an identical fashion. "No."

"Don't let this be the thing that fucks what you have up."

"I didn't tell Flora to move out."

"She's not moving out," Nestor said. "She's taking a breath. It's hard to breathe in this heat."

"You don't know what you're talking about. You don't have kids."

"Neither do you, yet."

"If she never comes back. I'll still be the father," Nix said, the thought of Flora actually leaving for good and taking the child occurring to him for the first time. "Why am I listening to you?"

"You're not, man. Did you know you're talking to the new Director of Composition at Carnelius College?"

"You're shitting me. What happened to Steve?"

"Nothing happened to him. Seems he took a long look in the mirror and didn't like what he saw."

"Where'd he go?"

"Tangiers."

"That's crazy. Why they give it to you?"

"I asked. I figured no one would consider an adjunct for the position. I stressed my lack of qualifications for the position and my unconventional teaching philosophy."

"That worked?"

"Yeah, it worked. Turns out everyone on the search committee hates Trout and couldn't wait to stick it to him."

"Funny how we always come back to you."

Nestor patted him on the shoulder and swung his legs on the floor. "Yeah, well, I think they call that charisma."

In the end, Nix not only helped Nestor find the clothes on the list Flora had made but helped him pack them into her carry-on suitcase. Nix was comforted by the fact that the clothes she had requested were only enough for a few days. On the other hand there was the mere existence of the list, the fact that she thought she had to send Nestor, that the very sight of him was unacceptable to her.

"I'm not going to call her," Nix said. "Tell her I really want to but I won't. Tell her that. Tell her I'm not going to call, but also don't forget the part about how I want to."

At the door, Nestor set the bag down and wrapped Nix in a bear hug. "Relax, my friend," he said, "No one's died."

22.

In fact people *were* dying. At ten the next morning, the temperature reached one hundred degrees at the earliest time of day in the history of the city. The old and poor, the ill and poor, the plain poor were dying by the hundreds. In burglar-barred flop rooms and in SROs, while the desk clerk dozed downstairs, nameless drifters boiled from the inside out. Childless widows too frightened to unlock their window latches lay down to sleep through the afternoon heat and never woke up. It was a cruel culling of the weak.

Flora called that evening, to Nix's great relief, just "Hi Honey, you okay?"

"Yeah," Nix said.

"Hot?"

"Yeah." He was sitting on the bed, close enough to the air conditioner to lay his ear on the vents.

"Me too," she said. "You sound glum."

"Glum? I sound *glum?*"

"Okay, now you sound like you."

It was hard for him to hear over the hum of the machine, but not hard enough for him to consider turning the knob to a lower setting. "Are you going to come back? When it cools off."

"Nix, I don't know," she sighed. "We'll see. I'm going to work now."

"Do you think that's a good idea?"

Flora laughed. "I do, but I'm the only one. Why don't I call you when I get home?"

"Sure, I've got no place to be," he said, aware only after he'd said the words out loud how pathetic they sounded, but then the phone rang again, and he was sure she had changed her mind.

"Are you alone?" the caller asked. It was Mrs. Fontaine, sounding not so much conspiratorial as tired. "I need you to come up here."

"Today?"

"Yes, today. I understand the weather is trying, but there is a meeting at FFS today that is likely to be auspicious."

Nix hesitated. There was no need in a memoir for live, on-the-scene reporting, particularly if the scene were one at which the ostensible memoirist was unwelcome. "There have been a lot of delays on Metra," he said. "The tracks are melting."

"I'll send Hector."

The car came in less than an hour. Hector was dressed in his summer livery and looked a little—with his mustache, driver's cap, and mirrored shades—like a field commander in some dirty Central American war. Nix barely had time to get his foot in the door before Hector hit the gas, rattling the pitcher of ice water on the mini-fridge in front of Nix.

The newspaper was folded in the rack, as always, but Nix didn't pick it up, knowing there'd only be stories about the heat. He decided as long as he was forced to live it, he shouldn't be bothered to read about it, and was content to look out the window at the slothful pace of the people on the street burdened by this scourge that had gripped them by their throats for four days and showed no signs of moving off. Had Nix been looking toward the curb as the car turned east on Irving Park toward the expressway, instead of at the green SUV darting across their path, he would have seen Flora at the corner, waiting for the light to change.

She stood at the crosswalk, feeling better than she had in days. This improvement in her frame of mind, she grudgingly attributed to her conversation with Nix of the night before—grudgingly, because she had been genuinely grateful to have time to herself and, more than that, away from him. She had been warned by city officials via the television news and directly by Nestor and Veronika not to leave the apartment, but she felt fine. She had a bottle of cold water and a cotton handkerchief to wipe away the sweat and wanted to show she could fend for herself, even in these conditions. For weeks she'd worried about everything she could think of to worry about. She worried about money, her marriage, the house, the baby, daycare, clothes, diapers, college, mental illness, and whether it skipped a generation. Nix wasn't well, in the most mundane, functional sense, but he wasn't stark raving mad like his father, either. But what if that meant her child would be? And now the weather, which was literally the only thing anyone was talking about. Flora never minded the heat. She preferred dog days to the dark days of winter, and had been able, particularly after moving in with Veronika and her central air, to avoid the worst of it. Still, she was frustrated by the extremity of the conditions and felt guilty that Nix might be suffering more than she, more than he should have to.

She'd already decided that she would go back to him. The deciding factor—if there was just one—had been a letter she'd received to the Reluctant Nurturer.

"Dear R.N." it read, "Is there any law that says I have to love my baby? because right now I don't.—And I'm not too crazy about his father either."

It was signed "Disappointed," and although this wasn't the saddest of the thousands of letters she'd received to her column, nor close even to being the most desperate, it touched her in a way that none had before. Since the letter's writer didn't say how old her child was, Flora hoped the condition was merely a case of post-partum depression. *Merely,* Flora thought, though she knew that can be fatal. Just as frightening, she believed, is to be sealed off from the love of others by impossible-to-meet expectations.

So, yes, she would go back to Nix and had known she would when he had asked her the night before, but had chosen to keep him hanging. That was cruel, really, and unlike her. Still she felt he deserved it. With what had been going on at FFS, he had become more intense and full of himself than he would ever have admitted. Nonetheless, she would go back to him, though she also knew he would disappoint her. Some men, she believed, brought very little to a relationship and gave all they had, some brought little and gave even less. Nix, on the other hand, had a great deal to offer but didn't know enough to offer what he had. His insecurities could drive him to monstrous acts of egotism. He seemed always so preoccupied with the possibility that he might be disappointing her that he had little time to see how disappointed she was. His work for Zira Fontaine had changed him in ways she didn't like, but that could be chalked up to this problem of fearing her disappointment. Of course the same couldn't be said about Flora being gassed at her corporate doorstep, though that had been her objective and not his idea. So she would take him back, for no other reason than her belief that, though he would certainly disappoint her, he could also be counted on as often to do the right thing, if only by accident.

She saw the light changing and had stepped off the curb when from behind her she heard a hiccup of tire squeal, followed by a tinkling of glass—the sounds of a fender-bender, sounds so common to the city that such bland commotion didn't cause Flora to turn her head. Had she looked, she would have seen, bearing down on her at an alarming speed, the forest-green Ford Explorer registered to Dominic Pelitieri of Winnetka, Illinois, a name familiar to anyone who'd passed a construction site in the Loop and seen it gracing the sides of the massive cranes that hoisted steel and concrete to the tops of the city's growing skyline. Neither Dominic nor wife Binny Pelitieri was in the vehicle at that moment but were instead at their Door County vacation home. The car was being driven by their son, Landon Pelitieri, 17, who had been compelled to stay behind to complete a summer course in geometry at his private day school. Though expressly forbidden by Armand to drive into the city, Landon had disobeyed his father and come down to Wicker Park because he was hosting a party that evening—also forbidden by the vacationing parents—and was keen to purchase a hundred dollars worth of crack. The only other time Landon had dared to buy drugs on the street had been from Juan when Landon and his friends had been down for the Smashing Pumpkins show at the Double Door, and therefore was returning to the block because he felt he and Juan had established a professional relationship. Unfortunately, when he arrived on the corner he remembered as being Juan's, Juan was nowhere to be found. Juan was taking a personal day, because, in his words—in everyone's words—it was "too fucken hot." When it came right to it, Juan had chosen drug sales as a profession because he had seen his mother slog off to work at dawn in all manner of crappy weather and wasn't going to take that shit himself.

Disappointed but determined, Landon had found what he was looking for a few blocks north, from a vendor who was grateful for the windfall on a low-traffic morning, and the Pelitieri heir was easing out the alley, triumphant, and heading for home, when he took the corner too tight and shattered the tail light of a parked Subaru with his own armored bumper. Fearing, correctly, that his ass would be grass if his father were able to place him in the city by way of a police report for a moving traffic violation, Landon pushed the accelerator pedal to the floor, causing the Explorer to buck and lurch into traffic, surging past a black town car with tinted windows and toward the curb at the intersection where he saw—too late to do anything as sensible as applying the brakes—a dark-haired woman in a skirt and white sleeveless shirt step from the curb in front of Mom's Explorer.

Commotion, voices—many voices. Flora thought that whatever had happened to her had happened to everyone around her, too, and wondered how long she would have to wait for help, even as she was unaware of what sort of help she needed. She could remember the sensation of all her limbs being off the ground, but no pain, no feeling whatsoever to explain what had hurled her into the air. Then she had struck the ground, again without pain. She was simply in the air one moment and on the ground the next, as though she had chosen this place to light, but she had not chosen to land here and worried before she was aware of anything else that she was going to be hit by a car, before she even understood that she already had been.

She couldn't see but was aware of the voices. Gradually, she came to be aware that those voices weren't talking about many accidents but only one, hers. Moved, embarrassed by the concern and help, she felt unworthy of the attention. One of the first on the scene was a house painter who had been waiting at the drive-through window of the Dunkin' Donuts, in whose parking lot she'd landed. Thoughtfully, he had covered her with a canvas drop cloth from the back of his truck, and then she was aware of the smell of turpentine and that she was very hot, that the asphalt—was she simply imagining this?—bubbled under her fingertips. She was conscious of not wanting to be misunderstood, of trying to talk very slowly, though she would be told later that she was actually reciting phone numbers in manic succession, her home number, Veronika and Nestor's number, Marcia's number at the office, Veronika's work number, her parents' number, and those of each of her siblings, while bystanders scrambled through their purses and pockets to find paper on which to write them all down.

The paramedics arrived at some point before Flora was aware of their presence. There was a shift in the urgency of the voices. Flora said, "Tell them I'm pregnant," expecting that this information would be relayed to the paramedics by the original Samaritans who'd come to her aid.

"How many weeks?" one of them asked.

"I can't remember," she said and worried they would think she was a madwoman who had invented a nonexistent pregnancy.

The hospital to which she was sped was four blocks away, the trip taking less than five minutes and further jumbling her unhitched sense of time. Her sight was returning, gradually, but somehow familiarly. She was aware of a bright circular light on the ceiling of the ambulance, then of the yellow sky as she was rolled out into the heat again, and then of the fluorescent lights of the hospital corridors. Her head had been taped in place between two pieces of foam, her body strapped to a wooden board of the sort she'd seen a gunshot victim loaded onto outside her home weeks earlier. She could see little to her left and right though enough to realize that the hallways were crowded with the heat afflicted. Sweat-drenched and hollow-eyed they stared without seeing, holding damp towels and ice packs to their foreheads and the backs of their neck.

The ambulance drivers left her along a wall in the emergency room, without a word of comfort or of explanation. She could not look around her, but she heard many voices, begging for help or simply moaning in their agony. I am one of them, she thought.

Hector opened the great oak door for Nix. Like a bellhop, he'd turned the key and the knob, pushed the door open, then stepped back to allow Nix to step ahead of him into the foyer. Rather than follow Nix in, however, Hector had gone away and left him standing alone in the Fontaine estate house. His footfalls seemed to echo on the marble even louder than they had in the past, as he walked through the grand rooms of the first floor, sitting rooms, dining rooms, the kitchen, even a utility closet bigger than their new bathroom, calling out for Mrs. Fontaine with a combination of hope and trepidation.

A maid appeared from down a darkened hall. "I am sorry, Mr. Nix" she said. "I was supposed to meet you." She led him down a corridor he had never seen of glass cabinets and closed doors, then through what appeared to be a utility room of pipes and gauges, and then to an outside door, which opened upon a broad patio. "Here," she said and closed the door behind him. He heard the sound of splashing and then voices and walked toward them. In the bright sunlight, Nix had a hard time making out the pool because it was shaded between a large tinted screen erected between the water and the sun. As he approached, Mrs. Fontaine called out to him. "Good day, Mr. Walters. Thank you for coming."

Nix's eyes adjusted, revealing a startling scene. Mrs. Fontaine sat in the pool, with her back against the side. She was wearing a swimsuit of a bright floral print and a white bathing cap. Claire sat beside her in a black suit, her hair, loose and wet on the ends where it touched the water. Maria was wandering along the deck, wearing a suit of the same pattern as Mrs. Fontaine, with a matching bonnet. She paused and looked at Nix though the heart-shaped lenses of her sunglasses, as she licked a red Popsicle. In addition to the tinted screen which was perhaps twenty feet high and thirty wide, her staff had rigged two hoses, one at each end of the pool that released a fine mist into the air, and a gardener sweating in his green coverall was shoveling ice from a plastic wastebasket into the blue water of the pool.

"Mr. Walters, there are swimming trunks in the change room if you would like to join us."

The idea struck Nix as so potentially awkward, he worried that he couldn't conceal his revulsion, he quickly said, "As much as I would like to, I don't think that would be appropriate—given my position."

Claire rolled her eyes and reached behind her for a pack of cigarettes.

"If you must smoke," Mrs. Fontaine said, "could you move to the other side of the pool?" Her daughter shook her head in exaggerated disgust, but glided on her back across the pool holding the hand with the cigarette above the water.

Mrs. Fontaine waited until Claire lit before she said, "This morning at 10:51, I lost a vote of no confidence by a margin of four votes."

"I'm sorry," Nix said.

"Don't be. It was a long time coming and far closer than I expected.
I submitted my resignation in advance of the vote."

He looked to Claire to judge her reaction, but she was gazing off
in the distance, oblivious as well to her daughter who had finished
the Popsicle and was leaning over the lip of the pool reaching to
float the stick on the water. Nix felt certain the girl was too young
to swim and was calculating whether he could, from where he was
standing, dive into the water and haul her out before she sank to
the bottom, when one of the maids hoisted her up and carried her
screaming into the house, an act of heroism that neither Claire nor
her mother noticed.

"Where's Anders?" Nix asked.

Claire stage-laughed.

Mrs. Fontaine smiled and pushed the water in front of her to the
side with the back of her hand. "Larson's gone over to the enemy,"
she said.

"I don't understand," Nix said.

"Are we starting?" Mrs. Fontaine asked. "Do you want to write?
You're sweating. Sit over here, at least, in the mist. We are at the last
chapter. Nowhere as we have been doing this did I have any idea
what form it would take."

Nix sat, pulled his notebook from his satchel, and tried with wet
fingers to pull the cap off a pen, realizing as he did that he wasn't
going to be able to write in this artificially induced rainforest. "As a
practice," he said, "the idea is to write down everything you think
might be important or relevant and shape all of that into the finished product."

"You are saying this may not be the ending?"

"Yes."

"What more is there to come? I said that I could not imagine an
ending. That is not the same thing as saying that I wished to go
on forever."

"Of course not."

"The reason I am not upset, the reason I resigned in advance of

a vote of no confidence, a vote—if you want to know my immediate impression—should never have been taken, given the fact that
I had already proffered my resignation, is that the vote was rational
and justifiable, if also unnecessary. It is a waste of breath to say that
the world that I was born into is very different from the one we
find ourselves in now. To have said that is to have said nothing. I
may surprise you, though, when I say that the business of currency
trading is more different from the field I entered thirty years ago
than this house is from the apartment in Budapest in which I was
born. What we did when we began doing it was to buy and sell in
small amount and small increments according to our observations
of trends and what we read in the newspaper. When we were right,
and we were right most of the time, we made a little money, and
when were wrong we lost a little less. Our sense was that we were
correcting errors in valuation—through our activity not through
the volume of our sales. Trades on the scale in which we were engaged were not of a size to have an effect on the valuation.

"People have said the British Pound crisis changed everything.
I was clear of the trading division and can't even tell you what our
position was. If we went short, it would have meant that everyone
was going short. As the sums became larger, reputations suffered.
Though I would hasten to point out that we were trading in currency, not coal or cigarettes.

"Currency is neutral. It is ornamental, forward looking. It's in-
novative. Coins meant more than an end to bartering, they signaled
order. Paper currency calls for an even greater act of faith. Money
cannot assert its own value. For that, one needs shopkeepers and a
centralized banking authority. The system doesn't depend on good
faith, it depends on the natural capacity for markets to offset bad
faith."

"People will not like being told that you got rich for their own
good," Nix said.

The sun must have moved beyond the screen because a bolt of
sunlight spread across her face. "Jorge," she said, shading her eyes,
and Jorge wearily, but with so sign of complaint, dropped the scoop
into the ice and walked over to reposition the screen. Nix looked
out over the hazy yard as from a bubble. "The aims of commodi-

ties exchanges and the public are often at odds. Stan used to say, 'If you're not making money, you're making a mistake.' It's glib but I always understood what he meant. I can understand that people are born poor. I do not understand they choose to say that way. Of course, no one chooses to be ill. And so I write checks. I do what I can. Good works are good business."

"Konrad Voigt puts it differently?"

Mrs. Fontaine's eyes flashed. "Does he?"

"You're familiar with his—principles?"

Her face softened and she smiled. "Confidentially, I wasn't aware he had any."

For the first time in her presence, Nix laughed. "You know—," he began, but then the maid who had let Nix in was hurrying toward them, the antenna on the cordless phone, shooting sparks of light as she came. "*Es para él,*" she said.

23.

A woman's thick Slavic-accented voice asked, "Are you Nix Walters?" "Yes." "Are you husband of Flora DiCicco?" "Yes," Nix said
again, annoyed then sliding swiftly into a blind panic, the sensation of all the blood rushing out his body. Before the nurse spoke
another word he'd imagined the worst, only to be told, when she did
speak again, something just short of the worst. Had he spoken then?
Had he said, "Flora's had an accident"? Obviously Mrs. Fontaine
had heard him if he had or, if he had not, had seen the same terror
on Nix's face she'd seen on her father's eyes upon learning of her illness. "Go," she said, "—go."

Hector said, "Just take the car, chief. Go ahead. I know where you
live."

"I'll get it right back to you," Nix said and jumped feet-first behind the wheel.

Given the plush indolence of the passenger compartment, the car
was surprisingly quick and agile, and Nix roared through Lake Forest toward the expressway, grateful to Hector and relieved that he
would be able to get where he was going with such speed and ease.

Then he reached the highway and was met at the on-ramp by
construction signs, followed immediately by a line of brake lights,
stretching as far as he could see. Dust rose into the hazy, jaundiced
sky erasing any trace of horizon, as the cars merged diffidently into
a single lane. Beneath his hardhat, the flagman had fashioned a
keffiyeh from his T-shirt. Nix always thought roadwork on steamy
summer days must be unbearable, today it seemed unsurvivable. As
proof of this thought, he rolled moments later past a row of men,
seated in the shadow of a massive earthmover, passing a bucket
down the row and ladling water onto their heads with a plastic cup.
Along the shoulder, every couple of hundred yards, a car sat, with
its hood up, belching steam, like beasts that had fallen prematurely
off of this single-file trek to extinction.

Then, for the first time really, he thought about Flora, or had he
been thinking of her all along? "Multiple fractures," the woman said,

of "vertebrae and bone in the arm," "serious condition," she said, "stable," she said, "pending further tests." What did that mean? that they could learn that she was worse off than they thought? Then for the first time—and Nix was certain this was the first time—he thought about the baby, about which the nurse had said nothing.

He sat for minutes, motionless, as cars edged up on both sides. They're dumber than rats, Nix thought. Rats encounter an obstacle and search for a way around it, while humans maneuver their cars to clog the approaches to every obstruction, as if solid barriers will yield to brute persistence. The sun reflected a searing glare off the tractor trailer in front of him. Car horns blared, just barely audible in the sealed cabin of the Fontaine limo. Pointless, Nix thought, dumb jackasses. His thumbs drummed the steering wheel and he rocked with frustration. The lane closure shifted from the right to the left. There was a sign for an exit a mile off. Seeing an opening, Nix swerved onto the shoulder and pressed the gas pedal, the force of acceleration pushing him back in his seat.

Drivers blared their horns, gestured obscenely—one threw a full beer can that exploded on the windshield. Their rage seemed to propel him faster. In this car, Nix was invincible. He pressed the button for the windshield washer. Nozzles elevated out of the hood and sprayed fluid across the glass. Two swipes of the wiper blades cleared any trace of the assault. Doubtless, those stalled in traffic thought Nix was some North Shore fat cat for whom rules the rest of them were compelled to live by did not apply, and Nix, in all his rage and fear, became that asshole. Who cared what anyone of these fools and weaklings who blocked his passage thought about him and his hurtling black bullet of an automobile? All he wanted was for them to get the hell out of the way.

At the exit, he turned off, forcing a car onto the shoulder, as the lane narrowed. As he rounded the bend at North Avenue, the broad side of a four-story building came into view. For almost all of the last year it had been painted with a sneaker ad featuring Michael Jordan but it had been replaced since the last time Nix had been past with the head and outstretched arms of Konrad Voigt. He was dressed in white in this likeness, in fact Nix thought at first that the photograph from which with the image had been derived was in black and white before realizing it was a color image of a colorless subject. His hands were out of the frame and thus it was impossible to know whether he was welcoming motorists into an embrace or he had been handcuffed to a rack. He was wearing black-rimmed glasses and bolo tie, the clasp for which sported the Voigt logo of the cross inside the V. And the caption whose font seemed to have been cribbed from that of the sneaker company, read simply, For Now. A lot you could make of that, Nix thought, but he was in no state of mind to consider the permutations. He was sure that this was a sign, even though he had no idea of what.

One right turn and he was on Division and a straight path to the hospital. Here the congestion lessened, but he had to put up with the traffic lights. On every block, the hydrants were exhausted. He saw a man kneeling at the curb to cup gutter water to his face. On the sidewalks pavement had buckled. Beneath a tree on a median a woman and a dog, lay in like postures of prostration. Nix thought, *This is the way the world ends,* people and animals brought low together.

Each block seemed identical in its affliction. Those braving the heat mopped their foreheads and carried water like oxygen. Nix, in the climate-controlled luxury of the car, felt none of it. In the future, he thought, the rich will take to their cars, their rolling eco-fortresses and forge a drive-through society, never having to do more than roll down a window to have their goods handed to them from a bullet-proof teller window, through the toxic air to the windows of their cars—until even that breaks down.

As Nix neared the hospital, more than an hour after he'd left Mrs. Fontaine's house, he realized that he had only a vague memory of where it was.

The lights ahead were out and cars were proceeding through a major intersection as though it were marked with a stoplight—every four or five cars, someone would jump their turn, prompting honks and shouted expletives. Nix rolled his window down to ask a man crossing the street if he knew where the hospital was. The man shrugged, said, "You look okay to me." An ambulance sped by seconds later another, and without thanking the man Nix sped off, following the flashing lights to his destination.

Piled at the pillars of the emergency room entrance lay bouquets of flowers, Mylar balloons, stuffed animals. It was the age of the make-shift memorial, vigilante shrines, spontaneous material representations of vicarious grief. Just as Flora had thought herself a victim among many, Nix saw these tokens left at the hospital's door and thought, *She's dead.*

He didn't find her lying on any of the gurneys in the corridor nor among the dozens more seated in chairs in the waiting room or lying on the floor along the walls. Nix hesitated at the nurses' station, thinking if he didn't tell them Flora's name, they couldn't tell him what he knew they were going to say, and she would still be alive.

When he did speak Flora's name, the nurse popped her gum and called up a screen with the indolent tapping of a single hand on the computer keyboard. "Seven sixteen," she said.

"What is that?"

"Post op."

"So—she's okay?"

"So—she's in room 716," the nurse shrugged.

Marcia, Veronika, Flora's parents, Nestor, and two brothers—all had heeded the calls from a half-dozen bystanders at the scene of the crime and hurried to the hospital. They stood, lined three deep against the wall opposite the door, as though preparing to pose for a group photo, but in fact were making space in the cramped room for a nurse to tend to the machine beside the bed, whose transparent tubes led to an apparatus on Flora's arm. Her lips had swelled into a pout, and the right side of her face was a single bruise that swelled her eye shut, so that she looked as though she were greeting him with a familiar coy expression. Her one good eye sought his, and when she found him, she looked at him for just a few seconds and then to the floor with what Nix recognized as a combination of sadness, embarrassment, and fatigue. "Don't look at me," said a voice he barely recognized as hers.

Last.

Dear Dis,

There is no law that says you must love your child. And if there were one that said you had to love your husband, half the married women in America would be in jail. However, most of the pertinent research suggests that an affectionate, protective bond will form between a mother and her child in the first weeks of life. Whether that instinct is a result of natural selection or of the natural occurrence of unconditional love is a question science cannot answer. In the meantime, I'd say that if you can't love your child, act as if you do, if only for the sake of her fragile, tiny soul.

Of course, what do I know? What do any of us?

RN

Thursday, after six straight days in the hundreds, the heat broke. The temperature fell into the nineties, seeming spring-like to the survivors of the previous week, and then, a day later, into the eighties. The evening was cool on which Nix wheeled Flora out onto the hospital grounds. The fiberglass brace, specially fashioned to fit over her growing belly, forced her into an uncomfortably upright position and tilted her nose to the sky. On the front of it, Veronika plastered a sticker that said, Mean People Suck. Although it was not certain, Flora would likely have to walk with a cane for the rest of her life, a price she would consider a small one to pay until she had to do it.

The operation to repair the damage done to her child in the womb had become the signature instance of survival among the ruin, the hook all the local stations led with, the incident they'd been praying for to shift the narrative from horror to hope, from the irresistible power of nature that it could be subdued by ingenuity. Frank Stuckey stared moist-eyed into the camera. "Out of tragedy—a miracle." Cut to three doctors, two men and a woman, sitting at a cafeteria table behind banks of fuzzy microphones. Outfitted with diagrams from the hospital's public relations team, the anesthesiologist from

Stockholm, the perinatologist from Islamabad, and the trauma surgeon from Tel Aviv described the child's in-utero encounter with American extreme medicine.

Lenny went to work. "Who writes a book where everyone gets what he wants, but nobody gets what's coming to him?" was what he wanted to know when he called Nix just two weeks later to tell him he'd sold *Clown U.* for a half a million dollars. "Or what I should be asking is, Who wants to read one?"

"Most of that is going to hospital bills," Nix said.

"You're breaking my heart," Lenny said like he meant it. "I might have news on the Fontaine title."

"When will you hear?"

"What I'm saying is I might have news."

"Don't be an asshole."

"Rules being rules I have to talk to her first. But I'm saying what I'm saying in case you want to rework your arrangement."

"It was a flat fee."

"Buddy, you sold yourself short."

"Who knew?" Nix said. "Meanwhile Voigt is taking a beating in the business pages. It turns out that cutting off the brand namesake at the knees is considered a bad business practice. And when that namesake is a woman, that makes you something like Bluebeard."

"Like I said, roses and rainbows."

"They're burying unclaimed bodies in a potter's field, Lenny."

"Kid, you're a black cloud on an otherwise sunny day. I want you to do something for me. Tell April to call me."

"Who? April March? You know her better than I do."

"In my dreams I do. I've called, written, sent tokens of my esteem."

Nix spooled in his mind through every conversation he'd had with Lenny trying to remember if April ever came up. Had Lenny taken on *Life During Wartime* just to please her? "You're out of her league, Lenny. Why would you want to set yourself up for disappointment?"

"Easy for you to say. You've got—what is it—Florence?"

"That's an open question, Lenny."

There was silence on the other end and Nix wondered if maybe Lenny had fallen asleep. Then the unmistakable sound of a nose blown into Kleenex. "Sorry," he said. "Allergies."

"In New York."

"Trust me, Kid. She'll be back."

"I'll call April for you, Lenny, and play Cyrano. I owe you that." He hung up and walked to the window. Minutes could pass on their new block without a car driving by. The quiet left Nix wondering what he was missing out on. The city that seemed capable of shrugging off any humiliation looked toward fall as a change of subject. Flora was at her parents' place. The reason she gave was that her folks weren't getting any younger and, after she was back on her feet, they would someday need the ramps and railings that her brothers had installed. Nix and Flora had named the girl Mirra, Italian for myrrh, an ancient harbinger of a miracle birth. Nix hadn't seen either of them in two nights. He stood by the open window, listening for the sound of tires on the asphalt, his outlook so uncertain as to be beyond reasonable speculation, his gods ancient and dead.